A USE OF RICHES

J. I. M. STEWART

PENGUIN BOOKS

Penguin Books Ltd, Harmondsworth, Middlesex
AUSTRALIA: Penguin Books Pty Ltd, 762 Whitehorse Road,
Mitcham, Victoria

—

First published by Gollancz 1957
Published in Penguin Books 1963

—

Copyright © J. I. M. Stewart, 1957

—

Made and printed in Great Britain
by C. Nicholls & Company Ltd
Set in Intertype Pilgrim

PENGUIN BOOKS

1960

A USE OF RICHES

J. I. M. STEWART

J. I. M. Stewart has been a Student of Christ Church, Oxford, since 1949. He was born in 1906 and was educated at Edinburgh Academy and Oriel College, Oxford. He was lecturer in English at the University of Leeds from 1930 to 1935, and spent the succeeding ten years as Jury Professor of English in the University of Adelaide, South Australia. He has published four novels and a volume of short stories, as well as many detective stories and broadcast scripts under the pseudonym of Michael Innes. His *Eight Modern Writers* is due to appear in 1963 as the final volume of *The Oxford History of English Literature*. He is married and has five children.

Cover drawing by Robin Jacques

PART ONE
THE CRAINES

CHAPTER ONE

RUPERT CRAINE walked out of Lombard Street and walked down the Poultry into Cheapside. Ruddy and iron-grey, clipped and brushed and polished, he might have been a general who had made the common move from commanding regiments to directing companies. He walked briskly, for the obstinate March frost gripped London. In the cleared spaces there was a sparkle of rime. The weeds and wild flowers that would later spread their threadbare rural carpet before St Paul's were still invisible beneath Goering's rubble.

On these walks – and he did more of them than his subordinates thought necessary – Craine had got into the way of filling the gaps with buildings of his own. But now there were real buildings going up, and nearly every site carried a coloured picture showing what the steel and concrete framework would be like when the achitecture had been added on. Craine looked at these shapes of things to come with misgiving. It would be reasonable, it would be modest, to suppose them much more splendid than anything his own fancy could furnish. After all, distinguished architects were designing them. But Craine's sympathies were with those other persons often equally distinguished, who formed obstructive committees and sent letters of protest to the newspapers. He himself mediated, patiently explaining this or that aesthetic plea to irritated associates. They listened with the open-mindedness of successful men; they acknowledged as a respectable circumstance that Craine's stake in the issue wasn't merely on the level of finance. They didn't see, indeed, that much could be done. When material interests are of a certain magnitude there really isn't much room for manoeuvre in front of them. But they tipped Craine to make a capital Lord Mayor. This was sagacious. He had never in fact had any other parade ground than London. Gog was his adjutant and Magog his A.D.C. His

7

feeling for the City covered both its life and its material fabric.

He was the more readily accepted as a man of taste because he had a modest disinclination to obtrude himself in that character. If he paused now to interpret through its scaffolding the new spire of St Mary-le-Bow it wasn't with any air of expertness. That he possessed a flair that way was something he had first come to acknowledge almost against the grain. The Medici, he had thought, were the last bankers not to look absurd when operating at all noticeably on such territory. But he had ended by accepting the bent, and he got a great deal of pleasure out of it. He thought and talked art when he felt like it, and when he didn't he didn't. This was one of his unabashed days. At this moment he was making a detour to be defended only on the score of aesthetic delectation.

Of course, he told himself, drum and dome were best from across the river. In the old days at Garsington there had been a Duncan Grant that gave you that – and all in browns and greens which might have been assembled on the artist's palette from Thames mud and slime. It was one very good way to paint, the way of the frugal Umbrians, who had dipped their brushes only in the olive grove and the vineyard. Walking down the chilly London street, Craine felt the tug of these things – Val d'Orcia or Val d'Arno – even as he thought of them. And then he paused, recalled to his surroundings. Yes – there it was: the aspect he had wanted.

He stood like a tourist and stared. The best thing would be almost no buildings at all. Open vistas, the great cathedral rising clear to Wren's intention, would be his own cup of tea. But – then again – wasn't that to allow too much to the artistic slant? Life ought to press up against a great church, not withdraw from it respectfully. A civic monument was what you wanted, if it was a question of closing or crowning a view. You could argue, perhaps, that St Paul's is just that. Go inside and you may feel the place doesn't contain much religion. Come out again and you may

8

acknowledge that what it expresses is a sort of mercantile grandeur. That was what its survival through the bombing had seemed to symbolize the toughness of: John Bull's England – or Soames Forsyte's. *Surely the Lord is in this place.* But the parsons aren't always right. With Him there's no 'surely' about it. To some offered dwellings He has never been attracted. And from others – perhaps immemorially august – He has removed Himself. Ravenna, for example. After century upon century of Christian worship San Vitale speaks only to German tourists, instructed in the art of Byzantium. No hint of the numinous remains. If you want anything of the sort, you must find some obscure church round the corner.

Craine turned away and walked on, questioning his own wandering mind. He recognized for the symptom it was this second cropping up of an image from abroad. If he could manage the time, it would be fun to get a spell in Provence or Tuscany. But that wasn't a practical proposition. Not now. He halted before one of the largest of the rising buildings. The labyrinth of steel constituted a hieroglyph which he was constrained to read. Companies, Groups, what they now called 'Organizations' went through his head. Poised on a girder, a spider-man sailed across the sky – but his wasn't the most hazardous position among those concerned with this colossal gesture of confidence. Craine knew where the headaches lurked. And he respected them. A cherished view of St Paul's or an unexpected glimpse of St Mary Woolnoth was something, but the first consideration was to pay your way. The Forsytes had accepted that – perhaps excessively. Now it didn't seem to be a piece of knowledge very widely diffused through the community. When it came to the plain business of paying their way, folk weren't practical. The Londoners brushing him at the moment didn't have a strong sense of economic fact ranged among the virtues that made him like them. They believed, bless them, that they could have their cake and eat it. They believed they could eat their cake and get another on the never-never or from the pools. You had to mind their p's and q's for them;

you had to accept as yours the whole headache of the nation's bread and cheese. Of course – Craine told himself – it isn't philanthropy, public spirit, any confounded impertinence of that sort. It's common sense and self-preservation – for if they go, I go too, and all my order with me. And it all applies particularly this year. My own interests – he thought – aren't in bottoms that will be the first to founder. All the same, I'm on the bridge until September at least.

Turning into Watling Street – it was absurd that men had taken to edging about the City in cabs: a flat degeneration, as bicycles would be in Venice – turning into Watling Street and hugging the narrow pavement, Craine repeated to himself *particularly this year,* and acknowledged some obscurely pleasurable sensation. It was different from his pleasure before St Paul's – and now he turned round on himself and asked whether it was nearly so reputable. The sense of responsibility was one thing, the lure of power was another – and the devil of it was that unobtrusive channels flowed between the two. God defend him from ever going into politics, from fancying himself on *that* bridge.

Still, one has to try to think ahead. The huge buildings will go up, but cement is tumbling all the same. Housing has had its boost and will have to accept a damper now. And what about the chain stores – the poor man's Army and Navy, the suburban housewife's Harrods? I own – Craine reflected – to a nasty feeling in my stomach when I hear of another half-mile of counter being opened in those admirably aseptic palaces. Miraculous brave-new-worlds, in which young ladies sell you tolerable vests and pants without a blush – but booked for a damper too. And then what? Another sixpence, even a shilling off – and at once a whacking sales tax all round? It doesn't sound too good, that, when you consider it dispassionately. You can't tell what may come unstuck, if you do a thing like that; only a Third Programme economist could fancy he had a clue. Devaluation, then? Everything coming into the office suggests that the whole world expects that. But then the whole world is something you mustn't give too much weight to.

Craine watched a telegraph boy shoot past. You never know what a telegraph boy may bring you, these days.

Damn the nation's headache, Craine said to himself, turning in at a shabby doorway. Damn most of the workers and damn all the shareholders. After all, why *not* get away? Why not take Jill to Naples, to Rome? The Pope had been doing something in a snow-storm, but spring couldn't be far behind him. Perhaps it would be possible to go in May. At the moment, even if he confounded business and ran for it, there were personal affairs that made a hobble. Jill's money was giving him thought; it was on an errand concerned partly with it that he was bent now. New money had come in – and what was to be done with it? The market had disintegrated. Sell five hundred of this and you were all right. But try to sell five thousand, and there might be a drop of shillings. As for buying . . .

Climbing narrow stairs, Craine shook his head. There was little in equities that he fancied at the moment. Probably one of the better discount houses was the answer. Yes, he said to himself as he passed a clatter of typewriters on a landing, a discount house. That's it. And not Naples, he added inconsequently. Rome perhaps, but not Naples. He paused, ruminating, before a glass door. It had been an association of ideas not hard to distinguish. There was a degree of poverty that moneyed people couldn't without indecency rub shoulders with. Rome would pass; Naples not.

For a moment he continued to stand still. Had he been challenged, he would have had to admit that he was considering his limited life, the narrow figure he would cut if juxtaposed with some quite ordinary saints, the oddity, say, of his umbrella and hard hat and the stripes and creases on his trousers as these would appear draping a donor in even the darkest corner of a canvas. It was unaccountable, in a way, that he had married Jill; that Jill had married him. There had been an element of rebound to it – an ugly word. However, it was all right. Craine opened the door.

A modest place; old-fashioned glass partitions with small

ineptly functional windows here and there. The commissionaire was peering at him through one of these now. Craine's father would have liked this set-up. But he had always snorted if you called a porter a commissionaire.

'Mr Groocock free?' Craine was aware of his own gentle voice and smile. These disconcerted people. They weren't felt to be right for either the banker or the Berkshire squire. Unfortunately they were genuine things that it would be affectation to monkey with, even in order to save people from feeling perplexed. The trouble was his being aware of them with the small annoying superfluity of self-consciousness he had carried into maturity. It was debilitating, he told himself. He would catch his own voice, his own look, and always a grain of assurance fell through the glass, as if more and more he was constrained to agree with his casual acquaintance that he didn't fit together too well. When his hour was up, it would be a soul without confidence who should present himself for judgement. But that, he added to himself with sanity, was just as it should be, after all.

There was no doubt about Mr Groocock being free. Framed in his stunted window, the commissionaire beamed a cockney beam, like a hard-working comedian on the cover of the *Radio Times*. He was aware that this visit of Mr Craine's was an affable thing; that Mr Groocock, although the power behind his own little scene, might well have been required to take up his brief-case and traverse the city himself.

Craine found himself knowing the commissionaire's name. It couldn't be called an effort of memory. Sometimes he commanded these felicities, and was grateful. Venturesomely, he asked after the man's wife. The question was a hit. An operation had been successful and Mrs Eggins was convalescing at Southend. Craine noticed that a shaft of sunshine had somehow penetrated this obscure place and was at play upon the glass partitions, turning them golden. He went into Mr Groocock's room.

Groocock made, or responded to, general conversation. It

wasn't for him to do the turning to business. And Craine talked cheerfully, although the remainder of the day was tight. He had to give a man lunch – and for that matter a cigar, which took time – and then he wanted to get to Weidlé's. He had his eye on an Amico di Sandro. In fact more than an eye. He coveted the thing, and it wouldn't be sold until he had decided. Amico di Sandro was a charming hypothesis: the unassuming friend of the painter of the Primavera. It had taken B. B. to think him up; and Craine didn't at all mind the same critic's later uncreating word in the matter.

Craine talked to Groocock about the Amico. In this dingy place it wasn't bringing coals to Newcastle; rather it was like taking warmth and light from his pocket and planting them on Groocock's well-ordered desk. Groocock knew who B. B. was; he knew whose buddy Amico had been – or would have been; he had been educated at the sort of progressive public school where there are lessons on art. So the talk prospered, and when they had finished talking pictures they talked land. Craine thought Groocock less sound – and rather a bore – on land. Groocock's line was to felicitate him on being a landowner. Well, that was all right. But Groocock brought his own angle to it; he expatiated on landed property as a hedge against inflation. Utter bosh, like talking of feather beds for farmers. Back in the old Queen's time, Craine's grandfather had bought land for more money that he himself could realize on it today. That was an anomaly outside Groocock's range. Craine moved on to his immediate affair.

His stepchildren and his children were still alike quite young – although Jill's two gave the effect of ticking off the years with a speed that surprised him. Tim Arnander was twelve and Charles Arnander eleven; sometimes you would swear that Jill couldn't be their mother. As for the joint efforts – Jill's and his – they were babies. He himself looked like their grandfather, he supposed. The present point was simple; one day or another the whole lot would come of age; and then money, advantageously tied up, must be waiting to carry them on. This was common prudence – particularly as some of them might declare for unprofitable pursuits: schoolmastering or writing poetry or composing symphonies. It was chiefly a matter for the lawyers. But there was an accountancy side to it, and for this Groocock was the man. Groocock handled Craine's personal taxation. He had a pretty good notion of the present family set-up.

Groocock flicked over papers expertly. 'Roughly speaking,' he said, 'Mrs Craine will continue to float her children by the first marriage, and you will be responsible for those by the second?'

'Certainly. It seems the reasonable thing.'

Groocock nodded. He had a professional trick of discussing affairs of this sort in a state of slight abstraction. Presumably it was tact. There was nothing wrong with two families. But in some circumstances they might be held to constitute at least a minor indelicacy. So Groocock kept on the safe side. 'Of course,' he was saying, 'the problems are different. Mrs Craine can't have more children by her late husband, but she can by you.'

A silence succeeded this bleakly obvious statement. Craine reflected that Groocock must do business for some extraordinarily stupid people. 'Quite so,' he said briskly. 'We expect more children.'

Groocock gave another abstracted nod. This time, he was acknowledging that with men at the top such an expectation is a public-spirited act. He accompanied the gesture, however, with words that were unexpectedly acrid. 'You'll get no thanks for it.'

Craine laughed. He was pleased when a chap spoke up. 'Fiscally, you mean?'

'From the universe at large.' Groocock pursued his theme firmly. He wasn't the first Groocock to have held down this job, and he talked as a fellow should. It was the absence of this capacity, Craine reflected, that made a lot of one's dealings with the new administrative classes tedious. 'Although

14

I'm a bachelor,' Groocock added in a vein of gloomy satisfaction, 'and oughtn't to speak out of turn.'

'Oh, I'm prepared for anything.' Craine took it lightly. 'Lear's hovel on the heath, and Tom of Bedlam in the straw.'

'Perhaps it won't come to that. You haven't got a kingdom to divide.' From gloom Groocock returned to geniality. 'Although you may end up with something near a principality.'

But Craine found himself not liking this. At bottom it was flattery over what only a fool would rejoice in. 'What we have to contrive,' he said, 'is fair shares – or something near it – for each of the little blighters as their several dates come along.'

'Exactly. And you'll want to avoid covenants, or anything like that. Nothing to be said for pitching large incomes at the heads of subalterns and undergraduates.' Groocock spoke with the assurance of one accustomed to address wealthy parents on this point. 'The Arnander boys – Tim and Charles, aren't they ? – might have a great deal, if there wasn't some careful disposition. As for your own children' – Groocock appeared to do a rapid actuarial calculation – 'you're more likely than not to be dead before some of the unborn ones come of age.'

Craine nodded. 'Yes,' he said, 'I've worked out that one too.'

'You won't be, of course. Still, it's probable that you will.' Groocock judged this an occasion for cheerful irrationality. 'As for what you should fix up, a trust's the thing, if you ask me.'

'Certainly a trust.'

'The trustees to have discretion to survey the field when the grandchildren thin out.'

'Thin out ?'

'When it's clear that they've pretty well stopped getting themselves born. Or say when the youngest existing grandchild comes of age.'

'That sort of thing's common, of course,' Craine said. He felt depressed. He wasn't all that wealthy, and surely he never would be. Nor did he fancy ending up as a dead hand from the grave. That would be a dreadful sort of immortality; not at all the kind he had once been absurd enough to imagine for himself when a young man. 'But I don't know,' he said aloud to Groocock, 'that one wants to conserve to that extent. After all, it would be for a world you and I can't guess at. Do we want to secure young men their manor houses and their hunters in the opening decades of the next century? Or even to put up a thoroughly cussed fight against the whole trend of social legislation – of history, if you like – in this one?'

'These are large questions,' Groocock said, and looked shocked. You could fancy him alarmed in case his client's irregular sentiments carried through the surrounding glass panelling to the innocent young accountants round about. 'And there are several things I haven't got clear. The Arnander boys, for instance: is there anything on the father's side?'

'Only genius.'

Craine had spoken promptly. It was a fence he could always take at once. And he was amused to see that it left Groocock quite blank. 'That's something, of course,' the accountant was saying vaguely. 'That's a great deal. But your stepsons will have nothing in the way of property from their late father?'

'Nothing at all. He had nothing – although my wife, when he married her, was already a wealthy woman. An aunt in Virginia, you know, who didn't have your sound views about pitching fortunes at undergraduates – even female ones. But Arnander had no money, and never thought to acquire any. He was a painter.'

'I see.' For a moment Groocock continued blank. He would have been quicker on any of the *amici* of Amico. Presumably the lessons at the progressive school hadn't come right down to modern times. But a second later he got there. '*Arnander*? Good lord! Do you know, I never connected up?'

'Well, you have now,' Craine said a shade shortly, for he

disliked being looked at with a new interest – particularly when the impact was vicarious. But the unworthiness of this response struck him immediately. 'John Arnander was a great painter. It isn't just his early death and the paucity of his mature work that has given him his reputation, and begun to produce some striking prices in the salerooms. It's the fact that he was right there. If not with Mantegna and El Greco, certainly with Cézanne and Picasso.'

'And he got nothing material out of it all?' Groocock assumed a properly sombre expression. 'Bad luck. It doesn't seem right . . . one who gave all that to the world.' He shook his head – a man of affairs who could yet sympathize with the artist's lot.

'A painter commonly has a certain amount of stuff in his studio when he dies,' Craine said. 'If he has any sort of market, it no doubt constitutes what you might call an estate. But the circumstances of Arnander's death were exceptional.'

'I see, I see.' Groocock appeared to judge that here was something into which it would not be profitable to inquire. 'It must be extraordinarily interesting,' he pursued, 'to have the boys. Do they show artistic promise?'

Craine was often asked this question about his stepsons, and he had a number of replies calculated to lead to a little speculative talk. On the whole, he liked things kept lively but impersonal. 'Don't they say,' he asked, 'that every child possesses the potentialities of an artist – of a painter? It's demonstrable whenever one looks at the walls of a kindergarten. But of course – unfortunately or fortunately – the survivors into adult life are few. My stepsons may survive in that sense – particularly Charles. It's impossible to tell.'

'Most interesting.' Groocock, who presumably had no occasion to inspect the walls of kindergartens, civilly took on the air of one under instruction. 'And I suppose it applies to music, too. Mozart, for instance.'

'That's a different thing.' These rambling chats, Craine thought, are seldom quite honestly time off. They size a man up for you, perhaps reveal some foggy area in his mind. 'It's a different thing,' he repeated carefully. 'In music one gets occasional prodigies, virtually abreast of the grown-ups while still in pinafores. But one doesn't get, in the infant population at large, the widely diffused ability and disposition to take the first positive steps. And the reason, if you ask me, is this: Nature has given the eye a big start over the ear. Ages ago, the ear was perhaps still exclusively on the alert for danger while the eye was already allowing itself spells at just having a nice look round. Or perhaps – and this is quite a different notion – there's a more effective group of primary industries working for the eye all the time.' Craine hesitated. It was certainly one of his unabashed days – but he wasn't sure that all this wasn't a bore. Groocock said nothing, contenting himself with an expression that acknowledged the other's deft touching in of a metaphor from the real world. 'You see,' Craine went on, 'the ordinary man doesn't, as he moves about, ever hear in Nature something uncommonly like a fugue or a symphony. But he does from time to time see something uncommonly like a picture. At least I do.'

'Most interesting,' Groocock repeated.

The conversation had turned disagreeable to Craine. To say *At least I do* was awkward. And Groocock was now regarding himself as humouring a client with an eccentric streak in him. It wasn't for Craine to say the fellow was wrong – and anyway one must tail the thing courteously off. 'I don't mean that one necessarily sees anything remotely resembling a significant work of art simply by looking out of a window. But objects – a tree, a door, a wall, a bowl of fruit – present themselves sometimes . . . well, with splendour. Their own essential quiddity shines out in them. And there you are. But I don't think Nature ever does that for one through the ear.'

'There might be exceptions. Wordsworth. Certain sounds, quite simply in Nature, haunted him like a passion.' Groocock had landed neatly on another set of lessons. 'A shock of mild surprise.'

'But Wordsworth didn't make music out of his mild surprises. He made poetry.'

'Well, that's a kind of music.' Groocock, an open-minded man, produced a concessive gesture. 'Although I've been told there's no correlation between the musical and poetic faculties. When we talk of the music of poetry we're merely using a figure of speech.'

That was enough – particularly if Groocock was thus left with the last pregnant word. Craine stirred on his chair, and presently they were back with the business on hand. In a week or two's time they would have a meeting with the solicitors, and Mrs Craine would come up from Pinn. But as he made these and other arrangements, Craine's mind continued to move in a different world. Where the deuce *did* music come from? What, for musicians, was the raw material equivalent to Rembrandt's armour and similar junk, to Cézanne's Mont Sainte-Victoire, to the wenches Titian would whistle up from a neighbouring bawdy-house? Come to think of it, he had never met a musician – and his sisters used to bring shoals about the place – who knew one bird-call from another. But now he must sign one or two papers, ask Groocock to look into this and that. He did so, quickening his pace; and in ten minutes was nodding to the commissionaire and making his way downstairs.

That had been as it should be. A family responsibility was on the way to being discharged. And at least he hadn't treated Groocock – a hard-working chap with a good deal below the surface – as if he were a piece of office equipment. Nevertheless Craine felt discomfort accompany him back into Watling Street. A shaft of sunlight – the same that had gilded the poky glass partitions of the office – was at play on a red bicycle by the kerb. Another telegraph boy.

And there, suddenly, was the experience – fleeting but indubitable. The bicycle seemed not a bicycle of earth. A city man, a reasonable shot, a farmer well known for his Gloucestershire Old Spots, he would always have these glimpses of this particular channel beyond sense. It was the ground of his proposing, that afternoon, to get old Weidlé down to a reasonable figure for the Amico di Sandro. A little analysis might reveal it as the reason for his having married John Arnander's widow. That was all right, But what walked at his elbow now, as he made his way to the chop-house where he was to give a man lunch and a cigar, was Arnander's shade. What would Arnander think of artistic talk in Watling Street ? Craine thought he knew.

CHAPTER TWO

THE Arnander boys were at a private school given to liberal policies. They came home at half-term. Their appearances at meals were civil and reasonably punctual, but they spent most of the time on the banks of the Pinn where it skirted the lower paddock. Tim fished industriously – sometimes with a worm and sometimes with a shamelessly childish net. Back at school, and questioned by other boys about how he had spent his time, he would say, 'Oh, flogging our bit of water, you know, for nothing very much.' This reply, judiciously combining modesty with an intimation of the right sort of background, gained him general approval. But Charles, who would say in answer to the same question, 'Just mucking around,' was equally respected, because nothing so much commends itself to small boys as reticence and veracity.

Here by the stream, Tim would lie on his stomach, peering into the water, and Charles would sprawl on his back, gazing at the clouds. Charles was an authority on clouds, and kept a diary in which their appearance and disappearance was recorded. In Charles's heaven the clouds were varied and abundant; they sailed past all day in every variety of form known to science. A cloud, unlike a butterfly or a bird's egg, is never there next morning, to be checked in a disenchanting light.

'Cumulonimbus,' Charles said. 'That's a cloud of convectional type.'

'I don't suppose you know what convectional means.'

'Yes, I do. It means formed by currents of rising air.' Charles thought for a moment how to retort upon this warfare. 'Why don't you get on with your fishing? Your schol. won't come any sooner just because you keep staring at the road.'

Tim was making an untidy job of getting a fresh worm

on his hook. With all the forces of his will he was striving to bring a red bicycle up the road from Pagan Episcopi. The telegram would say whether or not he was to be a scholar of Winchester. 'Naturally I'm impatient,' he said reasonably. 'And old Barker promised to send a wire.'

'Are you sure you want to go to Winchester anyway?' Thrusting back in his pocket the notebook in which he had recorded his latest cloud, Charles continued his challenging manner. 'When we went there in summer I thought it was a squashing sort of place. And Turk says a lot of artists' and writers' sons go to newer schools.'

Turk, a junior master much given to tickling and slapping his charges, was at present Charles's oracle. Tim disapproved of him. 'Turk's an ass,' he said. 'Although of course it might be different if our father was alive.' Tim was always fair-minded. 'He might talk to other artists and get ideas about schools. But I don't see what's wrong with Winchester. Rupert's a Wykehamist, and Rupert's all right.'

'Of course Rupert's all right – only perhaps rather a conventional person.'

'Don't you mean convectional – formed by currents of rising air?' Tim waited to let this jeer sink in. 'You've been eavesdropping again.'

Charles sat up indignantly. 'I haven't been eavesdropping!'

'Yes you have. You must have been. That was just not the sort of expression an eleven-year-old thinks of. You've been listening to some disgusting trog being beastly about Rupert, and now you're parroting him.' Again Tim paused and his glance wandered. 'Does the post office shut at lunch-time? And would that mean they'd telephone it?'

Charles pointed to the horizon. 'Nimbostratus. There's going to be rain. But if it does come by telephone, Mummy's sure to rush down and tell you. Unless she's taken the children over to the vicarage.' It was always as the children that the young Arnanders referred to the young Craines. 'I'd hate to be a vicar – or even an archdeacon. Do you think Rupert will want us to be bankers?'

'I suppose it's quite likely.'

'I don't think I want to be that, either. I've been into the bank in Newbury sometimes. Standing there, handing out wads of pound notes to farmers and shopkeepers, would be frightfully dull.'

Tim shook his head. 'I don't think that's quite what banking means – not for people like us.'

'You mean we'd be somewhere behind – and looking after the gold?'

'Well, certainly behind. But in London or New York, not Newbury. And we'd have to decide things. I mean, of course, after we'd learnt about it all. People would come asking for credit – a sort of loan, that is – and we'd say whether they could have it or not. It would be vital to decide properly, because it would affect the wealth of the nation.'

'Would important people come – a headmaster, for instance, wanting money to build a new gym?'

Tim nodded. 'Much more important than that. Men wanting to build factories and ocean liners and new sorts of experimental aeroplanes. I know Rupert had to decide something about a new sort of jet plane last week.' Tim had taken his eyes away from the road. 'It might be fun.'

'I won't have anything to do with it.' Charles spoke so decidedly that Tim looked at him in surprise, and he felt obliged to proceed to the sort of rational and decorous explanation that his brother was inclined to accept. 'For quite a long time the people who came would be older than I was. It would be embarrassing. I think I shall be a painter. I won the drawing prize, after all.'

'You know what Rupert says about that.' Tim met reason with reason. 'It's no good going after anything like that unless you're as mad as mad about it. If you're that, he says, good luck to you. But make sure first.'

'I don't see how you can make sure first.'

'Neither do I, really.' Tim always conducted discussions honestly. 'But I suppose people do. Daddy, for instance. I expect he was as mad as mad, and as sure as sure. The great ones are.'

'Of course he was.' The boys usually accepted each other's theories and speculations about their father. 'But how old was he when he began? And of course I don't expect he had anybody who was inclined to suggest making him a banker.'

Tim tossed his line rather absently into the Pinn; his gaze was back on the road from the village. 'But they'd have wanted him to be an assistant in a grocer's, or even a boot boy in a school. His people were quite poor. We must find how soon he knew he was mad as mad.'

'Altostratus – straight above the tithe barn. Warm moist air flowing up over a cold front. I've never explained cold fronts to you. But about Daddy' – Charles's voice grew elaborately casual – 'there's quite a lot to find out still, don't you think?' Clouds were the only subject on which Charles claimed even parity of knowledge with his brother; about their father as about everything else Tim must know a little more; his twelve months' start made that self-evident. 'Could he have been a conscientious objector? Turk says that conscientious objectors have to clean out the lats in lunatic asylums.'

'Turk's an ass.'

'Perhaps he *is* a bit of an ass. But it's queer, isn't it, that Daddy wasn't really fighting?'

'There wasn't anything queer about it,' Tim said impatiently. 'And I'm sure it's been explained to you. It was his health – not letting him fight. But he was on a commission. The commission went with the Army to try to keep churches and pictures and things safe during the war.'

'Did the Germans have a commission too?'

'Yes, they did. And Daddy was killed when he was trying to reach the other commission and persuade it to prevent the German soldiers from blowing up a very beautiful bridge.'

'There you are! That's more than they ever told *me*!'

Charles spoke without indignation. 'I suppose it's because I get nightmares and you don't. Was it that he was . . . very *badly* killed?'

Tim hesitated. 'Yes – very badly, I think. He was on the bridge when it was blown up. I suppose there was nothing left but hundreds of bits.'

'Of the bridge?'

Tim took a moment to deal with this. 'Well,' he said, 'of the bridge too, I suppose.'

'You mean, Daddy was . . . *gobbets*?'

Tim got hastily to his feet. 'You have disgusting words,' he said. 'And when you ought to be shocked, you're not. I don't believe in your nightmares any more. When you next pretend to be having one, I shall scrag you. Honest.'

'Well, I know now, anyway. And he seems to have been behaving quite sensibly when he got killed. I mean, if the bridge was really very fine. You don't think it was perhaps against the rules of war – going to find the people on the other side like that?'

Tim pulled in his line and looked gloomily at the worm; its appearance was unattractive. 'I *have* sometimes wondered. You see, it was pretty brave, walking across a bridge that was going to go sky-high. So oughtn't there to have been a medal? But I've never heard of one. And of course you have to be careful *not* to talk to the enemy while the war is going on just in the ordinary way.'

'But you say he wasn't a soldier.'

'Well, I suppose the people on the commission were half and half. I don't even know whether Daddy wore uniform. We could ask Mummy about that.'

Charles shook his head doubtfully. 'It might be embarrassing.'

'You're always thinking things would be embarrassing.' Tim removed the pallid and juiceless worm from its hook and threw it away in disgust. 'It's the phase of agonizing self-consciousness.'

'Who's been eavesdropping now?' Charles hurled this at

his brother in a fiercely triumphant shout – only to add without a pause, and in the friendliest manner, 'Here comes your telegram. I bet it will be all right.'

It was quite characteristic that Charles Arnander although his head was so learnedly in the clouds, had glimpsed the flash of the red bicycle first. The brothers raced across the paddock. But the house was nearly half a mile away, and the telegraph boy would beat them to it easily.

Tim drew ahead. Pinn, long and low and stone-roofed, with behind it the curved yew hedge that was the tallest in England, stretched itself in modest luxury to the clear spring sunshine, as if aware that cumulonimbus and nimbostratus were likely to spoil things later in the day. From each end of the house a column of smoke went up: one from the kitchen and one from the nursery. In between, they could see the line of dormer windows in their own domain: bedroom, schoolroom and the long attic that held only the electric train. Soon the children would be beginning to take a vexatious interest in that. And then, presumably, there would be changes. The children would move up, the nursery would go out of commission for a generation, they themselves would be promoted to rooms of adult diginity on the first floor. Ponies would become horses and bicycles would become ancient but presentable cars. Other boys would come from Winchester – if Winchester it was to be – and Rupert would mount them, would find them a rod, a gun. After that there would be two years in the Army – in the Coldstream, if they could grow tall enough – and then they would nearly all go up to New College. And after *that*, becoming a banker would probably be natural. Even for Charles.

Tim scrambled over a gate. He was still ahead. His legs had really been growing during the last few months, and perhaps he would be a long-limbed sort of person after all. He was in the big home paddock that some of Rupert's City friends politely called the park. Pinn bobbed up and down as he ran, so that it seemed to be nodding its agreement with the future that tumbled in quick pictures through his mind. Only the sun flickered on the dormer windows, and it was possible to feel that they were not nodding, but winking. You can't tell, the winking seemed to say slyly. You can't tell at all.

Jill Craine stood on the small paved space outside her husband's book-room. The open telegram was in her hand. She saw the boys come racing towards her as if on the wings of disaster. She frowned. Their sort of disaster, of course : the dinghy foundered, both wheels buckled, the old grey pony lamed. She had been startled when she looked up and saw them. But it could only be something like that.

They vanished behind a high hedge and then appeared again, perilously skimming the verge of the swimming-pool where the lichened statues postured patiently in cypress niches. Tim was ahead. They would neither of them ever be tall or notably athletic, but they were without their father's physical meagreness, his bodily insignificance which had been so extreme that he could carry it like a distinction. Rupert's world was claiming them; it could be read in their faces, which took more and more from nurture, gave prominence to the clear complexion, the good teeth, the straight glance, the promise of settling into firm lines and equable motions. Beneath this, John Arnander's features – pinched and skimped and plebeian in repose, yet so transformed at a breath of suffering or joy – showed only like a ghost haunting a fadingly familiar place.

Jill Craine folded the telegram and slipped it back into its orange envelope.

But they had zigzagged through the rose garden and tumbled to a halt in front of her. 'Is it – ' Tim began. He broke off, panting. The words he wanted were too big for him, too naked. He had another, an awkward, shot. 'Is it about – about my future ?'

She stared at him.

'He means his schol.' Charles spoke quickly. 'But it isn't. I see it isn't.'

She remembered. She smiled. 'Of course it isn't. That can't be till the afternoon. The Dong said so. What a shame, Tim – to run so hard and draw a blank! Go and wash and tidy – both of you.' She looked at her eldest child and gave way to something she rarely gave way to – the small propitiatory word offered to another whose being is the consequence of one's own act. 'Lemon sponge,' she said.

Tim flushed. He didn't think all that of lemon sponge; it was only a family convention that each child had a favourite dish; what affected him was something quite different. He had seen for the first time that his mother was beautiful, that her face was a strange and beautiful object. For a long time he had believed that because it was strange it couldn't be beautiful. Certainly it bore no resemblance to the photographs of fashionable women in weekly magazines in the drawing-room. But now he saw this as without significance. He saw too that his mother's head was entirely like what it ought to be like: the bronze bust which he could see at this moment glinting in a cleared wall-space amid Rupert's books. He felt an odd resentment towards the books, a jealousy. And suddenly he was visited by a quite extraordinary thought which he had an impulse to frame in words: that unlike the women in the magazines she would remain wholly beautiful if she stood on her head. But of course one couldn't say that, either seriously or as if it were a joke. It would be a wet weed's thing to say. So he said something else instead. 'And cream?' He used his tough bargaining voice. 'It's no good without cream, you know.'

'Quite definitely no cream.'

Their mother spoke briskly, and Tim found the reply entirely in order. But Charles had hardly heard it. His heart was thumping still at the queerness of the moment in which the scholarship had meant nothing to her, and in which he had glimpsed trouble in her eyes as she stood quite still in the sunshine, the unexplained telegram in her hand.

CHAPTER THREE

CRAINE'S secretary caught him at lunch-time with trans-forming news. There had been a cable from Washington. Mr Auldearn was coming home.

Over his chop Craine chuckled about it – silently, since he was entertaining a serious banker from Bonn. Hadn't he been telling himself that you never know what a telegraph boy may bring you, these days?

The cable had been brief, but Craine could guess what lay behind it. Old Mungo, like his father the judge, was a man of rapid decisions. And he was through with trying to hold their hands over there. His advice had been disregarded once too often; he had written a characteristic note to the P.M.; and now he was packing his bag. Once back in London, he would be spoiling to hog the whole show. He would take a single glance at Craine – if indeed he remembered to take as much as that – and pronounce him to be on the verge of collapse. He would disturb the calm of clubs by calling out to eminent physicians to come over and inspect a fellow member palpably *in articulo mortis*. By hook or by crook, in fact, he would get rid of his junior partner for a month, and indulge himself in a high old time. Everybody would be the better for it. Craine had no illusions as to that. There would be a general toning up, whether of gentlemen in Threadneedle Street or of tellers flicking their abaci in Aden or Hong Kong. But of course a month would be enough. For longer than a month, Auldearn without Craine wouldn't do.

The German banker was elderly, and two or three years out of date. He spoke of the wickedness of putting children into uniform – even, he would venture to say, uniform of the speciously civilian type which he understood to have been retained at Eton. In Germany children would never wear uniform again. As he lit his cigar the German banker warmed to his topic. His jaw squared and his voice barked. You may be all right in a board-room, Craine thought, but a barrack square is your spiritual home.

The coffee was taken away; the ash lengthened on the cigars. This sort of lunch, Craine said to himself, is a curse. My father always declared that, granted a single glass of decent madeira, one did best on something brought over from a pub. But there's no need to be impatient, all the same. Not now. For Mungo's coming back and I can get off that bridge whenever I want to. I'll celebrate by going down to Pinn tonight, after all. As soon as I'm through with Weidlé, I'll drive straight out of town. Yes, by Jove, and with the Amico di Sandro in the boot. We'll arrange our holiday, Jill and I, before we go to bed. On Monday or Tuesday we'll fly out. Malpensa, and a couple of nights for La Scala in Milan. And then . . .

The banker from Bonn had risen. '*Leider*,' he said – for blessedly he had an appointment with somebody much more important than Craine. Hats and umbrellas. There is something about Tim, Craine thought. Yes – his scholarship. The boy will get it, all right. The Dong is confident, and he's been shoving lads at these things for forty years. Jill's clever, and John Arnander must have possessed high intelligence. Artists of that calibre do. Pleasant to be back on the evening the news comes. Might I give Tim the Amico? Would there be any sense in that?

He didn't know. He shook hands with the banker from Bonn and walked west, realizing that he didn't know this small thing. Would the boy appreciate such a present? Or would he feel that he was being got at, was being nudged into remembering that he was a great painter's son? Wouldn't something more commonplace, more orthodox, be safer – say a gun? Although perplexed, Craine gently smiled to himself as he walked. A gun is safe in one sense. But Jill might point out it isn't so in another. Anyway, one gets nowhere in such matters on the strength of deliberation. To give this, to give that: the decision has to be intuitive if it's to be any good.

But Lord, he said to himself as he hailed a cab in the Strand, don't let's have this sort of thing again. It's settled that I have to guess about people – even about my wife, a little. And I oughtn't to have plans for the Arnander boys. For what do I know about them? There's not even the link of blood. Tim and Charles are two enigmas. Is it fair to hope that an enigma won't become an accountant like Groocock or a banker like Mungo or myself; that he will rebel, even, against the whole establishment? And the danger will be greater with my own children, even if a little less of them is concealed from me. It isn't so much the sins of the fathers that are visited on the succeeding generation. It's the grade the fathers haven't made, the challenge they didn't square up to.

He took a turn round the gallery before allowing the young man in charge to call Weidlé. The Amico was still there, and a ticket announced that it stood reserved. Whether for Tim or for himself, therefore, Craine looked at it with a proprietary eye. There wasn't much to be said for *that*; it was an irrelevant sentiment to entertain in front of a picture. On the other hand innumerable works of art would never have been executed if rich men had no fondness for possession, and the acquisitive instinct might surely exercise itself with particular harmlessness upon this small charming thing.

The Florentine lady looked out full face upon the few who stepped aside from Bond Street to hobnob with her. She had not made up her mind, one might say, about London. Indecisiveness indeed was her charm – and only the more so because one didn't determine whether the quality inhered veritably in her character or reflected simply the painter's uncertainty in modelling eyes and mouth. In the background's steep panelled and pillared perspectives sunlight tumbled through doors and apertures venturesomely drawn. The cramped space was all blond and golden, so that Craine was reminded absurdly of Groocock's office in its brief transfiguration.

But now Weidlé's young man was hovering. 'Reserved,' he murmured. 'For a regular client.'

Craine said nothing, and continued to look at the picture. He had schooled himself not to make kindly gestures in the face of incompetence. And in a place like this a salesman – were they called that? – was incompetent who didn't know Craine.

'Raffaellino del Garbo.'

Now Craine looked at the young man. 'What's that?'

'Of course it came to us from a private collection in which it was known as an Amico di Sandro.'

The young man produced a tight smile as he said this. It seemed designed as a gesture of admittance to some respectable outer circle of connoisseurship in these matters. Craine didn't care for it. 'Raffaellino?' he asked. 'That attribution hasn't lapsed too? I'm sure your client wouldn't care to be back with old *pictor ignotus*.'

'Ah – the *anonimi*.' The young man's smile was fading, but he remained confident. 'No, that's not in question. Quite a secure attribution. Raffaellino.'

'Really? But you know Vasari's life of Chimenti Camicia?'

'Yes, indeed.' Making an emergency effort, the young man put depths of quiet asseveration into this.

'Then what about Berto Linaiuolo? He ought to be allowed a modest canvas or panel here and there, poor chap. For instance, the first audience of Esther and Ahasuerus at Chantilly. And why not this? Do you see any relationship to the Haman and Mordecai in the Liechtenstein Collection?'

The young man was looking round for help. But for the decorum that had to be observed in this solemn little place, he would no doubt have hollered for his boss. However, he tried again. 'Most interesting,' he said – and Craine reflected that this was a verbal resource he held in common with Groocock. 'There's a large field for speculation, of course. But at least we can say – can't we? – that this painter is wholeheartedly a quattrocentist. And that's always precious, you'll agree. In fact, that's what makes it command the figure it does.' Having been thus led to touch on the commercial fringe of his priestlike task, the young man promptly made a compensatorily sensitive gesture in front of the Florentine lady's faintly faulty nose. 'Nothing at all that prefigures the late Bolognese. Austerely quattrocentist.'

The young man retreated in good order. His feet glided over Weidlé's expensive carpet. He was dressed in the same sort of clothes as Craine – but, unlike Craine, he wouldn't have been happier in knickerbockers. Not that he wasn't reasonably put together in a small compact way. A kindlier fate might have turned him into quite a decent scrum-half. But here the poor devil was, with his sacred books – Berenson and the rest – got as yet only imperfectly by heart, so that Craine remembered as much of them as he did.

Craine mooned around the gallery. He wasn't pleased with himself – celebrating his coming spell of freedom by playing ball like that with a scrum-half *manqué*. It was depressing that all day the Florentine lady had to look out on, and harken to, such ballyhoo. No wonder she was doubtful about London in the twentieth century; no wonder she was half minded to turn round and move off through these steep perspectives to whatever quiet *salotto* lay beyond. Craine continued to moon. But nothing much happened. Looking at a little Lorenzo Costa – the young man ought to have remembered he was peddling that before disparaging the Bolognese – Craine found himself thinking of Jill's awkward new money and comparing discount houses. Well, that was all right. You mustn't kid yourself about pictures. Sometimes they went to work on you and sometimes they didn't move a muscle. They were inert now. But was this, partly at least, because there was a paucity of good ones on Weidlé's walls?

Yes, the fact was undoubted. Craine found it interesting. London was full of markets that didn't figure in the *Financial Times*, and some of them were fascinating to keep an eye on. Was Weidlé up to one of his games? The old man's resources weren't enormous – he was no Duveen – and Craine knew how he enjoyed putting his shirt on a thing. What had he got in the farther room? Commonly it was eighteenth-century English portraits or landscapes, with Reynolds or Gainsborough or Richard Wilson authentically present to set the tone. You hardly ever saw modern painting there. It was possible to suspect that Weidlé had never met a living painter in twenty years, unless of the trade-fallen kind that had turned to restoring and copying. He was old enough to have fought the whole move to make contemporary works top-of-the-market commodities. Craine respected him for that. It was sound commercial sense. Persuade folk into paying the moon for great pictures by the incomparable Señor Negresco or Monsieur Le Blanc, and presently Negresco and Le Blanc will be asking answering prices for plates and pots splashed with pigment as they trundle past on a conveyor belt. Well, good luck to them. When the market comes unstuck through their industry, let the dealers take the knock if they've been foolish enough to buy heavily. Which, hitherto, Weidlé hadn't been.

Craine peered into the inner room. His first impression was of its having been hit by a bomb or in some other way demolished. There was nothing but piles of rubble. But they were all – of course they were all – on canvas. The rubble was unnaturally chunky and unnaturally harmonious. Somewhere in each canvas there would be a rectangular lump of stone the proportions of which had been conscientiously played upon through the whole design. To a seasoned eye the effect was comical. But Craine couldn't bring himself to laugh. He thought of the obsessed young man – whoever he might be – who had for months and years pursued this luckless vision. But why had Weidlé taken him up and filled a room with him? The answer wasn't far to seek. For the moment Weidlé was conducting his exhibitions on economical principles.

And here he was. All silver hair and elderly *élan*, Fyodor Weidlé emerged from his private room. But whence, more remotely, had he come? He had certainly been at Christ Church. There were people who remembered him there; and he still wore from time to time a tie with the little cardinal's hats used by that modest college to dissimulate the fact that it is a royal foundation. As an undergraduate he had possessed a number of icons which were asserted to be notable; there was a story that his father had been brought from hyperborean regions to form a collection of such things for Prince Schwarzenberg. Beyond this, not much was known about Weidlé. His business astuteness was staggering. Craine had heard informed people speak of him as a man of the strictest personal honour. It didn't, this, strain credulity. As one who could keep a good many balls in the air simultaneously, Weidlé carried conviction at once.

'Aha – so you've come for your lady?' Weidlé shook hands. 'I'm not surprised. An admirable Amico.'

'My dear Weidlé, Amico is no longer allowed to have existed. Your young man says the lady's a Raffaellino.'

'Well, well – what if she is? The important thing, surely, is that she's *amichevole* herself. And she's been looking out for you, Craine. I'll swear I've caught her at it. A wistful turn of the head. Moreover she knows, the sly baggage, that I'll take what you mentioned in your letter.'

'Then that's capital,' Craine wasted no more words on this. 'But what are you doing up here?' He glanced at the walls. 'A new departure, isn't it? And *they* haven't the advantage of turning a wistful eye on a possible buyer.'

As if he hadn't been aware of them before, Weidlé looked from one expanse of pictured rubble to another. 'You blocks,' he murmured, 'you stones, you worse than senseless things.' Then he raised a quick hand, as if deprecating his own irreverence. 'A most promising chap. A little restricted as to range, so far – but I've no doubt that will come. A wonderful sense of mass, wouldn't you say? Look at the one in the centre. Positively weighs you down.'

'Quite so.'

'And one owes something to the younger people. The mighty dead are all very well. But one should give a hand, from time to time, to poor devils who still face the grim business of keeping themselves alive.'

Craine didn't pretend not to be amused. He knew Weidlé quite well enough for that. 'Isn't it a realization that you've come to a little late in your career?'

Weidlé made a charming gesture. 'Of course,' he said, '*you* would guess. Call it a phase of concentration in the policy of my firm. Or say, less grandly, that I'm tipping my eggs into one basket.' He paused, and gave Craine the lightest of glances. But Craine, with his days given to negotiation, knew when he was being weighed up. He was no more than a small collector, and he was puzzled by his sharp sense of being the subject of intense calculation. 'Perhaps,' Weidlé went on, 'you've time for a dish of tea?'

'I'll be delighted.' Weidlé's tea was famous. Sipping it, one supposed it must have travelled by camel even on its last stage down Oxford Street. 'And perhaps somebody could ring up the office for my car? I'm going to drive that picture straight down to Pinn.'

'Then come in.' And Weidlé led the way to his inner room. 'I hope,' he said as he opened the door, 'that Mrs Craine is well?'

Craine made no reply. He had stopped dead on the threshold. As usual in the middle of Weidlé's room there was an easel. It generally carried what was reckoned to be the gem of his collection at the moment. Today, the canvas was a large one: a full-length painting of a man in a blue blouse, sitting on a high stool, with his hands resting idly on his knees. 'Good Lord!' Craine cried. 'It's an Arnander!'

Weidlé was beside him. 'It *is* Arnander,' he said gently. 'And I'd call it one of the great self-portraits of the world.'

Craine's first and inconsequent reflection was about the Amico. It was delightful – but it wasn't really worth lifting from one wall and transporting to another. It's only what they call great art that is, in a strict judgement, art. And here one had it. Of course it was indeed of Arnander as well as by Arnander. He could recognize that now. He had never seen his wife's first husband in the flesh. But photographs and Augustus John's sketch would have given him the truth unassisted. He turned away from the canvas. Just for the moment, he'd had enough of it. 'And anything more?' he asked.

'Actually here in this room?' Weidlé turned and pointed easily to a painting stacked against the wall. 'One you know, this time. The View from Cortona.'

It was certainly the View from Cortona. 'So it was you, was it?' Craine asked. 'And I suppose you got the La Verna too?'

Weidlé nodded. 'That's in the strong-room – with some other things.'

'You were run up to a pretty stiff price for them.'

'Yes, indeed. But it couldn't be helped.'

Craine wondered. If Weidlé had already got hold of more Arnanders than anybody knew, he was quite capable of seeing to it that he had to give almost spectacular prices for two more. And here, certainly, was Weidlé's basket of eggs. It was to be a sort of corner in Arnanders. 'I suppose,' Craine asked, 'there isn't such a large number, all told?'

'Not a considerable œuvre. In fact, I shall hold quite a fair proportion of it. And I'll make his reputation. As really one of the greatest, that's to say. It all depends, you know, on the marketing.'

'Whether a painter is of the greatest?'

'No, no.' And Weidlé waved an impatient hand. 'Simply the speed and finality with which his recognition comes.'

'My wife,' Craine said rather dryly, 'will be interested in what you're up to.'

Weidlé was at once gravely courteous. 'Perhaps she'd care to come in one day – say next week?'

'Thank you – but we're probably going abroad in a few days.' Craine turned back to the painting on the easel. He found that what he rather urgently sought when confronted with it was a handy speculative approach. And one presented itself readily enough. A self-portrait of this stature was surely an illuminating special case amid the general run of artistic productions. It was the limiting instance, as it were, of the successful fusion of inner and outer vision. John Arnander had been gazing into a mirror – or probably a couple of mirrors – and building with everything therein revealed to sight and touch. But at the same time – it was impossible not to be convinced of this – he had been projecting upon his canvas the conclusions of a profound introspection. The result was a triumph. Yet how imperfect as any sort of act of communication must it necessarily be ! The portrait must always and everywhere declare itself as a serious labour of art. But to Craine, to Weidlé, to Jill it must bring experiences of marked diversity – and who could tell what this canvas had been to Arnander himself as he laid his palette by ?

Weidlé was standing beside him again. 'Mrs Craine won't be acquainted with this one ?' he asked.

Craine shook his head. He realized there were things Weidlé wanted to know in the obscure history of the painter he proposed to set among the greatest. That was reasonable enough. But of course anything of the sort was Jill's business. All that he need himself do was to declare that Arnander's story contained nothing out of the way. It wasn't wholly happy. It held for several people some painful bits. Reticence about the recently dead, and about their relations with the living, is the decent and civilized thing. But there wasn't about Arnander, that he knew of, any strong prompting to sealed lips.

The tea came in and Weidlé poured it. 'What seems to me curious,' he said, '– and also rather a shame – is the fact of your wife's possessing so comparatively little herself. People will be surprised. There wasn't, after all, exactly a clamouring market for Arnander's work. And your wife, of course, is known to have been a woman of means.'

'She has the Maremma,' Craine said. 'And not even

this' – he nodded at the self-portrait – 'would incline me to say the Maremma isn't the best of the lot.'

'At least it's the biggest.' Weidlé was urbanely determined to resist any suggestion that the very finest Arnanders were not now his.

'And she has a good many drawings.'

'Ah – now, talking of drawings . . .'

As he said this, Weidlé rose casually. He had spoken casually, too. And Craine – it was again the faculty negotiation had developed in him – knew at once that the crucial corner of some manoeuvre was being turned. Weidlé had slipped from the room. Jill's two husbands, Craine said to himself, are left to improve their acquaintance. He put down his cup and walked over to the easel. The portrait would probably disconcert Tim and Charles. They would be inclined to call the sort of person represented in it a drip. Or would they at once see beyond the fact that here was a pretty poor physical specimen ? Craine didn't know.

But he knew why this picture was neither better nor worse than the Maremma or the La Verna; why it was simply of the same order of art. Brilliantly sensuous, it was yet suprasensuous. Even as it exploited the senses it bypassed them – letting in something that they commonly sieved out. At bottom the thing was visionary. But it wasn't in the least a mere ejaculation, a gasp, an *o altitudo*. It was a work of tremendous craft. Someone had likened the Maremma to late Turner. But that was entirely wrong. What remained the dominant characteristic of Arnander's brief maturity was the immense painterly resource, the range and sureness of technical accomplishment. Even with the flame out, the tap turned off, Arnander would have been one of the perfect painters.

It wasn't to advance such musings, presumably, that old Weidlé had left the room. Craine looked at his watch. He was impatient to jump into his car and drive off to Jill. For the moment – he said to himself with one more glance at the painting – it's an advantage that I have over that immortal thing. I can join Jill.

Weidlé was back. He had half a dozen sheets of drawing-paper in his hand. They were small, and might have been torn from a sketch-book. 'Look at these,' he said, and put them down on his desk.

Craine looked at them, one by one. The implication seemed to be that they were Arnander's work. But they didn't look like that to him. 'I don't make much of them,' he said.

'You've seen nothing of the sort before?'

Craine shook his head. They were exiguous drawings done with a thick black lead. For the most part they seemed to do no more than sketch uncertain arabesques. Here and there, perhaps, they hinted a volume, essayed to define a form. 'You think they're by Arnander?' he asked.

Weidlé nodded. He was looking not at the sketches but intently at Craine. And Craine found this irksome. 'Well, even if they are,' he said, 'I don't see that they're of the slightest interest or value.'

'Value? It's not in question.' Weidlé spoke with a flash of impatience. 'You don't think I go peddling stuff out of people's waste-paper baskets, do you? But interest – that's another matter.'

'How do you know they're Arnander's? What's their provenance?'

Weidlé shrugged his shoulders. 'They haven't any – worth speaking of. They came to me for an opinion, an expertise. Well, I've studied and I've compared. It's my opinion they're by Arnander.'

'I see.' Craine knew that Weidlé, unlike many of his kind, spoke in such matters with authority. He looked again at the sketches. 'But, dash it all,' he burst out, 'they're all wrong!'

Weidlé nodded. 'He didn't go off his head? Something didn't go slowly soft in his brain?'

'Nothing of the sort.'

'It sometimes happens. For instance, it happened with Utrillo.' Weidlé picked up one of the sketches and turned it over and over. 'I'm inquiring about the paper,' he said.

Craine was puzzled. 'What the devil are you after, Weidlé?'

'Nothing I haven't a fair claim to know. But you must snub me, of course, if I'm being tiresome. Would your wife resent my seeking information?'

'You have only to put your questions to her, and you'll get your answer.'

Weidlé accepted this for the ambiguity it was. He shrugged his shoulders; it was a gesture, one fancied, he had deliberately allowed himself to inherit from his father, the henchman of Prince Schwarzenberg. 'I am unforgivable,' he murmured urbanely. 'Will you have more tea?'

Although he wanted to be off, Craine passed his cup. He might as well find out, if he could, just what was in Weidlé's head. 'As you know,' he said, 'John Arnander died in the mid-forties. So we're talking about fairly long-past history. As far as I'm concerned, it's scarcely even that. I never met him. And my wife doesn't talk about him a great deal.'

'She wasn't with him during the last six months, or thereabouts, of his life?'

'No. They were all right in Italy during the earlier part of the war. Various things helped – Jill's possessing American citizenship, knowing the Princess of Piedmont, and so forth. The Italians themselves tended to have a comfortable eighteenth-century slant on what constituted an enemy. But when it appeared that the Germans would probably come down, Arnander insisted on getting her out of the country. He was absolutely right, for things did eventually, as you know, get pretty grim. Jill had her baby, and was already carrying her second child. What happened to him in the succeeding months, I've never heard properly sorted out. But eventually the Fifth Army came up with him, and he was given a job. He's said to have died while trying to save one of the finest bridges in Italy. It was a pretty good end.'

'Decidedly.' Weidlé took a turn about the room. 'Of

course I know how their home was bombed and a lot of his work destroyed. An appalling disaster, that. It's the later period that seems obscure. He got his wife and child away. But what then? Was he in hiding? One supposes it must have come to that. But what about the conditions? Could he paint under them? And, if he could, is there no doubt about his being fit to?'

Craine got to his feet. 'You seem to come back to that. I repeat that there's not the slightest reason to suppose that he was off his rocker, or anything of the sort. If he was physically fit, he may well have kept on painting.'

'They sometimes paint when they're not that.' Weidlé gave this the air of a rather shocking communication. 'You remember "A Second Innings"?'

'No, I don't.'

'It was one of Mark Lambert's last short stories. It's about a painter called Ainger. He isn't represented as of any consequence; he's just a pompous old donkey of an R.A. He'd made his pile – which was what he'd been born to do – long ago; and for years and years he'd painted nothing at all. Then something went wrong with his inside – lungs or liver or lights, we're not told. His relatives packed him off to a clinic. It's a high-class, *Magic Mountain* sort of place, very entertainingly described. Through years of senile idleness Ainger had been a terrible pest – maid-servants couldn't be kept in the house, and so forth – so they were all thoroughly glad to be rid of him. Something over a year later, he died. The family went out to Switzerland or wherever for the funeral. They found a studio absolutely stuffed with masterpieces.'

Craine laughed. 'Really with masterpieces?'

'Good Lord, no. Just with the familiar Ainger stuff, as it had been piously represented for thirty years in all the municipal art galleries of England. The tale ends with a girl, Ainger's grand-daughter, who wants to paint, sitting among all these things helplessly, while the snow falls softly outside.'

'Clearly a very amusing story. That was how his approaching dissolution took its hero – a phrenetic return to professional activity?'

'Just that. Maidservants no longer deflected his energies, and various other distractions were happily out of the way. So he piled up canvases as he never had before. In the story, of course, it's represented as a little more than that – as a sort of fever that was a natural concomitant of the particular morbid process his body was harbouring. I've sometimes thought that Lambert's story may have given a hint to Thomas Mann.'

'A beguiling hypothesis, Weidlé. I hadn't known you were a bit of a literary historian too. And the story's given you a hint as well? It's suggested a fantastic sort of threat to your proposed near-monopoly in Arnanders? What a wary fellow you are!'

'Come, come – I appeal to you, as one merchant to another. For I suppose a banker is a merchant?' Weidlé had his most charming smile.

'Certainly a banker's a merchant.'

'Then you know how it's one's business to have a reasonable care to one's profits. No one, believe me, would rejoice more if a dozen further canvases like *that*' – and Weidlé waved at the self-portrait – 'should be discovered cached somewhere in Italy. But when you get into the present century – which is a thing you know, I don't much do – and are dealing, say, with a painter who died young, or who for some other reason left a very circumscribed body of work, then the sudden popping up of a lot of unsuspected stuff would be thoroughly tricky. Think, for instance, of Christopher Wood. There were certainly several years during which, had anyone come unexpectedly on another score of important paintings – '

Craine nodded impatiently. 'No doubt, no doubt. I don't question your knowledge of your own market. And I can see that this obscure phase at the end of Arnander's life may make you begin to wonder. But if you regard these

drawings as evidence that he went in some way to pot – '
Craine broke off, and stared for a moment at the topmost
of the drawings. 'Drink?'

Weidlé shook his head. 'No, no,' he said. 'Not behind
that line.'

'Well, the enigma's yours.' Craine reached for his hat.
'Did you know I'd picked up a small Van Stry?'

'Of course I knew. I hear all these little things.' Weidlé
instantly acquiesced in the change of subject. 'And you're
hoping it's really a Cuyp, eh? Well, I hope it is, too. Make
up for the Amico's being a Raffaellino.'

Craine nodded and shook hands. 'A protean crowd, the
painters,' he said. 'You never know where you have them.'

CHAPTER FOUR

It was only when Tim's celebration was over, and both boys were in bed, that Craine spoke of his day. 'I've had news,' he said. 'A cable.'

'A cable?' Jill didn't look up, but for a moment her right hand paused over her work. Then she drew the silk softly home. 'I had one too.'

'Mine was from Mungo. One of the old boy's bombshells.'

'Does he want you to go out?' Jill might have been bored, so that he couldn't help catching her eyes and smiling. She hated his flying the Atlantic, and her skill in dissimulation was unimpressive.

'Nothing of that sort. He's handed in his check. He'll be home tomorrow morning, and giving the Chancellor a bit of his mind in the afternoon. And I think we can do one of our Box and Cox turns – he and I.' Craine knocked out his pipe. 'I suppose everything's all right with the children?'

She laughed. 'Of course it is! An almost Edwardian order reigns in your household, Rupert. Nannie is satisfied with Jane, Mrs Moore is satisfied with Nannie, I'm satisfied with Mrs Moore, and I believe you're satisfied with me. Of course none of it may last.'

'None of it?'

Jill tossed aside her embroidery with a subtle luxuriousness that was its own answer. She raised her head so that her features were softly lit by a flicker of firelight from below. They were features so strange that he still through the mounting intimate years felt what he had first felt before her: a fascination having its substantial basis in alarm. Looking at her, a stranger might assign him the position of a man who marries a prima ballerina, a famous executant on an instrument, a poet, a fanatic of some

45

social or political cause: a position interesting, perhaps, yet not likely to comprehend any large element of repose. But it would be no more than a conjecture founded on the way the bones built themselves together in Jill's skull. There was nothing of happy accident in the fact that order reigned at Pinn; nor was that state of affairs likely to be impermanent. Jill's instinct was entirely for the equivalents, here in England, of the life of the South in which she had been bred. Glancing up now at John Arnander's visionary unquiet Maremma which hung over the chimney-piece before them, Craine understood the attraction Arnander had held for her. It had been the polar attraction that the textbooks recommend as the basis of a satisfactory sexual relationship. And no doubt the textbooks were right – as a matter of short-term policy. But perhaps there was something to be said for the old-fashioned persuasion that community of tastes affords the best buy in the long run. It was conceivably the desuetude of this idea that had resulted in long runs being not much the go nowadays.

'Then if everything's all right' – Craine's tranquil marital reflections had led to his stretching out his legs towards the fire – 'let's go to Italy. I don't mean for long. Say a fornight, three weeks.'

'Italy? You haven't had any other cables?'

Something made him draw back his legs, as if it might be necessary to sit up. 'I've had scores of cables. They pour in all day, prophesying woe. But we don't worry about them.'

Jill took up her embroidery again. 'You know I don't mean that. Nothing's put Italy in your head – as a place where we might have private business? Nothing about John?'

He stared at her. 'John? Well. Weidlé's been talking to me about John this afternoon. But my thinking of a get-away for us has nothing to do with that. Weidlé's planning big business with Arnanders. He's got hold of a lot, including the View from Cortona, and the La Verna, and a tremendous self-portrait I'd never seen. And he

46

wanted to know about John's last months. He thinks he may have been painting away through all that chaos, and that somewhere or other there may be treasures it would be nice to get in on.'

'I see. Well, that fits.'

This time Craine did sit up – although covering the action by bending forward to give the fire a jab with the poker. 'Fits with just what ?' he asked.

'It doesn't – really. Only my cable was from Italy too. And it's about what Weidlé's interested in. John's last months.'

'Good Lord!' For some reason that he couldn't distinguish, Craine felt himself at a relaxed tension.

'John did, it seems, continue creative work almost to the last.' Jill paused and carefully selected a fresh silk. 'In collaboration, I think it must have been, with an Italian girl.'

For just a second Craine simply didn't take it in – perhaps because Jill, although she loved faint mockery, hadn't the habit of expressing herself in an oblique or sardonic way. Then he asked, 'Just how does this appear ?'

'There's a boy. Doesn't it seem odd ? Another posthumous child. He must be just a few months younger than Charles.'

It didn't seem at all odd to Craine – or not the mere fact of it. That such information should pop up now, and only now, was another matter. But presumably there would be a speedy explanation. He wanted to ask Jill whether she was surprised. But he didn't. He mustn't go blundering about. Whether or not she was surprised, she was considerably stirred up; he could divine that. And he didn't feel any longer alone with her in the room. He looked up at the Maremma – there wasn't a single figure in it, but it was in essence a sombre statement about the human condition – and he felt Arnander walk. They talked about him seldom – it had never occurred to him that it was perhaps too seldom – which was the reason, no doubt, of Arnander's retaining a certain power of joining in when they did. And now Craine felt that he must say something. 'It's not anything staggeringly out of the way,' he tried. 'Not as things go. Not, certainly, as they were going in Italy then.'

'Oh, quite. And I'd quit, after all.' Jill spoke dispassionately – so that he was surprised when she added, although in the same dispassionate tone, 'Of course he was a most unreliable – a quite thoroughly unsatisfactory – person.'

She had never said anything like this about Arnander before, and for a moment he was disconcerted that it came from her now without the slightest emphasis. She might have been voicing a piece of knowledge they already held in common : that the vicar's wife was having a great struggle, or that it had been a wonderful March day.

This was his mind, for a moment; then, as so often, he convicted himself of obtuseness. He did, after all, know a good deal about Arnander – and even about Jill's life with Arnander – that had never come to him in set words. It was Jill's taking this for granted – taking for granted the play of implication, the depth and volume of silent communication between them – that informed her manner of speaking now. He lay back in his chair, once more at ease. 'Artists,' he said, 'are often disconcertingly egoistic.'

She laughed – and her amusement didn't astonish him. It was a joke between them : his disposition when facing tricky ground to find a jumping-off place on some tump of incontrovertible platitude, of solid generality. But now she raised her fine head and gazed seriously into the fire. 'Simple egoism wouldn't have made John what I've called him – unreliable and unsatisfactory. Or not both. For with a simple egoist, I suppose, you do at least know just where you are – which is nowhere, in a last analysis. He's insulated, entirely. But John was an egoist who was very delicately aware of everything around him – and not merely of things that touched him. He knew about the play of your feelings even when they had no concern with him, or he with them. He had antennae, you might say, that he just couldn't command to let be. It must have been frightfully wearing, poor chap.'

'It certainly must.' Craine realized with dismay that discomfort was attending this conversation. He would have supposed that, when things were all right, your wife's late husband would be no more awkward a topic than, say, the children she had borne him. But it wasn't so. You found yourself listening for you didn't know what and indulging responses coming you didn't know whence. Jill's 'poor chap' was lingering on his ear now. It sounded considered. And he found himself resenting what had the air of a correction in her speech – as if she had been saying that there had been more to Arnander than he was allowing; that Arnander had been rather a special sort of person, whose quality a solid banker might entirely miss.

Craine's thought had got as far as this when – so to speak – he stopped and stared at himself. He was strict with his own mind. He didn't, for instance, license a large disparity between thought and speech, between fantasy and what was conceivable and decent in act. And always, for him, there was a peculiar horror – a terror, almost – in all that ambivalence of the emotions which the age had rediscovered with such an air. It wasn't so much the large operation of the thing that could shock him. It was rather the little domestic exemplifications. Love and hate revolving on their monstrous axis was one thing. If caught in that awful revolution there would be some sort of dignity at which one might have a chance of clutching. But when it came to small irrational jealousies, to the sense of unappreciated merit, to sulking, as it were, over the breakfast bacon; then, certainly, one's spiritual state was desperate.

He had supposed long ago that he was through with all danger of a touchy reaction to any of the residual consequences of his wife's having formerly been married to a genius. But now, for a moment at least, he felt not sure of it. At least his mind had gone off at a useless tangent when it ought to have been considering a specific situation, and how that situation was best to be handled in Jill's interest.

Essentially it didn't seem to be – this of Arnander's having had an illegitimate child in Italy long ago – Jill's business at all. But the circumstances were still obscure to him, and he was wasting time until he got hold of them. 'How has this turned up?' he asked. 'Just as information, or as an appeal for help, or what? Have we to act?'

She stretched out her hands to the flame between them, and gave him a smile of such confidence that he knew she was going to balance up by saying something mocking. 'Are you stepping into the breach, Rupert,' she asked, 'and saying "This had better be left to me"?'

'That's possible. It depends on the facts.'

'They're not abundant, as yet. It's different, I suppose, with bankers. But among common mortals, cables are apt to be on the skimpy side.'

'No doubt.' He was smiling back at her – and at the same time he was conscious that this again wasn't quite her style. Whatever the form in which her news had come to her, its impact had, for the moment at least, stirred, opened, quickened he didn't know what. And how much – he always came back to it – he didn't know! For instance, with what force, and to what effect, would it strike her that the child whose existence had just been revealed was not merely the son of the dead Arnander but the half-brother of the living Tim and Charles?

He watched her rise and walk across the room to her writing table.

PLEASE COME AND TAKE SHARE ARRANGING FUTURE LIVING NINO ARNANDER ELEVEN YEARS HE IS NOW IN MY CHARGE BUT NO LONGER POSSIBLE

MARIA FORNI

Craine read the cable and handed it back to Jill at once. He mustn't seem to be baldly taking command of things. 'Who is this Maria Forni?' he asked. 'Is she someone you know?'

'I used to know her. She must be an old woman now.'

'Where does she live? There's no address.'

'Look at the top. The cable comes from Castelarbia. I think that must mean that her husband is still alive. But quite long ago he was an invalid, and she managed the place.'

'You mean they're landed folk – aristocracy?'

'He's the Marchese Forni – and what you might call an impoverished landowner.'

'I see.' Craine felt impatience and anger unwisely rising in him. 'Or rather I don't. That sort of Italian isn't commonly impoverished nowadays. He's right back on top again – and about the smartest tax-dodger in the world.'

'I don't think these people are like that.' Jill was looking at him intently, as if trying to decide what prompted the harshness of his tone. 'I've heard they're in a far from flourishing way.'

'Then they're rapacious.' He snapped this out. 'Rapacity is the absolute keynote of an impoverished aristocracy.' He barely paused. 'Do I understand that this is a woman who made your acquaintance years ago, and that nevertheless this cable is a bolt from the blue?'

Jill nodded. 'Just that.'

'Then its motive is mercenary, and its form is an outrage. If this little Nino has waited more than ten years, he could clearly wait another week. The woman could have written, with proper consideration and proper explanations. As it is, she's patently trying to bounce you into scurrying off to Italy and signing a large cheque. She probably thinks of Master Nino as a scandal you'll pay to have suppressed.'

Jill was silent for a moment. 'It's possible,' she said gently, 'that you're being unjust.'

'That's true.' Craine found that he had got to his feet – and now he abruptly sat down again. He was shocked that his conviction of being in the presence of a calculated assault on his wife had betrayed him into harsh speaking. Whatever was the motive of Marchesa Forni, she had disclosed the existence of something to the handling of which there must go quite as much of gentleness as of strength.

'Look,' he went on, 'we can start – can't we ? – from the quite certain ground that we *don't* think in terms of a scandal – that if that's what's in this old lady's hopeful mind, she's entirely barking up a wrong tree ?'

Unexpectedly, Jill laughed – so that, absolutely, there wasn't a shadow between them. 'Darling,' she said, 'you should have been Archimedes – or was it Euclid ? With your passion, I mean, for starting from self-evident truth. Of course Nino's not to be kept dark. Tim and Charles would take him in their stride tomorrow.'

'And if it's best to bring him home, I'll address him like the chap in the advertisements.'

' "Let me be your father" ?' Jill laughed again. 'You'll have to say it in Italian, Rupert. Let me see. I think you'd have to say *padre adottivo*. But I shall be something different.' Suddenly she was thoughtful. '*Matrigna?* But of course not. Nothing at all.'

'We won't stumble over words. Now, let me see.' Craine was on his feet again, and this time pacing the room. 'We know nothing about the mother, and she may have been a fool. Even so, it's fifty-fifty that the boy has brains. And he's younger than Charles. He can have decent English in under two years, and pass Common Entrance as well. And I'd be prepared to bet that Winchester – ' He broke off – aware, without dismay, that Jill was once more amused. 'That's all nonsense ?' he asked.

She came up to him and kissed him. 'Probably. But at least it's positive, and confident, and . . . and a line. Whereas I'm bewildered – really.' She looked at him candidly. 'I don't know what this strange news is telling me. And, alone, I don't think I'd know what practical steps to take.' She paused. 'But you were talking about an Italian holiday. That means you'll have time to go with me ?'

He nodded. 'We can fly out any day. But when we get there, will you let me have first go ?'

'At seeing the boy ?'

'At seeing the whole set-up. I still think this old woman has behaved in an uncommonly odd way. It may be the impulsive Latin temperament, no doubt. And instant suspicion is, of course, as ignoble as you please – '

'But I don't please. I'll be absolutely as suspicious myself as you care to direct. It's up to the Marchesa to prove that she's not a monster. So there.'

He made a comical face at her, feeling that she was wonderful. But he held to his point. 'And I'll do a reconnaissance?'

'Agreed.'

CHAPTER FIVE

FOUR days later Craine motored out alone from Arezzo. The car was powerful; its chauffeur had all an Italian's pride in driving fast and well; nevertheless it seemed a long run to Castelarbia. Craine had forgotten – if he had ever known – that this part of Tuscany held such fastnesses, and eventually he felt that they would certainly get lost. But the chauffeur had no doubts – and finally, when a wide valley opened before them, broke into speech. He was, it seemed, a local man; it was for this reason that he had been assigned to the trip. The volume of the *torrente* – later in the year, indeed, it would shrink to no more than a muddy trickle among stones – was something by which his passenger must necessarily be impressed. The olives were admitted to be the finest in the province; even their kernels gave you twice as hot a fire as any gathered in Val d'Arno or Casentino; and never in all Italy had there been such alfalfa as he had used to harvest when a boy !

Craine, although he had distracting thoughts, listened with pleasure to as much of the vivid Tuscan as he understood. It was a perfect day, with the sky one clear vault of blue, and he found it hard to believe that, only a few weeks ago, this had been a bare and bitter land, whipped by the *tramontana*. From late spring to early autumn spans the Englishman's Italy; he can't believe his eyes when he sees a snow-plough; confronted by a whole olive grove that the frost has stricken, he forgets his Virgil and dimly supposes a forest fire.

'*Cinquantuno.*'

'*Come?*' Craine's mind had slipped away.

'*Cinquantuno poderi, signore.*'

Craine looked about him. However good the alfalfa was or had been, these were miserable little farms. But by owning fifty-one of them you could presumably do quite well.

54

'*Ecco la fattoria.*' The chauffeur pointed ahead. '*Molto, molto grande.*'

They were certainly substantial, the barns and granaries into which Marchesa Forni garnered her due proportion of what the estate produced. It wouldn't do in Berkshire, Craine reflected, and it mightn't get you far with Gloucestershire Old Spots. But as a system of land tenure it was older than anything known in England. So there must be sense – good business and good human sense – in it. He'd like to learn about it. Only he wasn't here on any inquiry of that sort. He was concerned with the future of a small boy. And very much more – he told himself – with the boy's future than with his past. There must of course be explanations. Without a satisfactory modicum of these, the possibility of a mere deception couldn't be ruled out. But after that the thing became a matter of plans, of foresight. What would be the best future for this lad, who had been brought up, with a status as yet unrevealed, in the heart of Italy? Perhaps he lived with one of the gardeners, or perhaps he considered himself as virtually a Forni. The Marchesa's cable hadn't given much clue. But that sort of thing didn't greatly matter. What was crucial was the nature and strength of the affections involved. The Marchesa might be devoted to Nino Arnander, and her message have been wrung from her by some powerful start of conscience. Or she might be an indifferent woman, briskly addressing herself to one of a number of dispositions required by some change of circumstances. Craine realized that he didn't commonly go into a piece of business equipped with so little in the way of bearings. Even his chauffeur, having been born in the valley, probably knew more than he did. And this was a good reason for questioning him now – rather late in the day, since the walls of the villa could already be glimpsed behind a screen of ilex.

The Marchese Guido Forni had been an old man, and now he was dead. The chauffeur announced this with confidence. It was known that the Marchesa was going away, but whether the new owner would live on his estate was quite uncertain. Very likely not. Very likely all would be in the hands of the *fattore*. The new Marchese – he was a young man – might well live in Rome. Most people of that sort did, and extraordinary things appeared about them in the picture papers. Did he know anything about the late Marchese? Certainly he did. Everybody did. The old man had always been strange, and during his last few years had been mad. *Pazzo*. The old lady had controlled everything. She was a woman of strong mind, who had possessed her own ideas about Castelarbia. So probably there would be great changes there now.

Craine listened to all this – both to the facts and to the tone in which they were delivered – with interest. He liked, as he went about, to feel the pulse of the Continent. The chauffeur, a man in early middle age, had broken free from the life of this valley. His companions must be artisans – Communists, for the most part – and his job was driving round Italy the sort of wealthy foreigners who put up in the biggest hotels. What did he think about the immemorial peasant world from which he had emerged, and which, today, he was revisiting? He had spoken with pride about the fertility of the soil, but was that simply a sentimental turn, whether for his own or Craine's benefit? Questions like this were of high general interest. . . . Once more Craine had to remind himself that it was a different kind of concern he had on hand.

But now the man was continuing to be communicative. Castelarbia was impossibly remote. Even the coming of the Vespas and the Lambrettas had scarcely altered that. Twelve kilometres from even a tolerable *strada provinciale*! In winter one came to it over ice, in spring through mud, in summer and autumn amid clouds of disagreeable dust. Conditions of that sort were intolerable. They lacked all modernity. If one had a good car, it was folly to live other than on the Via Emilia or the Via Aurelia. Or in the north there were the *autostrade*. He had a friend who, having the happiness to drive a new Alfa-Romeo, had made a quite remarkable time from Torino to Brescia only the week before.

Craine's interest in the chauffeur lapsed. He was suddenly eager, as he had not been before, to see the child who was to be – if only loosely speaking – his stepson. Had he been away to school ? That, at eleven, would not be in the Italian manner. The villa and its surrounding life – the stables, the oil-presses, the various offices of a small, self-contained community – would constitute his present world. And now that was going to break up on him. Whatever his condition, it must have seemed secure and unchanging. For the chauffeur was clearly right. The age of the motor-scooter had brought little of modernity to Castelarbia as yet. One would suspect here a manner of living almost as antique as the façade now presenting itself beyond a formal garden and a series of terraces – a façade of the *cinquecento*, not in very notable repair. Or there would be a mix-up of old and new. A Marchese Forni filled in, it might be, as many Government forms as any harassed landed proprietor in England. But in all sorts of ways he could hold up the clock as he pleased. He could be eccentric as an English aristocrat in the eighteenth century could be eccentric. Possibly the late Marchese had been *pazzo* after that fashion.

The car stopped and Craine got out. On his left there was the gloom of a massive loggia, and on his right sunshine on the long terrace. And suddenly his heart gave an unexpected jump. He had seen a child. But a moment later he realized that it was a girl – a peasant girl who, in a fashion entirely Italian and unaccountable, was driving a young pig down this august vista, where urns and statues cast alternate shadows on the flags, and beyond which, across the valley, one saw a hillside scored and scratched in an anxious cultivation that presently lost itself in the chestnut forest softly closing the horizon.

Craine turned towards the house. An old manservant, white-gloved and with a silver chain round his neck, already stood prepared to admit him. He took a last glance down the terrace. Through some trick of perspective, or of the light, the child and her pig appeared to have made no progress since he first glimpsed them. And he felt an obscure and absurd alarm. It was as if time really could stand still here – could arrest itself, and then spring.

The family might be in a poor way financially, but at least they hadn't been reduced to eating their stuffs and furnishings. If they had parted with anything to the great predatory collectors at the beginning of the century, it had not been in a big way as far as square or cubic feet were concerned. He was to be received, it seemed, in some remote apartment. But as he was led through the long series of rooms – restlessly intercommunicating in the ancient fashion – he hadn't the sense of anything missing. Massive or finely elegant, dull or gleaming, in marble, bronze, pigment, leather, wood, the superimpositions of centuries cluttered the cold floors and climbed the walls to mingle with obscurely sprawled mythologies on the ceilings. Basically it was domestic and familiar and muddled, as if many generations ago people had here ceased condescending to any planned effect. In this it actually had its resemblance to Pinn, so that even if he had never been in such places before he wouldn't have felt largely out of it. But he smiled to himself – treading unobserved behind the old servant – as he thought of the Amico di Sandro, recently acquired from Weidlé after so much careful thought. Here such things lurked dimly in a shadow, unvisited except by the perfunctory duster. Or so it was easy to feel.

But it was in a different sort of room that the Marchesa Forni awaited him, an office entirely bleak and functional, in which Groocock himself would have found little out of the way except perhaps the huge German stove. Although the day was so mild the Marchesa had been sitting close by this, and Craine saw at once, as she rose and held herself rigidly erect, that she was indeed a very old woman. Gaunt but not shrunken – so that one guessed her to come of some race that did not run to fleshy abundance in its prime – she had a face so pale and lips so drained of colour that there was violent and painful contrast in a single broken vein streaking her temple. Her eyes were black and piercing, yet heavy-lidded with her years; her clothing was an unrelieved black; her only ornament was an ebony cross. She might have walked straight on a stage, Craine thought, and there enjoyed perfect acceptance as a figure of conventional gloom, with a role confined to the harbouring of some secret highly discreditable to the illustrious name she bore. But with associations of this sort the office with its commonplace desk and filing cabinets didn't at all cohere; the old lady would have her more appropriate *décor* elsewhere in the villa. The mouldering accoutrements of *condottieri*, St Laurence on a canvas all keyed up to the brisk fire on which he was roasting, devotional objects giving robust prominence to scourges and nails; it would be with these that any active dramatic instinct would fit her up. But at the moment she was standing beside a typewriter, and the only picture in evidence was a large diagram showing how to dismember an ox. It didn't escape Craine that this choice of meeting-ground was by way of defining what the Marchesa conceived to be the nature of their relationship. He therefore opened the exchanges with a bow the formality of which would have been distinctly comical across the Channel.

She barely acknowledged it. For a moment he even thought she proposed to conduct their interview standing. But she slightly moved a hand – it was a hand to paint or draw, he noticed, despite its chalk-stones and its tremor – and pointed to a chair. Then she sat down and spoke, rapidly, confidently, and in an English so bad as to be virtually unintelligible.

For a moment the effect was merely disconcerting – for it didn't go with the dignity the old lady was evidently concerned to consult. But it also seemed clear that in this medium communication was just not going to be achieved – or not more of it than was represented by Craine's distinct

59

sense that he was being disapproved of. He was puzzled to know why, for it could hardly be because he didn't display, in the manner of persons attending conferences or assemblies, some species of pedigree dangling from a lapel. Even the most antique Continental grandees hardly now went in for that sort of exclusiveness – or not in regard to presentable elderly Englishmen. But however that might be, it was assured that no progress was to be made this way. So Craine interrupted, in his careful Italian, with a plea that he might be allowed to practise himself in a language he greatly loved. The Marchesa acquiesced in this with perhaps greater relief than she showed, and went on to express – in Italian and with an effect more icy than Craine would have supposed readily compassable in that language – the hope that Mrs Craine was not unwell. For it had certainly been Mrs Craine whom she had invited to honour her with a call.

Craine replied – on his part as briskly as he could bring out the words – that his wife was happily in the best of health, and at that moment no farther off than Arezzo. He had judged, however, that, the business in hand being what it was, he had better in the first place come over himself. Perhaps he had been wrong in insisting on this. But a certain suddenness in the Marchesa's summons – not to speak of a sparing quality – had persuaded him that the first approach had better be made by one thoroughly conversant with the conduct of affairs. *Eccomi qui!*

This was perhaps slightly heavy – it wasn't the less so for striving to close on his notion of a colloquial note – and the Marchesa received it in silence. Then, abruptly, she asked a question. 'Mr Craine, have you ever been a faithful son of the Church ?'

'No, Marchesa, I have not.' Craine was to reflect afterwards that he had missed something in the implication of this question. At the moment it came to him simply as a very obvious light on the way the old lady's mind was working. 'I was brought up as a Protestant. That, you know, in England, is the common thing.'

'No doubt.'

'And I attend – say, I have the habit of attending, certain of the services of the Church of England. But to a serious inquiry like yours, I must reply that I'm unable to make any formal religious profession.'

'Quite so. It is what I would have expected.' The Marchesa gave a sombre nod, which Craine found himself not taking very well. Perhaps unreasonably, he was annoyed that she should suppose there was a presumption that an Englishman of his sort would be agnostic. 'And Mrs Craine ?' she asked.

'I'd say her position may fairly be called much the same.'

'And may I ask, Mr Craine, what, in these circumstances, is to be the fate of your children ?'

'Certainly. It's a fair enough question, in view of what we have to discuss.'

The Marchesa looked at him stonily. She might have made nothing of this. 'Yes ?' she said.

'They will go to church, and so on. Roughly speaking, they will be brought up to attach a good deal of weight to the simple fact that people have been doing just that for quite long time. Later, they will have to decide for themselves, find their own feet.'

The Marchesa was silent. Her mind might have been wandering. Certainly she didn't give the impression of much taking in what he had said. Perhaps, he thought, he had been a little too ambitious in the way of Italian idiom. And now she stirred on her chair. The small movement was noticeable, because she had the art of sitting quite still. She might be said – if she wasn't so stiff already – to be squaring her shoulders. And he had a sudden, almost alarmed, impression of immense fatigue.

'Mrs Craine,' she said, 'is doubtless the last person to whom I ought to appeal.'

'Dear me, no. I see no reason to say that.' Craine was surprised at what he interpreted as evidence of extreme consideration in one whom he had been regarding as thoroughly hard. 'My wife is most anxious to do what she can. And so am I. There's nothing, surely, that can't fairly readily be sorted out.'

He was conscious that he spoke with what might appear a rather easy confidence. And perhaps it was too much the confidence of money. Tutors, prep. schools, a word here or there where he carried weight, Groocock, trusts, a ready entry to half a dozen professions; all that side of the thing belonged to a world he commanded. Perhaps he was rather grossly putting it in the forefront, while the old lady was facing deeper – or at least more personal – issues, where difficulties weren't so effortlessly overcome. He thought he had better take up at once what she had begun with, and explain that the child would of course be brought up as a Roman Catholic if his young mind was already inclined that way. 'For instance,' he went on, 'the religious issue. There's certainly nothing we can't manage there.'

Again it wasn't perhaps a felicitous manner of speech, but he was downright astounded when the Marchesa rose as if she had been stung and walked the length of the room. When she turned, there were small spots of colour on the dead pallor of her cheeks. 'I am distracted,' she said.

Distratto. She was only apologizing for absence of mind. But in fact she did give the appearance of something like desperation. And she was looking at him as if he were a monster. He could think of nothing better to do than produce a sympathetic murmur. It's effect wasn't happy. Conceivably from a monster it was a disconcerting move.

The Marchesa made a gesture round the bleak room. 'My nephew inherits. I retire to Florence. The house there is large. But there are my late husband's sisters, and other members of his family. There is thus a problem – a practical problem. It has seemed to me proper that Mrs Craine and yourself, living as you do, should take some part in solving it.'

'My dear Marchesa, it is a point on which we perfectly

agree.' He had a vision of a small forlorn private Hampton Court, standing secluded and decayed on a slope below Fiesole, and cut up into apartments for an army of aged Forni ladies. Certainly it would constitute a problem where a small boy was concerned. 'We are absolutely,' he went on, 'the natural people to take over. There can be no doubt of that.'

She was standing in front of him, so that rather awkwardly he had to rise. She made one of her rare movements, placing a hand on her ebony cross. The gesture didn't register with him as idle. 'You are to understand,' she said, 'that this act of – of charity and asylum was the Marchese's. There were difficulties, legal difficulties, which he had to exercise his influence to overcome. It was the influence, you must know, not of his personality – for he was too much of an eccentric to possess that – but of his rank and name. I acquiesced in it. I acquiesced in it, once certain assurances, the nature of which you may readily guess, had been given me. I have never been troubled by the legal aspect of our conduct. There have been a good many centuries during which my own family, equally with my husband's, have not always taken kings and princes and policemen very seriously.'

'I wouldn't doubt that for a moment.' Craine, who was rather startled by this sudden gleam of grim humour, spoke with unforced conviction. Colloquially, he would have expressed his feelings by saying that the Marchesa now struck him as a thoroughly spine-chilling old girl. At the same time he had a sense that she was really making unnecessarily heavy weather of it all. And perhaps there was a way of dropping to a less dramatic tone. 'But what about Nino himself?' he asked. 'I'd say he deserves consulting. Has he any notions on what should be done with him?'

There was a moment's silence – or near silence, since the Marchesa was distinctly to be heard in it as taking a deep breath. 'Nino,' she said, 'doesn't say much. In fact he doesn't often say anything.'

'I see.' This was in fact on Craine's part a doubtful claim.

Anything he saw was by way of distressing conjecture, and proceeded more from the Marchesa's tone than from her words. He had suddenly glimpsed the possibility that the child was in some way not normal. It seemed, as he turned it over rapidly in his mind, only too likely, for it would explain the old lady's overwrought manner of dealing with her problem. There would be something a little stiff, after all, in confronting Jill with the fact that her first husband had fathered, say, an idiot boy. But at least Craine wasn't disposed to linger in a doubt like this. 'Hadn't I better meet him?' he asked briskly. 'After all, as far as I'm concerned, we're discussing an unknown quantity till then.'

The Marchesa bowed – at the same time looking at him with an intensification of the sort of regard by which he had already been a good deal perplexed. It was as if he were something preserved in a bottle. Then she turned and, with a motion to follow her, left the room.

They climbed. They climbed – as it seemed to him – in a way the old lady oughtn't to venture on. Driving up to the villa, he hadn't been struck by it as notably lofty. But this, he now realized, was because it was on a large scale throughout. Taken on the flat, it would certainly be a place to get thoroughly lost in; you could have whole suites, rather than mere cupboards, for your family skeletons. Perpendicularly, it just couldn't be negotiated without a prodigal expenditure of breath. First they climbed a staircase that was broad and imposing – and moreover thickly carpeted in a fashion suggesting that some late-nineteenth-century Forni had been disposed to unworthy concessions to bourgeois spirit of his era. Up this, nevertheless, they moved in single file, for it was somehow unmistakably the Marchesa's sense that he should keep a tread or two behind. And presently there was no alternative. The place, so to speak, got into its stride. The staircase took a slant, or twist, into the medieval mode, and spiralled upwards through solid masonry. Every full turn there was a narrow window, through which Craine glimpsed a landscape which, thus viewed, appeared to lie under an intolerable blaze of light. He hadn't anywhere earlier noticed in it — it occurred to him — that sort of ruined fortification which often, near a great Italian house, represents the original *castelletto* in which the family began. Perhaps the Forni had adopted another plan, and simply surrounded an ancient structure of the sort with what struck them as adequate in the way of Renaissance expansiveness.

It was at least clear that the Marchesa had conducted him to the oldest part of the place, and that the young Nino was accommodated in what might fairly be called an aerie. Perhaps it was assured that he had a sound heart, and desired that he should develop his leg muscles and his lungs. Otherwise, it seemed to be rather an out-of-the-way — and even a slightly grim — place in which to keep a small boy. At Pinn, it was true, Tim and Charles lurked under the stone slabs of the roof. But their quarters couldn't be called remote; when their trains were going, or they had a row, you could hear them all over the house.

The Marchesa had stopped at last. She opened a door and made, without looking at him, one of her small commanding motions. He obeyed, and walked through the door before her.

He was in a turret chamber. It was circular, with a conical roof into which a large skylight had been inset; there was a stove opposite the door; and midway between these, on either side, a modern window. It was a pleasant room, comfortably if sparely furnished in an undistinguished modern way. Apart from its basic shape, there was nothing striking about it except its single occupant.

Near one of the windows a man sat at a bench, weaving a basket. For a moment, after the door opened, he had continued his work, as if there was some small manipulation he wished to complete. Then he turned to face his visitors, and as he did so his hands fell idly on his knees.

Craine took a long look, and realized that this was John Arnander. He took another look, and saw that Arnander was blind.

CHAPTER SIX

IT was afterwards Craine's impression that, during the first moments of facing his strange disaster, mere intelligence had made all the running. Marchesa Forni's cable repeated itself in his head, and he realized the grotesque misconception that her wretched English had started. It was not a child's age that she had set down, for there was no child. It was the length of a man's sojourn in her house. And Nino was good enough Italian for any John – the more so if the person named was of the standing of some rather humble domestic familiar. Perhaps with a very good reason for having himself taken for dead, Arnander had presented himself to the late eccentric Marchese, and had been received – they were the old lady's words – as an act of charity and asylum. This might be wrong in detail, but it clearly gave the outline of the present formidable situation.

And Craine realized too – with a sharpness that would have penetrated to something funny in it, had not the whole revelation been so little that – the extravagant cross-purposes at which the Marchesa and he had lately been talking. He had himself come to Castelarbia, it must appear to her, prepared to do something about the husband of the woman with whom he lived – and he had spoken blandly of sorting matters out. He had even airily told this oppressively Catholic lady that in regard to religious issues there was nothing that couldn't be managed. It was true that the Marchesa's own conduct rose up before him as being – at least in default of much explanation – absolutely monstrous. But he himself, by jumping to conclusions, had accepted the part of a fool. He disliked appearing a fool, and his mind took a second's breathing space to acknowledge this before addressing itself to the substance of his and Jill's – and John Arnander's – plight.

For Arnander too had his plight, his disaster, his claim.

This, objectively regarded, was obvious. But – again when he came to look back on those first definitive moments – Craine was to be surprised at the absoluteness with which the fact established itself in his own mind. It was true that Arnander, unless he were not blind merely but demented as well, had everything to answer for. His conduct, when probed, would almost certainly illustrate Jill's assertion that he was a thoroughly unsatisfactory person. Nevertheless he was John Arnander, with that one of his senses gone in which all his riches had consisted; was John Arnander, forgotten, weaving baskets in an attic in a back-of-beyond of Tuscany.

It was all in Craine's head as he stood in his moment of revelation, as yet hardly advanced into the room. And – although so much was already in fact decided for him – he believed for a further moment that he simply didn't know what to do. He might have been a child on the brink of a party, wondering. And then he walked forward. 'I suppose even Englishmen sometime shake hands,' he said.

Arnander didn't speak. His right hand, idle on his knee, seemed inert and dead. Craine found himself watching it with intense anxiety. And then the hand stirred.

Perhaps Arnander hadn't a notion of who had been brought into the room. Nevertheless Craine had a small, secure sense of triumph, mingled with desolation, as their hands touched.

But it was virtually as far as they got. The man existed, it seemed to Craine, in some deeply introverted state, and one couldn't tell whether it reconciled itself with sanity. He wasn't hostile. Once or twice he smiled. And the smile was transforming, as it must always have been. It even lighted up his eyes. And they were eyes which – strangely – were already striking; were the only striking aspect of his features. His blindness seemed to be one of the disconcerting sorts that scarcely appear. And now when he smiled his eyes were beautiful, and all his features redeemed themselves momentarily from meagreness and meanness. In repose he gave the impression of one who has prematurely aged and shrunk. Yet even if he hadn't a presence he had – all the time – an identity. He was the man whose self-portrait, body and soul, Craine had seen in Weidlé's room only a few days before.

It didn't seem an occasion for evasive chat, or yet quite for an orderly entry upon the situation in its aspect as a problem to be solved. As if he were making a customary periodical report, Craine tried telling Arnander about his sons. And the man knew he *had* sons. That much became clear. But it emerged only from muttered responses to what, on the subject, Craine could cast into the form of questions. And the mutterings, he felt, were the product not of curiosity but of courtesy. Courtesy lingered – a sort of forlorn unreliable handle – in Arnander: partly the native courtesy of a man who owns somewhere some very large domain, partly the wary courtesy of a man who has picked up manners rather late. It wasn't, Craine felt, worth twopence, either way. And there was something disagreeable in trying, so to speak, to sell Tim and Charles to their father. They were a damned sight too good to need selling. . . . Craine was surprised when, just for a moment, this feeling in himself was shot through by another. It happened – again just for a moment – that he seemed to catch Arnander's interest with something he recounted of Charles: the boy's absorbed contemplation of clouds. And instantly Craine distinguished in himself something which, although sharp enough, he had to grope to identify. When he did so, the thing didn't look pretty, for it was jealousy. He accepted it, soberly, as a first small mark set on an uncharted future.

And presently it had to be over – this interview with a husk of genius. It had to be over without what, from Arnander, could fairly be called intelligible speech. His mind had simply drifted away – as his hands had strayed back to his basket – and the Marchesa had made a sign that Craine should follow her from the room. He obeyed, but not before he had gained one further, and almost shockingly poignant, impression. Directly under the skylight, so that he had to pass it as he moved to the door, there was a table with a litter of papers. And these were scrawled over with arabesques in thick black lead. He wondered whether the medium meant that Arnander could still just dimly see – or whether he continued in total blindness an exercise formerly remaining feasible at an earlier stage of whatever disease his eyes had suffered. Anyway, it was some of these papers – call them drawings or documents – that had, heaven knew how, come Fyodor Weidlé's way. And Craine understood why Weidlé had murmured something about having the paper examined. It had appeared to his skilled eye not as old as it ought to be. There was glimmering in Weidlé's mind the notion that he had come into the possession of – so to speak – posthumous drawings. It was a minor – it didn't seem to Craine at all an important – queerness in the situation.

They descended from the turret in silence. But at the head of the broader staircase the Marchesa paused. 'If you will be so kind,' she said; and he realized that she proposed to take his arm. Certainly she looked done up. But he understood that he was favoured, that his monstrosity had in some way been mitigated for her as a consequence of the interview just concluded. And he found that he wasn't led back to the office, in which, no doubt, she was accustomed to discharge the business of the *fattore* and the tenants. They went into a small high room of more hospitable suggestion, hung with faded silk and containing a little French furniture hinting the possibility of at least moderate relaxation. There was a modern oil portrait which Craine for a moment supposed to be that of the late crazed Marchese, but which he then saw to be of the present head of House of Savoy; on a table in the window there was a signed photograph of the Pope; opposite this a half-open door gave a glimpse of an oratory. He had been abruptly promoted to the most private part of the house.

The Marchesa made the familiar small motion with her hand and sat down. 'I am afraid,' she said 'that I have received you under the influence of a mistaken impression.

I am very much afraid that this has been a shock to you; that your – your wife told you nothing, until my cable made it necessary to do so.' She paused and looked full at Craine. He was never to know what his expression had been in that moment. But whatever it was, it brought her instant comprehension. 'No,' she went on quietly. 'That too is wrong. Your wife has not known either. This is terrible.'

He said nothing for a moment. He hadn't sat down, and now he walked to the window and looked out over the terrace to the distant chestnut woods. The old lady might judge this an improper lack of formality, but it was his instinct to try for something easy between them. Even with people rather remote from her, and whose habits and assumptions could do no more than glimmer on her horizon, she must be called quick on the uptake. 'Jill – my wife – certainly didn't know,' he said as he turned back to face her. 'And the discovery had been, for me, more abrupt even than you now realize. It was kind of you to cable in English, but it set us oddly on the wrong track. When I entered that room a few minutes ago, Marchesa, I didn't expect to find a man. I expected to find a small boy. And our first conversation – which seemed so strange to you – was conducted by me on that false assumption.'

What the Marchesa would have found by way of reply to this never appeared, for the door opened to admit a small procession of servants. The first was carrying a silver lamp with a flickering yellow flame, and it was an index of Craine's disturbed condition that for a second he supposed that something of a religious character was about to transact itself in the adjoining oratory. But presently he found himself drinking tea – and separated from his hostess by an expanse of silver and china that stood in a rather striking disproportion to the actual quantity of refreshment provided. He caught himself reflecting that, although you can't dine like a prince in Arezzo, there is a catacomb-like restaurant where you may fare quite well and appropriately on *funghi*. In a few hours' time he and Jill would sit down there. Indisputably, it couldn't be *tête à tête*. There would now be a ghostly third – and one whom the two of them had rather inadequately entertained in the past. It was true, for instance, that he didn't feel himself at all fully to know what sort of marriage Jill's first marriage – her legal marriage, as presumably for the present it must be called – had been. Of course he knew its factual, and even its overtly emotional, outlines. He knew what Jill supposed to be her own judgement on it when she had closed the door and applied the seal. But even when Arnander had appeared to cease to be, the marriage hadn't ceased to be. Behind the door there must have remained a large shadowed chamber of which some of the dimensions might still be unknown to Jill as well as to her second husband. And it had to be opened up again now – to be opened up that evening over *funghi* and acid Tuscan wine.

'He lied.' These were the Marchesa's first words when her major-domo had securely withdrawn.

'I suppose he did.' Craine paused. 'Unless,' he allowed himself to add, 'you and your husband took rather a casual view of its mattering – the difference, I mean, between a woman's husband being alive and dead.'

'I spoke earlier of an assurance.' The Marchesa's tone was sharp for a moment. 'I required it, and it was given. Nino told us, in some detail, how he had managed to let his wife know what he proposed.'

'To let her know that he was disappearing and allowing himself to be supposed dead?'

The Marchesa inclined her head.

'No doubt he had his reasons – of which perhaps you'll be able to inform me now. And they may well have been cogent, from his point of view. But didn't the immorality of the thing strike you at all?'

The Marchesa accepted this as a permissible question – and indeed Craine felt that she was schooling herself to accept quite a lot. 'He assured us,' she said, 'of word having come back that his wife concurred in the plan. He said that she was rich and attractive and would console herself.'

'I see.' What Craine was literally seeing as he said this

happened to be the photograph of the Pope; and it occurred to him that he must make as much allowance for the Marchesa's alien climate as she must make for his. 'And her consolations might include bigamous marriage and illegitimate children?'

'Children? But, yes – I know you have children. And I scarcely know what to say, Mr Craine. You must understand our situation. We weren't dealing with a believer. We were dealing with a pagan – a persuasive and charming and desperate pagan. And my husband believed him to have genius.'

'So he has. It was one particular, at least, in which you were right, Marchesa.'

'That may be so. But it was my husband's conviction, not mine. I have little knowledge of painting. Of – of his wife we naturally knew less, although I had met her. Nino assured us that her views were similar to his own. The arrangement would only be a kind of divorce – as divorce is conceived of in Protestant societies. Not indeed a legal divorce. But I have remarked before that we are not much concerned about policemen. Even if Nino's wife contracted another seeming marriage, in the full knowledge that Nino was alive, it would be no affair of ours. In our hearts we should disapprove – but only as we should disapprove of some savage ritual in a jungle. It would be her own responsibility.'

There was a short silence. Craine had again caught the Pope's eye, and it occurred to him that it was a pity the Forni had not consulted him. He suspected that his Holiness would have rather briskly corrected their moral theology. However, that was neither here nor there. 'But last week,' he said, 'you felt constrained to summon the savages from their jungle? Well, here I am.'

'We must not give way to asperity.'

The Marchesa uttered this gently, so that it rather took the wind out of his sails. 'That's very true,' he said.

'Although I now realize, Mr Craine, that you and your wife have every reason to reproach us bitterly. And my

73

own fault is very great. For it was my instinct from the first that Nino is utterly unreliable. And now, too late, we know the truth. He has cheated and betrayed us all.' She paused, and he was suddenly sure that she was indeed moved and shaken. Yet it was with a steady hand that she took his cup and poured more tea. 'But not, after all, too late,' she went on. 'Or not if your beliefs are as I take them to be. I suspect that there has been a guardian angel at work.' For the first time, Marchesa Forni smiled. 'A wholly pagan guardian angel.'

'I don't think I understand you.'

'A guardian angel that controlled my pen, and made me invent a child where there is no child. Return to your wife, Mr Craine – for she is that, according to your secular persuasions. Make suitable explanations. You have seen the boy, and discussed his future with me. He is happy in his Italian surroundings, and it would be a mistake to think of any drastic change. I am arranging for his care and education. All that will be proper is the payment, through me or through some lawyer, of a small annual sum.'

There was again silence, in which he heard the tiny hiss of her silver kettle. Just how to take her proposal, in what terms to answer this counsel offered to the jungle, he seemed for a moment not to have an idea. When he did speak, it was like somebody in a play – somebody more concerned to screw out a few extra lines of effective dialogue than to get on with the business of the piece. 'It would hardly work,' he said. 'Jill's a woman, after all, and humanly curious. She'd hardly consent to return to England without taking a look at John Arnander's child.'

This time the Marchesa didn't smile. She was wholly serious. 'There is no difficulty,' she said. 'I can find a suitable child in ten minutes. And as for Nino, you and I can arrange matters.'

Craine at this point was glad to pick up a minute cake and make a business of biting into it. Marchesa Forni as an ally took quite as much coping with as did Marchesa Forni as an adversary. And now she improved upon his silence by pointing out – unemphatically, as one might do with a self-evident proposition – that it was his duty to protect his wife from a dilemma which might well prove intolerable to her. Happily, in so acting he would also be protecting his own rights – which was something a gentleman was bound in honour to do.

He finished his cake – with nothing better occurring to him than certain unprofitable reflections on the nature of Italians in general. What – he asked himself – are you to do with such people? Mendacity is their element. The Marchesa, who only a few minutes before had been sincerely distressed, was perking up as she invented for him this proposed course of monstrous deception. How she could logically reprobate John Arnander for *his* lie was something he couldn't penetrate to. But it remained true that he was coming to find the Marchesa rather a sympathetic character, and he didn't want inconveniently to indulge an outburst of Anglo-Saxon rectitude. So he said, very gently, that John Arnander had rights too. In fact, he felt it was just there that it was necessary to begin.

The Marchesa didn't resist this way of regarding the matter. Her position – he was beginning to see – was delicate. When she had believed that he and Jill had built their life in deliberate disregard of Arnander's continued existence she had been against them – as her brusque cable and her first reception of him had made clear. Now that she could see their conduct as having been, in intention, innocent and legitimate, she had swung round for the moment, and was prepared to approve, or tolerate, a future course for them that wouldn't be innocent or legitimate at all. It wouldn't be kind to drive such an amiably prompted confusion to expose itself. And he mustn't be impatient with her. For she knew things he wanted to know, and which there might be no other means of his knowing. So he began by asking her about Arnander's blindness. What was its nature, and for how long had it afflicted him?

On the first point the Marchesa wasn't precise. *Amaurosi*

was the only technical-sounding word her explanation ran to, and Craine supposed it merely to describe that sort of malady in which the organ has suffered no visible damage. But certainly the trouble was incurable; this had been the pronouncement of a family doctor for whom the late Marchese had owned the highest regard. And its origin was no doubt in Nino's wartime experiences. Its effects, as Craine must have been able to observe, had penetrated to the roots of his being, so that his whole personality was transformed.

Craine agreed that this was no doubt so. He had never known the earlier Arnander – the painter of the Maremma and the La Verna – but presumably he had been distinctly unlike the withdrawn being who wove baskets in the Marchesa's turret chamber. She had earlier remarked that Nino never said much. But did he ever, in fact, say enough to make it appear assured that his mental processes were approximately the same as other people's?

The Marchesa replied emphatically that Nino was sane. Her own life had given her certain standards of comparison in the matter. Nino existed in a dejected condition. But it wasn't a pathological dejection that spun itself outward from within. It was a state one might readily imagine for oneself if one had a single passion and a single power – and if that passion and power had been rendered functionless at a stroke. No one could face such a deprivation uncrushed who was unable to find repose in a conviction of the infinite mercy of God.

Craine could produce nothing to say to this. No doubt – he was thinking – she had set priests at the poor devil. Indeed, from her own standpoint, she would very imperfectly have discharged her duty if she had not. But Arnander, it could be guessed, knew only one priesthood: Piero's and Giorgione's and Vermeer's – or call it Amico di Sandro's. The pious Italian voices, subtle or urgent, would have come to him without effect through his latter darkness; it might have been while he listened to them that he fingered out on paper those arabesques that he would never see. There was no question that the Marchesa knew all about this, and it puzzled him that her compassion could accommodate itself to planning a course by which Arnander would be cheated. Arnander hadn't played fair by his wife – but he would be cheated if his wife weren't given the opportunity of deciding what, now, would constitute playing fair by him. And fortunately there wasn't for Craine, at present, any need to decide just where fairness to Arnander stopped. That lay all in the future. It lay equally with Jill and himself – and as the Marchesa didn't come into it there was no need to hold any debate with her now. But he still wanted information. 'Is there any absolute reason,' he asked, 'for his remaining dead?'

'I don't know. My husband had formed an opinion on the matter, but it may not have been well founded. And I have scarcely known where I might safely go to find out.' The Marchesa raised her head and looked at the portrait of the royal personage which did its best to dominate the room. 'We are not, you understand, quite where we were.'

'But at one time, certainly, the law would have been after him?'

'That was our belief. But it may have been some sort of impermanent military law. I spoke of my husband's having come to a conclusion on the matter. He believed that Nino's affair had been so buried beneath the chaos into which our country fell that there was little likelihood of any authority's wishing to dig it up again.' The old lady paused. 'Would that be your own opinion?'

'I'd be less unable to reply, Marchesa, if I had any clear notion of what his affair was.'

'You know nothing?'

'I know that he wasn't simply reported missing, believed killed. His death was accepted by the International Red Cross. Well, there are several possibilities. He may simply have decided, for reasons of his own, to profit by a chance mistake that had been made. But that doesn't sound to me a likely explanation. I suspect that the mistake was a consequence of – well, call it some decisive evasive action of his own. I know what he's supposed to have attempted – and to have been killed attempting. Perhaps his nerve failed him.'

'Would you blame him if it did?'

'No, I wouldn't. But sometimes a man who loses his nerve goes on to do things that won't – from a soldier's point of view – at all do.'

'Nino was not a soldier.'

'I understand that.' Craine looked at the Marchesa curiously. She might be prepared to abet Jill and himself in sidestepping the consequences of their situation, but she had sheltered Arnander for too long not to have an instinct to continue to do so. 'A commission like that,' he said, 'is, of course, no more than a quasi-military affair – and, even so, Arnander was only very loosely attached to it.'

'You know about the bridge?'

'Yes, I know about the bridge – in a general way.'

'It was already mined – and at the same time it was the only link for any effective communication with the enemy. But it was known that the German commandant had an excellent record in such matters, and some sort of contact was established by wireless. There seemed hope of a parley on the bridge itself at midnight. A staff captain was sent. But Nino was sent too – indeed, there can be little doubt he volunteered to go. He was sent, you may say' – and the Marchesa paused – 'as representing what was above the battle. It was a responsibility.'

'It was certainly a responsibility.' If Craine's tone was grim, it was without irony. 'Particularly for a man who had, perhaps, his unreliable side. It's a fair guess that he parted company with the captain and made himself scarce. But that doesn't quite account for his being subsequently so definitely declared dead.'

'The bridge was destroyed. It was blown into a thousand fragments. That is one fact. And another is this: Nino is extremely intelligent. He was no doubt much more intelligent than anybody else who was making calculations and taking chances that night.' The Marchesa's voice was harsh, but somewhere in it Craine thought he heard lurking admiration. The old lady, he saw, relished intelligence, even when

it was allied to reprehensible courses. 'And I think that –
perhaps quite suddenly – he *knew*. The captain had penetrated to the farther bridge-head; Nino himself was in the
middle, alone. And he suddenly *knew*, I say, that the gamble
was hopeless. At any moment the bridge was going to go
sky-high. And at that realization, although he kept his intelligence, he lost his head. I believe it had something to do
with vanity.'

The Marchesa paused again, and there was complete
silence. The silver kettle had ceased to hiss. Craine found
that he didn't want to stir. It was as if this silence were
echoing another silence – silence in a velvet Italian night,
with men striving to catch some tiny indication of death
crouching in a crater, crawling on a belly. 'Vanity?' he
forced himself to say.

'Vanity, certainly. We can scarcely, I'm afraid, call
honour into court. Indeed, I don't suppose that Nino's tradi-
tions much allowed for anything of the sort.' The Marchesa,
who had lately been proposing so large a deceitfulness,
threw this in with a passing arrogance that Craine found
engaging. 'He could, no doubt, simply have walked away or
crawled away – have returned to barracks, as you say. One
can't believe that anything very terrible would have happened to him. His cleverness would have had no difficulty in
spinning an admirable story – a story, it might be, quite
worth a medal. An American or English medal, if not an
Italian one.'

Craine didn't say anything. He took this mild insolence
to be a sign that the Marchesa was now, in some odd
fashion, enjoying herself. But whether she was giving him
actual information perhaps acquired from Arnander himself, or whether she had simply embarked on speculation,
was something that didn't appear. Perhaps it didn't matter.
In all this, indeed, it was going to be something to hold on
to that the past didn't very much matter at all; that there
was going to be a sufficient job of work in addressing oneself
to the future. 'I don't imagine,' he said, 'that Arnander
would much think about medals. Not even Italian ones. But

79

that doesn't mean that I don't see the point about vanity.'

'But now there comes another fact about Nino. He is an artist. That, I may say, was the basis of my husband's admiration for him. I do not admire artists myself.'

'I don't think I'd have supposed you to.' Craine was looking at the large portrait. It made a shocking business of a not unattractive seventeen-year-old boy. 'Which renders the more admirable all you've done for the unfortunate man upstairs,' he added.

He thought that the old lady flushed. Certainly it was with some haste that she resumed her theme. 'Nino's intelligence remained serviceable, but his imagination took control. It dramatized his plight. He couldn't stay; he couldn't stay another five minutes in that dreadful spot. At the same time the bridge was a symbol. And he was on the bridge in a representative character. You follow me?'

Craine had no difficulty in following her. And he was reflecting that she was quite as intelligent as John Arnander could be. She was contriving all this tolerably precise communication with a due regard to the limitations of his Italian. 'You suppose,' he said, 'that he saw himself humiliated?'

'Indeed he did. And he wanted to die. But at the same time he wanted *not* to die. If he hadn't so much wanted the second, he wouldn't so much have wanted the first. It was a dilemma. Fortunately – shall we call it that? – there were several bodies on the bridge.'

The Marchesa's dislike of artists, Craine thought, didn't inhibit her from playing for a certain amount of artistic effect. But he needn't go out of his way to encourage it. 'Civilian bodies?' he asked prosaically. 'Peasants caught on the road?'

'I see that you understand what followed. And one sees two facts about Nino's deed. It wasn't exactly sane. The bridge might *not* have been blown up. And, even if it was blown up, a body in his uniform, and with his papers and so on, might still have been recognizably not his body. I

80

don't know enough about high explosives to make a calculation myself.'

'Probably he didn't either. But it was, at the least, a risky bet.'

'So I should have supposed. And the other fact one sees about Nino's proceeding must be called, I think, its spiritually conclusive character. To do just that, to make that exchange of clothes with a dead body, in the dark, and listening perhaps for the return of a companion with whom one had set out on a dangerous and honourable enterprise ...'

'Quite so.' Craine felt that this was all a matter on which one should keep to the bare bones. 'But it came off?'

'It came off. Once away from the bridge, he had only to make his way to us.'

Craine waited for a moment. But the story appeared to be concluded. 'I can understand,' he said, 'that the Marchese had little difficulty in sheltering him at the time. But didn't it become a problem later?'

'Certainly. When things settled down, and we gained a Government of sorts, a nameless Englishman without papers was an anomaly to some minds. There is a great deal of impertinence in the world nowadays. But, as I said before, my husband had only to assert his position and Nino was left discreetly alone. It was no doubt acknowledged that a blind man was scarcely likely to be a dangerous monarchist agent.'

'A blind man?' Craine was startled. 'It happened as long ago as that?'

'Yes. Nino was already in distress about his sight when he reached us.'

'And his coming to you was final? He never put himself in communication with the outer world again?'

'Yes, he did. He had a friend called Morrison, an American painter who had managed to remain in Rome throughout the war. Nino sent for him, and he came two or three times to Castelarbia. It was through this Mr Morrison that

Nino claimed to have communicated with his wife, and to have settled matters with her. But when Mr Morrison died, Nino seemed to feel that his last link with what you call the outer world was indeed broken.'

Craine nodded. 'It appears to be our business,' he said a shade grimly, 'to forge it again. And at least I can't see that we are dealing with a fugitive. I take it he told the story of the bridge to your late husband?'

'He told it to me, Mr Craine.'

'Thank you.' He glanced swiftly at the Marchesa. She had spoken with sharp pride, so that he wondered why she was proposing to disburden herself of Arnander at all. Probably the marching orders she had received were pretty stiff, and the mode of living that lay ahead of her quite as straitened as she had represented. 'And he must have told it,' he went on, 'to this man Morrison?'

'No doubt he did. Mr Morrison was devoted to him.'

'Then it appears to me, Marchesa, that Arnander can come publicly alive – or be brought publicly alive – with little risk to himself or anybody else.'

'I am relieved that you should think so. But it is not, of course, a fear of legal consequences that has – well, ingrained itself in Nino's mind. Nor is it the point of honour – of vanity, as I think we were agreed in calling it. What he has not reconciled himself to is simply his affliction.'

'I'm very clear as to that.' Craine got to his feet. He had no impulse to linger at Castelarbia, or to do anything other than carry straight to Jill the cold fact they must confront together. The one issue he didn't want – it queerly came to him for a moment – was to get himself killed on the road back to Arezzo. If that befell him, there would be things about himself that he would never know. And to know pretty fully about himself represented the scope of his ambition and the twitch of his tether. Other people weren't for him. He wondered, he admired, but he didn't – he was sure he didn't – penetrate. What was it like to be John Arnander – now, at this very moment, up there in the turret room? He couldn't do more than touch the rim of that darkness.

82

Whereas there were men who would know. And no gift, it seemed to him, could be more wonderful than that.

The Marchesa too had risen. 'Mr Craine,' she asked, 'you will consider my plan?'

'I'm afraid not.' Without being aware of it, he smiled at her as one might smile at the quaintness of a child. She was inconsequent; it was for Jill that she had sent; and yet now – simply, it seemed, because the Craines were revealed as having acted in innocence – she wanted Jill kept out, wanted Jill absurdly and monstrously deceived. It struck him that her second thought in the matter wasn't perhaps after all a consequence of her discovery of that innocence; it represented in her a more settled disposition than her impulsive cable had done. Yes, that's it – Craine said to himself still smiling – that's exactly it. The old lady doesn't, at the pinch, really want to share that poor chap upstairs with any other woman. But she wouldn't mind sharing him with me. 'I'm afraid not,' he repeated. 'In fact I shall explain the situation to my wife this evening.' He said this as flatly in the English manner as he could contrive. And he gave the words 'my wife' no air of asserting a claim; they represented a mere commonsense of linguistic usage. 'She will no doubt want to come over tomorrow. I hope that will be convenient to you?'

The Marchesa acquiesced with a bow. She didn't like being crossed, but he suspected that she didn't wholly detest his manner of doing it. 'I am seldom engaged,' she said dryly. 'Later, it is true, I shall be a little taken up with my removal.'

Craine uttered his hopes that this impending event would not prove too fatiguing; he added a few sentences on the pleasures and conveniences of living on the outskirts of Florence. These were civilities that echoed nothing very urgent in his mind. But he'd be a little failing, he thought, in the matter of showing the flag, if he didn't take his leave with some regard to a code. And the old lady accepted his words as constituting the entirely proper concluding note.

His last impression was almost his strangest, and it came to him simply from the reserve into which she withdrew as she said good-bye. He had made – totally unlikely as it seemed, he had made – a hit with the Marchesa. But it was a hit which a great deal in her disapproved of. She might be returning to her earlier attitude long before he left the last of Castelarbia's fifty-one farms behind him.

CHAPTER SEVEN

JILL was still asleep when Craine woke up next morning;
was sound asleep despite the racket that had brought him
awake with a jerk.

He got out of bed and went over to the window. It wasn't
cosy in the hotel bedroom, and it must be chilly outside.
Perhaps it was simply to warm himself up for his day's
work that the man Craine now looked down at was be-
labouring his horse with a shovel. It was the sound of these
blows, and the man's angry shouts, and the rattle of the
cart-wheels on rubble as the horse backed and swerved, that
made the racket – a racket reverberating from the great
blank wall of San Francesco against which these primitive
excavations were going on.

There was a further – this time a mechanical – clamour.
Two men appeared to be engaged on the modest task of
undermining the church. The second had a motor-tricycle
with a barrow hitched behind; he had backed this into the
courtyard with a roar, and at once – having no horse to
discipline – fallen to work with a pick. He was already
stripped to the waist, and his back was glistening. The men
worked side by side, ignoring each other. They were rival
contractors, employed, it seemed, to demolish and carry
away by a sort of ant-like effort the very foundations upon
which were reared, in the dimness of the building beyond,
Piero's majestic evocation of the history of the True Cross.

Of course nothing dramatic was actually happening. The
foundations of San Francesco went fathoms deeper than all
this feverish scratching – which would be in the interest of
leaning a new garage or cinema against so admirably massive a rampart of stone. The men worked with a strong concentrated energy that Craine could feel in his own muscles.
The second man filled his barrow, flung himself across the
saddle of his tricycle, kicked the engine into life again and

vanished in pandemonium and dust. The first man worked on; he had a bigger cart which it took him longer to fill. He exacted as much from himself as from his miserable animal; he was paid, no doubt, according to the weight of what he shifted, and if short on his day's stint might himself be flailed at home by a desperate wife with children to feed. Certainly at the moment the horse was having the best of it, nuzzling in a meagre nosebag with no sign of apprehensiveness. From beating to beating the creature carried, conceivably, no more than a dim sense that the universe has its unkindly moments. In humans, Craine thought, we call that displaying a good nervous tone. It's how one gets along – more or less ignoring or forgetting until the great shovel is again about one's head and flanks.

Against the side of San Francesco a rope quivered and flapped. High up, what looked a very small bell wagged in its belfry. The brazen syllables tumbled briefly, hastily on top of each other; they meant something to the monks; but the man with the shovel laboured on. Craine turned round. Jill was awake.

She smiled at him through a sleepy grimace from the farther bed. Everything became her, he thought. Once you had realized it, her beauty would hold you, were she in the middle of sweeping a chimney. And it was a beauty that would shine out in sorrow and be more precious in pain.

He saw her shoulders move, and he knew that she was stretching out her limbs beneath the bed-clothes. Then her body went still, and he could see the pupils of her eyes contract. He felt his heart contract as if through some organic link with them. For he understood. It was the moment of recollection – the strangely unfair moment at which the awakening mind has to accept, again and anew yet with a special quality of suffering that haunts this hither fringe of sleep, some deprivation, some burden, upon which only dreamless nights will henceforth have any power to scatter the poppy. You could put it that way. You could put it – quite brutally – that he was watching the instant in which she became aware again of the raised shovel.

He was about to speak – heaven knew to what sombre effect – when she forestalled him with three or four murmured words. She was still smiling – as a married woman will smile at her own innocent prescriptive call to love. Her smile belonged with the fact of their having been married a thousand years. But when he went over to her, jumping over his own bed like a boy, it was rather swiftly that she put out her arms to him.

They had been cautious the night before – tacitly agreeing to turn out the light on unresolved bewilderment. She hadn't, after the single strange cry his news had drawn from her, moved towards anything that could be called decision or even exploration. And this, he realized, was right. He'd have been shocked if she'd said, 'This makes no difference to us' – as shocked as if, on the other hand, she'd promptly packed a bag and said good-bye. It isn't in every situation that the heart can speak at once, and in some a ready word is likely to be a shallow one.

Her reserve – he'd said to himself in the small hours – was of the kind she'd have maintained in any crisis. It went with the breeding – as aristocratic as Marchesa Forni's – that she'd received in the paradoxical democracy he'd found her in. She'd maintain it, for instance, were one of the children suddenly taken to hospital, and the two of them left waiting with reason to fear a dire diagnosis.

But no – he'd then gone on, as he turned with due caution on his pillow – there really wasn't much of an analogy in that. Or, if there was, it was only to the extent of their holding in common, in the one case as the other, emotion they must both repress. With the sick child it would be fear. But now, to put it mildly, the situation was less simple. In each of them it must arouse a complex of emotions, only parts of which overlapped. And the elements even of what they thus had together might be so difficult to give a name to that there would be folly in not acknowledging the need to wait for them with a strained ear. Which didn't mean that it wasn't a good idea to go to sleep – and Jill's being asleep while he lay sleepless he simply took as an exemplification of what he liked to acknowledge as her generally superior talent for life. That sort of ear didn't go off duty while one slept; it sometimes became hypersensitive then.

But Jill hadn't wakened up and announced any clarification; she had wakened up and called him into her bed. Perhaps that *was* a clarification. Yet he suspected that it just wasn't – and that there would be naïveté as well as arrogance in supposing the contrary. And now, when he had picked up the telephone and ordered coffee and *panini* from the *cameriera* at the other end of it, he felt that his vigil had put him ahead after all. He could, in fact, name something. He could name a response which John Arnander's resurrection had elicited alike in Jill and in himself – a response, an element, which, however obscure now and subsidiary to other emotions, would in both of them play its part in any explosion that the affair was fated to produce. He could name it, although to name it was perhaps scarcely to understand it. It was excitement.

Perhaps there was no need to distrust this feeling as much as he found himself doing. It might be called, in either of them, a biologically healthy response to their new situation. When anything firm comes unstuck, when the static turns fluid, when not the sun but a question-mark sails up over the horizon one day; then this undertone of excitement – distinguishably pleasurable even if what one largely faces is calamity – represents simply the wholesome knowledge that one isn't dead, that one has powers to call up and perhaps even quite surprising possibilities to explore. And now, through whatever labyrinth of feeling he and Jill must follow their several threads –

'Do you think he'll see me ?'

He had been clearing a table for the tray that would be brought in. Now he turned round. Jill was lying back in bed with her eyes shut, and her face suggested so gentle a repose in their recent moment that it was difficult to believe she could be feeling forward into the future at all. But, as he was thinking this, her eyes opened and she looked at him in a way he could interpret at once. She was experiencing her affectionate amusement at his ruminative way of going to work on whatever confronted him. He had a second's irritation in which he said, 'He certainly won't *see* you.'

'You know I don't mean that. Why should he want to start bothering with me again? He made up his mind, it seems, long ago. About me, and Tim, and an unborn child. Why should he want to see me? He'll send down a message by that old woman.'

'I think that's very unlikely.' He paused, because there was a knock at the door and their breakfast was brought in. He remained silent until he had poured out a cup of coffee and carried it to her. 'I didn't feel he was antagonistic.'

'You chatted about me?'

It would have been fatuous to tell her she was upset. But her words showed him a new dimension of the thing. As far as he was concerned, John Arnander had simply come alive. But for Jill he had not merely done that; he had revealed himself as once having decided to sham dead. 'No,' he said. 'We didn't mention you – as I thought I'd made clear last night. I simply tried to tell him a little about Tim and Charles. That seemed the best way in. And all that happened was that his interest just stirred. He's in a queer way, but I don't think he's in the least mad. And I didn't, as I say, feel any current of hostility in him.'

'So you feel that, if I try hard, I may just stir his interest too?'

He was suddenly very much troubled, for he had caught himself tumbling into the feeling that she was being horribly perverse. And yet the truth was as formidable. For he saw what it was from which she had been taking refuge in him ten minutes ago; it was her sense of bitter humiliation at having once been let pass, without word or sign, out of John Arnander's life. 'I don't know,' he said, 'what he will feel about you. But you're going to find out.'

'Whether he'll be prepared to forgive and forget. More coffee, please.' She watched him pour it. 'The bastard,' she said.

He set down the coffee-pot abruptly. The mere word had startled him – rather as it would have done if suddenly used by a bishop about a contumacious curate. His mind even tried to take it literally – in its application, say to one of his own children. Jill hadn't given it any accent to stagger him. She hadn't attached it to Arnander as a covert term of indulgence or endearment. She meant it – or thought she did. But – just as a bit of vocabulary – it didn't belong to her. He remembered how, when the Marchesa's cable had come, she'd dropped in an instant into what wasn't her, what wasn't their, tone. No doubt Arnander talked about bastards – and used, when talking to women, any words that came into his head. Plenty of perfectly decent men did, and Craine had no particular notion that it was nicer to be more refined. But they had a habit, the two of them, and when Jill came out with the statement that Arnander was a bastard she was in fact dipping back into Arnander's world. 'You'll have to find out,' he repeated. 'What he feels about you, and what you feel about him.'

'Clearly.'

'And whether you mean much or little, either way, by talk of forgiving and forgetting.'

'He let me down – didn't he? – going to earth without a word. I mourned him – in hard desolate fact and not just by convention. Do you realize that I even visited what they told me was his grave? What he did was a bloody thing to do.'

It was certainly that, Craine thought. 'Yes,' he said, 'it was bloody, all right.'

For a moment Jill looked surprised, much as if he had produced this summary unprompted. 'He'd have called it that,' she said, ' – John would. If he'd heard of it, I mean, in any other man. He was unsatisfactory, but I never found him lost to decency.'

'Not many people are that.'

'After all, he had children: Tim born and Charles coming. That's what makes it seem so utterly strange to me.'

'It certainly increased the responsibilities he was deciding to evade.'

She shook her head. 'That's not what I mean. There's something natural in a man's walking out on a woman. When a man flies off the handle that way, there's an obvious centrifugal force at work. There's the tug of another woman – or just other women – who he hasn't had. It's primitive – but there the excitement is.'

'The excitement?' Craine put down his coffee-cup.

'Yes. But as a man walks about the streets, or works in his garden or lies in his bath, he isn't liable to be prompted, from deep within himself, to the notion that it would be fun to take over his neighbour's children. That's one direction in which Nature doesn't set promiscuity working. There wouldn't be any society if it did.'

Craine said nothing. He walked to the window and looked out again. The man with the horse and cart had tied a handkerchief round his head and was labouring on – was acknowledging, you might say, the burden of fatherhood in the sweat of his brow. And John Arnander hadn't acknowledged it. Jill's deepest feeling was of that. She had given him sons and he had turned away from them. It was that – it wasn't his having turned away from her after heaven knew what woman or women in those obscure disastrous months – that she believed she couldn't forgive.

He turned back into the room. It was his urgent impulse, for her sake and, as he instinctively knew, for his own, to get some of this bitterness dissipated. 'Look,' he said. 'There's something you must face. Arnander's is, was, a special case.'

'What do you mean – a special case? We're talking, surely, about quite damnably universal things.'

'He's a powerful painter – a very great artist. That's a cardinal fact.'

'To hell with art.' Suddenly, and not wholly to his astonishment, she blazed out at him. 'You're always paddling around in art, Rupert. But, for God's sake, don't start splashing me with it now.' She sprang out of bed and strode to the wash-basin, as if her one concern was to get into a fit state to leave the room. Then she turned and came towards him, with tears in her eyes. 'We've had this for just twelve hours,' she said, 'and already it's made a bitch of me.'

'Rubbish. And of course you've had enough art. It's a deplorable habit of mine – collecting it and staring at it and talking about it. I'll quit. We'll have nothing at Pinn but prints of foxhunts and steeplechases, and daguerreotypes of great-uncles and aunts.'

She laughed, rather uncertainly, and began to dress. 'Tell me what you were meaning,' she said. 'Although of course, I know.'

'You took him on. You knew what he was – an obsessed and compelled artist – and you took him on. Of course it isn't true that artists are inescapably prompted to let their fleshly children starve while they labour to beget nurslings of immortality on their canvas. That's no doubt vulgar twaddle. Still, when a man has that sort of creative temperament, and bows to it, there are certain to be very special strains upon his marriage and upon all that naturally flows from it.' He hesitated. 'You may find this infuriating too.'

'Bits of the address that, unfortunately, the parson didn't deliver at my first wedding.' Jill's head emerged from the dress into which she was scrambling. 'Of course your mind's beginning to move down the right lines, Rupert. It always does.' She pulled down a zip, and put her hands to her hair. 'Just to look at you makes the world seem manageable for a while. And nothing else does. I'll always, you know, be quite, quite clear about that. Now, go on.'

'It should be easier to forgive him for letting you down, and yourself for letting him down . . .'

'You know about my feeling that? I must always have felt it – and yet I never quite fully knew that I felt it, until last night.'

'Quite so. It's part of the devil of the whole business. And if all the regrets are to be got into a proper proportion' – although he didn't pause, he heard her give a little sigh, as of helpless satisfaction, at the banal phrase – 'you have to remember that it was a hazardous sort of marriage. And that's not a disparagement. It's a fact.'

'I oughtn't to have left Italy.'

'As you know, I don't know about that. We've never gone over it, you and I – not in detail.' Craine had managed to set himself shaving. 'But I can give a guess. He'd been impossible.'

'Oh, yes – of course he'd been that.' She sounded impatient.

'I'd say he had very conventional feelings, really.' Craine brought the razor down his jaw. 'Even after a good many showdowns, he'd have a solid lower-middle class conviction that one's adulteries ought to be concealed from the wife.'

'You don't like John.'

He turned and stared at her. 'Of course I don't like John. Despite anything I've maintained, I think there's almost nothing to be said for him. But I like Arnander. He pleases my taste tremendously. Or – to speak more honestly – he fills me with absolute awe. But let me go on. He'd think it clever – and even respectable and morally beautiful – to conduct his infidelities in secret. But probably he was no good at it.'

'He wasn't.'

'And when, with his eyes on some slut or stunner, he began making a pother about your safety amid the horrors of war – '

'And the children's – Tim's and the unborn child's.' Jill's eyes were suddenly blazing. 'He had a lot to say about that.'

'Well – then you'd had enough.'

'For a lifetime. But I didn't like it when I heard that he was dead.'

Uproar from below made it impossible to speak for a space. The man with the tricycle affair was excelling himself. 'In this country,' Craine said presently, 'they think that the chief function of the internal combustion engine is to make as much row as possible. And yet you couldn't have better engineers.'

'Rupert, how utterly fair you are. I believe I can trust you even to be fair to me.' She was sitting before a looking-glass, holding a lipstick. 'Whatever happens.'

'Why "even"?'

'It might be more difficult with me than with the Italian people.' She paused, frowning into the glass. It was as if she had spoken in a sudden abstraction so deep that she couldn't be certain of what she had said. 'Must I go?'

'Yes.'

'Hadn't you better come too – or at least part of the way? There are some interesting things near Castelarbia. Etruscan tombs.'

'Nothing would make me fair to Etruscan tombs. I think them utterly dismal. In fact they frighten me quite a lot.'

She had been ordering her few toilet things carefully on the dressing-table before her, and now she turned round. 'I can hardly imagine anything frightening you, Rupert.'

He was taken aback. He believed that she trusted his judgement, his devotion, perhaps some other qualities. It had never occurred to him that she might see in him a symbol of strength. 'Lord, yes,' he said. 'Sometimes, for instance, I have a child's fear of death.'

'Like John on that bridge.' She didn't say this at all as if she was making any sort of point. Then she rose. 'Had we better be going to see about a car? There's no advantage in putting it off.'

He walked to the door. 'None at all. The sooner you set out, the sooner you'll be back again.'

CHAPTER EIGHT

FOR a long time he sat in the café opposite his hotel, reading an Italian newspaper, making a business of drinking a tepid *cappuccino*. He could have taken a bus to Sansepolcro in time for lunch. But it would have been an artistic excursion and he was chary of that – for what Jill had flashed at him about artistic paddlings had left, if not a scorched, at least a small singed area in his mind. Of course there was Perugia. Perugia was even more replete with art; nevertheless one could make for it with nothing but gastronomical designs. But Perugia was too far away unless he hired a car, nor had he any impulse to regale himself. He would spend most of the day, he foresaw, prowling about Arezzo. Until restlessness overcame him, he had better stay put.

So he sat measuring by how much all this wasn't his sort of crisis – for he felt that in sizing himself up without illusions he would make the best start towards what might prove to be adequacy after all. It wasn't his sort of crisis, and only grotesquely could his own familiar idiom be twisted to fit it. Rupert Craine had suffered a sharp and unexpected contraction of credit. But had he ? He didn't know. Jill, being driven alone now towards Castelarbia and Arnander, might be more aware of him, Craine, as her principal asset than she had been twenty-four hours earlier. Certainly he might have been excused for thinking it was so when she had put out her arms to him that morning. But these moments – he said to himself – aren't moments of knowledge. It is only the ironic genius of language that has attached the word to them. They may be profoundly treacherous, wrong.

He wanted to do the decent thing. It was a discovery he'd made rapidly, but he continued to be surprised at the strength of the simple fact. The feeling went deep – there was the sense of an anchor and cable in it – and he had to remind himself that anything going deep went into an obscurity where the emotions keep queer company. Still, it stated itself in his consciousness as a firm desire. Ordering more coffee, and pushing his newspaper aside, he tested this firm desire as an engineer in a laboratory might test the strength of materials. He stretched it out in stilted phrases – telling himself that, having been placed in a trying situation, he was anxious to comport himself like an English gentleman. And at this – he reported to himself – there wasn't as much as an ominous creak. He recalled a friend who, in an acrid moment not long before, had assured him that, like all Wykehamists, he regarded virtuous discomfort as the *summum bonum* achievable by man. Again there wasn't a shiver. Decency held firm. He could credit it with being really there. Unless his personality strangely transformed itself, he'd get no change out of doing other than trying to behave in a civilized fashion.

There was a stir on the steps of the church. A Franciscan had appeared from the interior, leading a scraggy brown dog. The dog had got into the church and was being expelled. Several old women – bent, crumpled and in pervasive black – came out at the same time. They regarded the case of the dog as one of some scandal, and debated it vociferously. The Franciscan paid no attention to them, but addressed the dog, wagging an admonitory finger at it, making a reasoned point, gesturing with an explanatory palm. The dog nodded – or at least to Craine it appeared to nod – and walked away. The Franciscan turned to the old women with a swift practised geniality, joked with them, picked up his skirts and retreated into the church. How well – Craine thought – they know their job. But trying situations – at least of an unexpected kind – seldom come their way. The rope slaps against the wall, the bell rings, the next stage in the day's long gentle discipline has started.

But to discover the decent thing as almost a physical need was no occasion for sitting back in an ethical glow. Blundering good intentions, an insensitive high-mindedness;

these might be the real villians of such a piece as he had been handed a part in. What he lacked the power of achieving was a view from well back in the stalls. It would only be by finding some means to distance his spectacle that he would have any chance of controlling it. He thought of other husbands and wives. He tried to think of this extraordinary thing happening to the Hallidays, the Dilgers, the Petford-Smiths, the Voyseys – couples drawn at random from his acquaintance. He tried to think of it as happening to old Mungo and his wife twenty years back; he even tried to think of it as happening to the Groococks, although this necessitated his inventing a Mrs Groocock on the spot.

For nearly an hour he continued to sit in the café, watching these shadowy people and listening in on them as they talked out just such a predicament as his and Jill's. But the effect was blurred and unsatisfactory; he was a banker and not a writer; it wasn't any sort of interior peepshow either that was his line. Yet, when he told himself he was an ass and had better cogitate on other principles, his mind didn't wholeheartedly acquiesce. Some of these people continued to flicker in his fantasy, although the effort to involve them in a relevant situation had faded out. The husbands and wives remained for a ghostly review – and presently it was only the wives. Diana Voysey, Jane Petford-Smith; he knew more about them – about their manner of regarding and phrasing things, about how their minds worked and their bodies moved – than it had ever occurred to him to notice. And particularly Jane Petford-Smith. He was certain that she was a woman whose actual acquaintance he would never develop in any significant degree. But here and now, as a phantom hovering in his head, her conduct might turn irresponsible at any moment. In that event, moreover, Diana Voysey wouldn't consent to linger far behind her.

He got up and, as he had foreseen, wandered restlessly about the town. He was shocked and shaken, but also curiously relieved. The excitement which, almost from the first moment of revelation, had companioned his dismay, had at least now unmuffled itself and revealed an honest unassuming face. He had been given a wink from the simple, ever-hopeful eye of plain male promiscuity. Well, that was all right. It would be merely sinister if, with his whole system of life given a sudden damnable jolt, the bleak wind whistling and the windows rattling and the doors swinging on their hinges, there was absolutely no accompanying disturbance in the cellarage. He summoned up Jane Petford-Smith again for the purpose, as it were, of briefly expressed gratitude for the clarification she had supplied; he was perfectly willing to acknowledge their brief spectral familiarity by dismissing her with an admonitory smack.

He bought a couple of picture postcards – they were of uncompromising artistic objects – for Tim and Charles; he bought a third, a cat with a saucer of milk, which he thought might be within the grasp of his own elder child. When he had provided these with appropriate messages he climbed up the hill and entered the cathedral.

He'd paddle, he told himself, if he wanted to; and with this resolution he walked straight towards Piero's Magdalen. But his attention was distracted by a woman with an imbecile child who had entered just before him. She had brought the child for what was perhaps a daily exercise, the attempt to teach him to kneel and cross himself before an altar. The child was finely formed, but his head moved without reference to his surroundings, and he made a low gobbling sound. Patiently, intently, again and again, the mother moved his hand from forehead to breast. Craine wondered from just what Limbo she sought to preserve him through this minimal endowment of religious comportment. What would the priests teach her about the fate of a soul unfit for Judgement? He had no idea; he only believed that it was a question heavy with centuries of theological debate. Very probably it was some mild doctrine that now obtained. But whatever it was, it didn't abate the mother's intense concentration on her task. She wanted the same felicity for her child that she was herself instructed to hope for; not a special compassionate sort laid on at a remove. Craine still had his three picture postcards in his pocket, and they spoke to him of hostages of fortune. He wanted to put out his hand to the imbecile child, to please him by offering him some small bright object. But the discomfort of an intruder assailed him, and he made to leave the cathedral. Then he thought better of it. In these places, after all, one was entitled to what one could get. He turned back and sought out his Magdalen.

And there she was – sculptural and massive in her mysterious world, wafer-thin on the plaster wall. Once upon a time somebody had hit on the notion of tracing round the shadow of a man, an animal, as it fell on the rock. And now there was this: a head held so, discourse in the volumes of a robe.

For some minutes Craine studied the fresco. Then he walked away, recalling relevant things: the Masaccios in the Brancacci chapel, Donatello learning to lay great folds of bronze between parted knees. But he was aware of something factitious in these reflections, as if he were entertaining himself to a patter reminiscent of Weidlé's young man. It wasn't that the object he'd been looking at hadn't moved him. It had. It had moved him after a fashion which he was exploiting these artistic musings to dodge.

There was now a pleasant warmth in the sun. He wandered into the public garden and sat down beside a large monumental composition of the sort in which the municipal genius of Italy delights; its subject appeared to be Petrarch with allegorical trimmings. His mind went back to the cathedral. It would be inapposite to say that Piero's picture represented a beautiful woman. There were things you thought about his Magdalen: for example, that she knew all the burden and the pride of being part of a story not invented by man. She was even a little insolent about it; she knew your place. But her pride wasn't in being any sort of stunner; and it hadn't remotely been part of the painter's intention to commemorate some special instance of what in a woman attracts the desire of a man. Yet in actual women, or in an actual woman, he must have discerned a disposition of sensible matter that gave him his hint beyond sense. As, humbly in a smoothed pebble, a broken shell, an eroded log cast up by the tide, there may lie the first prompting to exploration of a world with which such debris has little to do, so in a specific human face or body there can be that which prompts the contemplative as distinct from the appetitive energies of certain men.

And that was where Jill came in. For of course it was Jill that was all the question. If, today, looking at cunningly daubed pigment raised in him any genuine response at all, Jill must be mixed up in it. He would be heaven knew what – say one of Nature's ninnies or eunuchs – if it were otherwise.

There was a Jill who must be admitted – to put it with a stark directness – John Arnander's by right. An accident of the way she came from the womb, of the fashion in which her limbs, her features waxed and formed themselves under the skies of Virginia, had produced beauty of a strangeness beyond or aside from what may be discerned and desired by any sensually cognizant man. And that strangeness had been the catalyst of Arnander's art.

It didn't mean that Arnander had obsessively planted his easel before Jill. In actual fact, he had tried to make a big thing of her only once – and the effort hadn't been a success. Nevertheless there had been in her that which held and sustained him as an artist. It had been – strangely but absolutely – the mystery of Jill's beauty that compelled him when he managed such a declared triumph as the View from Cortona. Craine was sure of this. He was also sure that it all hadn't made Arnander the better husband – or at times, perhaps, any sort of husband at all.

The queer fact – perhaps the grand complicating fact – was that Craine's own Jill was in part this Jill too. If Diana Voysey and Jane Petford-Smith discussed his wife, their charitable agreement would be that she was striking if they were feeling catty, they would say something quite different. And Craine's relation with her had its origin – it simply had to be confessed – in his flair; in his very real capacity for what, in anger, she had called paddling. Crudely put, he shared Arnander's eye for Jill.

But there was so much more – there was unspeakably so much more – to his own marriage! When everything was said, Jill was a hundred miles from being a mere object of his contemplation. There was, there continued to be, all the mystery of the body in their marriage; and no number of Janes and Dianas, however oddly peeping out from the wings of his consciousness, would persuade him that he wasn't rather a monogamous type. And in the children – hers, theirs – and in what the children could be surrounded with and trained and tempered to there was creation which, if not of the grandest, had its honest place on the line. So it wasn't even true that a grand difference between Arnander and himself lay in this: that he would never create as much as a tea-cosy or milk-jug on the strength of Jill. He could create, he was creating, a whole texture of life that wouldn't exist without her.

In short – he said to himself, getting up and walking away – if his marriage had to be defended, there could be a pretty confident appeal to the traditional human sanctities. Only it would all be simpler – at least from his point of view – if there wasn't, in the solid wall of his own common-place personality, that small imaginative chink or cranny through which he could catch a glimpse of the obscurely crucial function which Jill had performed in the chemistry of Arnander's vision.

And yet Arnander had walked out on her. However much of reticence there still was in Jill's account of their parting, it was clear that he walked out on her as definitely as he had walked out of his assignment on that damned bridge. The bridge had been too big for him, and she had been too big for him too. He wasn't much of a chap, Lord help him, and she had simply owned an awkward overplus of human qualities, not readily concealed, which had ended by putting him out of conceit with himself. What compelled him in her as an artist, he had perhaps exhausted – or fallen back from, baffled; Craine didn't pretend to guess. What attracted him as a man could be had all over the place. So he had walked out – and in such a way that he had deftly left her with a lurking sense of guilt and responsibility. There was a sort of revenge on her in that. What, if anything, he had at that time planned for the future, one couldn't tell. Actual crisis had come along; the bridge had come along, and then blindness; and after that something in Arnander much deeper than impatience or resentment or promiscuousness had taken control.

For Arnander had his depths. Even as a man he had them. Finally they had drawn him to his present condition. Indeed, he had his qualities. His marriage, despite its appearance, had been no more mercenary than Craine's; and there didn't appear to have been any subsequent time at which the fact of Jill's fortune had formed any part of his calculations.

CHAPTER NINE

WALKING down the hill, dropping his postcards into a box, returning to his café for the glass of vermouth which would fill in, after a fashion, the last half-hour before an early lunch, Jill's second husband – if he could be called that – continued to give Jill's first husband his due. It had, of course, to be nearly all a matter of what Arnander had achieved; and even of what he might further have achieved, had matters gone with him otherwise than they had done.

That this last consideration had any place or weight in the scale seemed doubtful, but Craine did his best to toss it in. It was a counter in the affair which he now knew Jill herself was going to claim to have no patience with. That it had been so profoundly to the artist in Arnander that she had appealed was a fact that Craine couldn't conceive of her having been blind to. Yet she wasn't going to allow anyone to import into the present situation an atom of talk about Arnander's immortal genius; she was going to take her stand on the proposition that anything of the sort only darkened counsel. If the man's return from the dead was at this moment a weight about her heart, a problem of which the very terms, let alone the solution, had to be groped for in the recesses of her being, it had nothing to do – she was going to maintain – with the fact that he had once painted La Verna. At the same time she must certainly be vividly aware of the special poignancy of his case; the difference there would be, say, if Arnander's art were the art of music or poetry.

And here something stirred in Craine's mind that he couldn't quite catch hold of. It was a glimmering that there was a point at which, merely in virtue of being an intelligent man of the world, he could at once effectively act. He had been aware of it when talking to Marchesa Forni, and he guessed that its eluding him now was a manoeuvre of that part of his mind in which a fair hearing for Arnander didn't get much of a show. But it would come back – and probably in a few minutes, as he was eating his lunch.

There was a car with an English registration in the square. It had been there when he sat down, and he had noticed the porter from his own hotel lifting out a couple of suitcases. The owners weren't visible, and he supposed that they were inspecting the treasures of San Francesco while the light was still more or less that recommended in the guide-books. One hardly expected to see one's fellow countrymen in Arezzo at this season; the tourists were in the main indefatigable Germans, whose *Sehnsucht* for Latin civilization marched with the circling year, or Americans convinced that they were making a last inspired dash through Europe before things got too bad altogether. These reflections accompanied Craine down to his subterranean restaurant, and almost into the alcove in which Jill and he had eaten their ashen dinner on the previous night. It was thus that he came suddenly upon two people he knew. They were Jim Voysey and Jane Petford-Smith.

The position didn't in the instant, strike Craine as difficult. There was an inner room, and although it wasn't in use at midday he knew that he had only to stride into it, with a significant glance meantime at the attentive proprietor, for a table at once to be prepared for him in tactful obscurity. And in passing his acquaintances, as pass them he must, he need only nod to Voysey as casually as if this were a London restaurant; so casually, indeed, that his eye wouldn't travel on to Voysey's companion at all.

But he'd forgotten what an inept creature Voysey was. The man had got to his feet, his face beneath his iron-grey hair flushed like a detected schoolboy's. And now he was making a large pleasurable fuss over the meeting. What they call – Craine thought – brazening it out. Voysey was even drawing up a chair for him, and as he was himself demonstrably alone he couldn't very well decline it.

He looked at Jane. She was sitting quite still, her eyes

bright with mingled apprehension and triumph. Her appearance would have afforded no satisfaction to a moralist; she looked younger and prettier than she had done for years. Her escapade – for this somehow instantly betrayed itself as that – was in some enormously agreeable phase. And Voysey too was in high spirits which weren't much marred by his confusion; if he was awkwardly tongue-tied as he sat down again it was only because he couldn't decide whether it would be quite the thing to offer Craine a sort of invisible wink. Deciding against this, he occupied himself in giving unnecessary guidance in the ordering of a third lunch, and when he did venture an expressive look it was directed at Jane. Craine, although this meeting was disturbing him strangely, couldn't help being amused at it. Poor Voysey was signalling that she had the quicker wits of the two, and had better launch out on the explanations.

'Rupert, darling, how amusing this is!' Jane looked at him with conscientious wickedness – she had decided on a bold line – and arched her back like a tart in a film. 'And isn't Jill with you?'

'Oh, yes. We're together. But she's gone off for the day.'

'Lots of jolly day trips round about here,' Voysey appeared to feel that he had been given a cue too good to miss. 'Jane and I ran into each other in Florence quite early this morning, and found we both had it clear till dinner-time. So I drove her over. There's said to be a lot of good stuff. I've never been in Arezzo before, as a matter of fact. Nice place. But a bit out of the way.'

Craine nodded. 'It's quiet. You'd hardly expect to meet anybody you knew.'

'I suppose not.' Voysey's cheerfulness was waning. He must be thinking – Craine thought – that Craine wasn't the fellow he'd have chosen for an awkward sort of encounter like this.

Jane again did something with her body – gave it a lift and a twist at the waist. 'But you never know,' she said, 'who you'll rub up against on the Continent. That's what makes it such an exciting place.' She raised a wineglass in a hand that trembled slightly. 'Cheers, Rupert,' she murmured. 'Thousands of cheers.'

Craine said nothing. It hadn't presumably been a coincidence that an hour or two ago these people had begun to run in his head. Probably Voysey's car was obscurely familiar to him, and a glimpse of it had been the reason for his choosing the particular *dramatis personae* he had for his speculative musings on husbands and wives. Still, the resulting effect was very queer. Two of his puppets had promptly turned up – and in a combination that hadn't occurred to him. Moreover they brought dead into the centre of his vision something that he acknowledged as having been disreputably hovering on the fringes of it. Here, in fact, was divorce-court stuff – call it the sort of situation that may develop with anyone once things come unstuck. And here, in Jane Petford-Smith, was eminently the sort of person it may develop with. His musings – even more than he'd acknowledged – had discovered that for him earlier on.

'What happens when Jill gets back?' Voysey spoke with lumbering casualness. 'Do you stop, or go ahead?'

'We're stopping for a time, at the hotel across the square.'

Craine saw a look pass between his companions. They must be called, he supposed, the guilty couple. Certainly their adventure wasn't all before them. A glance at either rather brutally told you that. Jane's expectations had been fulfilled. And Voysey already had much occasion for an uneasy conscience. One could see that he gave it an airing from time to time; he felt a little bad, perhaps, that he and poor old Hugo Petford-Smith belonged to the same regiment. Still, it was only a small fly in the ointment. Voysey plainly couldn't glance at Jane without experiencing the sensations of a man who has done, and is doing, a marvellous job. To one less unsympathetic than Craine he would murmur that these things are a matter of technique. But meanwhile he faced a practical problem, and he was trying to canvass an answer to it in Jane's eye. Must they have those damned suitcases back in the car and drive on somewhere else? But Jane seemed to put the question aside. She turned to Craine and talked to him in a manner which – he realized with discomfort – he might have taken, on a less disenchanted occasion, for amusingly daring.

And at first Voysey liked it. He liked having a woman to exhibit who was all keyed up like this. But when Jane produced certain sallies that couldn't be called decent he grew uncomfortable. There was some book of rules, no doubt, in which he'd read that a woman in her situation preserved without difficulty a more than common modesty when in public view. So he was wondering whether, after all, she came from quite the right stable. The simple sensual man in Voysey was at odds with the rather elementary social being who had been told you didn't, if you could help it, sleep with a fellow's sister. There was sweat on his forehead – he had been eating in nervous haste – and now there was a thin lock of hair across it. Craine looked at this and made a discovery.

It was the small discovery that, when he called Voyseys and Petford-Smiths and Dilgers and Hallidays to mind in the sort of context he had lately been creating for them, his fancy took them for granted as a good deal younger than they in fact now were. And he would somehow less have disliked the insignificant intrigue upon which he had stumbled if Voysey's hair hadn't been touched by middle age even more than his own, and if Jane – in spite of all that her adventure was doing for her looks – hadn't hollows to conceal in her neck, and certain small but unobliteratable lines round the eyes. It wasn't a logical feeling, but it was certainly an instinctive one. An aesthetic rather than a moral sense was in question. If these two people were – what Craine didn't for a moment believe – in some deeply passionate relationship, their state might speak powerfully to the imagination and the sympathies. But it couldn't speak directly to the senses, simply because it came to one as a vagary unsupported by the heyday in the blood. One preserved towards these matters, it seemed, the judgement of one's adolescence – the judgement that the amative ceases to be agreeable or even excusable when it exhibits itself in the parental age-group. And yet clearly – clearly, Craine repeated to himself, looking at his companions – one can make no end of an ass of oneself at an age when one's grandchildren might well be at one's knee.

'Do you say Jill is visiting friends – Italian friends ?' Jane Petford-Smith was sharply curious. 'Didn't she once live in Italy quite a lot ? Wasn't she in with the nobs ?'

'I don't know about the nobs.' Craine hated the affectation that used such terms. 'But she certainly spent several years in Italy. It was before I knew her, and during her first marriage. And yes – it's an Italian acquaintance she's visiting, Marchesa Forni.'

'Somebody you don't know yourself, Rupert ?'

'Somebody I met for the first time yesterday.' Jane, Craine could see, was in a state to scent intrigue anywhere, and she had formed the notion that there was something odd about his being alone here in Arezzo. So, for that matter, there was. He did, for the present at least, quite substantially have something to conceal – for he couldn't dream of communicating to these casually encountered adulterers the first intelligence of John Arnander's being alive. So he said a few words about the Marchesa's present situation and a few more by way of speculation on the manner of life awaiting her in Florence. If he gave the impression of being close he didn't at all mind. And Jane couldn't positively push, since he could give an overtly awkward twist to her own position by himself asking some of the simplest of questions. Presently, indeed, she gave up, rose with a word, and vanished.

If she wanted to powder her nose, presumably the small restaurant had at least primitive accommodation for the purpose. It was Craine's sense, however, that it was with malice she had left the two men together. She got some amusement from the thought of their sitting in uncomfortable silence. Yet it was somehow just not this that happened. They didn't, indeed, for some time speak; but they did – if only metaphorically – breathe more freely. They even exchanged a glance. This couldn't be called collusion, but at least it signalled sympathetic intelligence. They might have been two males escaping unobtrusively from a drawing-room on the simple lure of a game of billiards.

And presently Voysey spoke. 'I say,' he asked cautiously, 'how d'you like the look of oil?'

'I think oil looks better than some of them are running about saying.'

'Do you, now?' Voysey was impressed. 'It's the devil of a business knowing what to do with people's money, all the same. They have such a damned lot of it.'

Craine considered. 'There are the Scottish trusts.'

'Yes, of course. Get you a bit of spread in dollars, I agree. But I've had a fly out over that stream for some time. . . . By Jove, better get a bill.' Voysey waved to a waiter. 'Put you in with me, old chap.'

'No, no. I'll pay for myself.'

'Eh? Oh, I see.' Voysey looked awkward, as if he now felt there had been some indelicacy in proposing to treat Craine as a guest at his guilty board. 'Well, we must be getting along. Back to Florence, that is.'

'But you're going to look at a few more things here first?'

'Oh, I don't know. Perhaps Jane will want to take a walk round. Care to come along? I realize you know a devilish lot more about it all than either of us do. Quite a line of yours, I've heard.'

Craine shook his head. 'Letter to write, I'm afraid. Don't miss Santa Maria della Pieve. It's half-way up the hill.'

'Some good stuff, eh?'

'Well, there's a Madonna by Pietro Lorenzetti. But the great thing's the façade.'

'The façade.' Voysey appeared to take adequate mental note of this circumstance. 'Here's Jane again. We'll be off.'

And in a couple of minutes they had gone. Jane Petford-Smith spoke only half a dozen further words to Craine. But she parted with a look that shook him. For it was a look – there was no other way of interpreting it – that told him mockingly and triumphantly that he had been too slow and too late. The insinuation was, it couldn't be other than, a monstrous and insolent fabrication. He had never, in the vulgar phrase, made the ghost of a pass at the woman. Yet how queerly she had been hovering in his mind only a couple of hours ago! He sat for some time frowning at this – at what, once more, may bob up when things threaten to come unstuck. He smoked a cigarette. He even ordered a brandy, and then thought better of drinking it.

Even with this lingering, he found he had miscalculated his time. He came up into the square to see his late companions climbing into their car, and a discontented porter shoving a couple of suitcases in the boot. They drove off with a wave, and he strolled to the corner and watched them down the hill. The car went straight on beneath the winking traffic light at the bottom. Wherever they were going, it wasn't Florence. Perhaps they had decided that Siena was the best place to spend the night. Craine turned away, and stretched his legs to some effect in the other direction.

CHAPTER TEN

ABOVE the old town squats a fortress big enough to play football in. It was being so used when Craine returned that way in the late afternoon. For some time he watched the play. Those who hadn't boots, he noticed, made do with gym shoes, and he had to admire an energy that didn't seem very substantially based on an intake of calories. But he soon turned away to circle the ramparts – to circle them again and again as a chill wind began to blow down from the Apennines and the light faded across the Valle di Chiana. One had here at least the illusion of commanding the approaches to the city. There would have been no diffi-culty in spotting an army, a large troop of horse, even a railway train. But a motor-car was another matter, and he had to acknowledge as irrational the prompting that took his gaze so often into distance. He was familiar with sus-pense; there were times when he sat, alone or in a small group, waiting some sufficiently fateful word from Tokyo or New York or Rome. But this felt different. Part of the strain came from his inability not to strive to persuade himself that there wasn't, that there wasn't really any occasion for a feeling of suspense at all.

His lunch-hour encounter nagged at him – only the more so because it had, after all, no clear relevance. He wasn't going to run away with anybody and Jill wasn't either; and this was sensible, since they would neither of them make much of it. If Jim Voysey and his mistress were having a wonderful time – and they certainly were, although there might be headaches later – one wished them luck and moved on.

Craine moved on. He made, that is to say, another circle of the battlements; and in the course of it, sure enough, his late experience did at last drop out of his mind. But this wasn't to his comfort; it left nothing except the urgency of his wish that Jill should come back to him. Or just that she should come back, that he should catch a glimpse of her before night fell. Arezzo thrust lengthening shadows at him as he stood looking into the west – shadows like exploring fingers intent on getting him where it hurt. For a moment he was frightened of the simple fact that it would soon be dark; as frightened as a child might be when left alone.

But you looked these unweaned moments straight in the eye and they retreated rapidly. If they didn't, it was just too bad and you betrayed yourself, as John Arnander had done on that abominable bridge. He'd take another turn round this gloomy place – the footballers had departed and it now lay deserted – and then go back to his hotel. He could reasonably calculate that Jill would arrive as he himself had done on the previous day, for a rather late dinner.

Lights were coming out in the city. He paused a moment or two to look at them, and for some reason thought of the watch-fires of the Greeks kindling on the plain of Xanthus. On ramparts vaguely like these a young man had lingered, waiting for the return of Cressida. Craine shook his head. It wasn't a good comparison. Indeed, it couldn't be called a comparison at all; it was an almost random image fished up in him by some lurking taste for pathos or self-pity. He was no Troilus, the young lover of a night. He was a maturely married man. At home he had two children and an umbrella and a bowler hat. Jill had four children, and pearls which she put on for his birthday. Neither of them had anything to do with windy Troy. They couldn't have. They simply couldn't. He turned away and walked back into Arezzo.

Hours later, he dined alone. The little restaurant was empty. Its evening clientele, at this time of the year mostly unattached business men, had departed, and for entertainment he had the choice of either a television set or his own thoughts. The television offered a boxing match – which in any circumstances he would have judged poorly of as an aid to digestion. On the other hand he found that his head no longer admitted any succession of fancies tenuously tied to his situation. His mind was now concentrated on Arnander, concentrated on the blind man who had turned from his basket-making to put himself in some small degree of relationship with a visitor the day before.

He wondered in the first place whether he had himself achieved at all an accurate and adequate impression. To what extent, for instance, was Arnander in command of his own moods? How much fuller and more definite a communication with others could he manage if he were minded to it? Craine couldn't be certain that the man had even very securely identified his visitor, or understood that visitor's relationship to Jill. Perhaps then he himself in his recital – here in this restaurant the night before – had altogether understated Arnander's mere strangeness, and so sent Jill unprepared to the full shock of it. After all, it was she who must take the brunt of comparing then and now. Perhaps, for her, nothing that she could call John Arnander still existed. Perhaps this would be the definite result of that day's meeting.

Certainly it was what he found himself hoping for. He was entitled, in his heart, to do that – but not entitled to go on doing so if his intellect told him that he was thereby deluding himself. And there remained another, and quite different, possibility. It was that Arnander *did* command his moods, and that yesterday he had, in a sense, been foxing. Whatever his feelings for Jill had been during these absent years, when she was round the corner he wanted her – as he certainly didn't want the man who had set up as her husband. So he would be a far more positive person today than he had been yesterday. Craine glanced at his watch – an action he was managing to avoid except at substantial intervals. It seemed indeed as if Arnander might have been progressively a more positive person into the late evening.

The restaurant door opened, and he looked up quickly. It was the porter from his hotel, and he knew the meaning of his appearance. He had arranged to be summoned if a telephone call came through, and in a moment he was crossing the small square. The shuttered façades, uncertainly suspended under a black velvet sky, seemed as flat as a back-drop, so that one almost expected to see them stir in the thin chill wind. He heard a faint sound of cheering, as if his appearance against this *décor* were being applauded by some audience of interested dwarfs. The sound came from behind the glass doors of the café, where the televised boxing match was providing excitement for a dimly distinguishable fuggy crowd. He passed through the lobby of the hotel and picked up the telephone receiver. What he heard was Marchesa Forni's voice.

She spoke, harshly and rapidly, in English. It was the language in which she had contrived grotesque misapprehension before, and he at once tried to change to Italian now. But she would not be deflected, and he had to put up with a message the bare sense at least of which was clear, although the implications of the tone in which it was conveyed baffled him. Jill was staying at Castelarbia for the night. She would be back in Arezzo by noon on the following day. What more the Marchesa said before ringing off was unintelligible, and he had a sense that it wasn't meant to be otherwise. If the old lady had been for a brief space potentially an ally, she was that no longer. He put down the instrument, thanked the porter, and went slowly up to his room.

He hesitated for a moment before undressing, for it came to him that he ought to find a car and drive straight over to Castelarbia through the night. But that wouldn't do; it had been the understanding that Jill should find her own line. If she had been in any way knocked out by the situation, the Marchesa would presumably have said so – and it was an inherently improbable conjecture, anyway. Only the fact that Jill hadn't herself done the telephoning was queer.

Thought upon, it proved to be queerness of a numbing

114

order. Half an hour later, and against all his expectations, Craine had fallen into deep sleep.

But very early he woke up – before the labourers had begun their excavations beneath his window. He had no fancy for a solitary breakfast here, and as soon as he had dressed he left the hotel. There had been a drift of rain at dawn, and the smells around him, although urban, suggested spring. He walked down to the railway station and bought a newspaper; sitting in an Espresso bar he turned over its damp sheets, forcing himself to read. Then he walked back to the square. The front of San Francesco lay in shadow, cold and uninviting. But people were coming and going on the steps, disappearing through, or emerging from, the small leather door in an ant-like activity, straggling and irregular but purposeful. When he had watched for some time he went into the church himself.

The business of the place already went forward. A little knot of people knelt before the Tarlati chapel, and as he walked up the nave he heard the sanctus bell. At the same time a lay brother was at work with a broom; he plied it in a practised circle round an old man who knelt in isolation before some waxwork contrivance against the west wall. The whole church stood chill and dim, with only a pale light striking through the high disorientated windows beyond the altars. Opposite the waxwork a bustling functionary was opening up a booth; he flicked a feather duster over the authorized guide-books, the beads and bangles and medals, the *quattrocento* reproductions that were stacked indifferently with the popular iconographic monstrosities of contemporary Catholic devotion. It all seemed to Craine alien and meaningless, like some old mouldering volume in a language to which he hadn't the key.

He edged round the worshippers and went into the choir. He sat down on a meagre bench. He was in the presence of a decayed harmonium, badly in need of dusting, and suggesting to his Anglican mind the utmost dismalness of dissent. He was in the presence of a pile of tattered music, several broken chairs, and a tangle of electric flex so perished and casual that one would have expected the high altar to which it led to have gone up in flame long ago. He was in the presence, too, of what he had now for many years considered to be the supreme achievement of Western art.

It had been apparently without design that he had drifted here – but he supposed that he must really have come in to see if these things were any good; if Piero's frescoes had any virtue for a London banker in a great state of personal anxiety. And of course they had none at all. If he made a firm effort of the will, he might succeed in exploiting them as a distraction – as in some degree he had managed to do with the same painter's Magdalen the day before. But in that role they would come, surely, a poor second to the cinema.

He looked at the Torture of Judas. The officer conducting the interrogation was, in his impassive way, entirely benevolent; it was unexpectedly that he had one hand in Judas's hair and the other grasping a cudgel. And why did he have a ticket in his cap, like the Mad Hatter? This was something to the explaining of which, surely, the learned had never got round.

Craine sat for a long time in a sort of nadir of sensation. There had been times when he judged the fine arts to be famous nonsense. But now he just wasn't attending to them. Perhaps it came to the same thing. And it was sensible enough to feel that he had, at the moment, other things to think about. Or had – if he *could* think. He didn't now seem to be doing much in that way either. He was simply sitting in the choir of San Francesco in Arezzo. That seemed about all that could be said.

And he would have to sit some time longer. He made this discovery presently, just as he had made it on several occasions here before. The Minor Friars were demons – if one might put it that way – for non-stop devotion; and no sooner was a celebration finished in the Tarlati chapel than another began either in the Guasconi or – as now – at the high altar itself. And that made one a prisoner here in the choir, unless – what indeed nobody might much mind – one emerged rather awkwardly as from the wings upon the ritual. Craine didn't care for that. He would wait here until he could leave without a sense of apology. The choir was cold, but he didn't mind a little external chill. It matched the way he felt inside.

He stayed for a long time, with no more than a hovering sense of what was around him – as if, almost, he had been a corpse laid up in some austerely splendid tomb. Even when the mass was over he didn't stir. An old man entered the choir, and climbed painfully to a low scaffolding against the east wall. He was engaged – whether for purposes learned or artistic or commercial it was impossible to say – in making a water-colour copy of the head of St Helena. Then came a woman with a guide-book. Although the morning was not yet far advanced, she had the air of one who is bored and tired. But her face brightened a little when she saw that something was going forward; she paused beside Craine and watched for a moment the old man arranging his brushes. Then she spoke in a cautious whisper. 'Is he touching them up?' she asked. 'They do look as if they needed it.' Her voice became aggrieved, baffled. 'They look so old, so mouldering!'

The woman drifted away. Italy was letting her down badly, it must be supposed. Craine shifted his seat. He'd take one look at the Death of Adam. He did so, and again without much conscious sensation; only he was obscurely aware of a sort of phantom scene-shifting at the back of his mind, a change of stresses and proportions and perspectives accomplishing itself behind a curtain that might presently rise. He stood up and walked down the long nave of the church, pausing only to put a small sum of money in a box. He had a notion that he owed the place something – and a notion too that he would never enter it again.

Clear sunlight filled the square. The woman with the

guide-book had sat down outside the café and put on dark glasses; through these she was looking about her with regained poise. Craine felt his own vision to be improved – or at least he'd brought back into focus the salient features of his scene. A job he could get down to without delay, for instance; it had oddly slipped from him but now he had hold of it again. He walked over to the hotel, collected some letters and went up to his room. There was still a clatter going on outside. He crossed to the window and looked down. The man with the horse and cart was at work; he had just thrown aside his pick and was shovelling up earth and broken brick; dust rose in clouds around him and changed to gold where it caught the sunshine. Craine turned to his letters. He had opened the first of them when he heard a step – Jill's step – in the corridor. A moment later she was in the room.

When she saw him she stopped – as if their moment had come minutes earlier than she had expected. Downstairs, the porter couldn't have told her he was in the hotel. She made as if to speak, stopped, and sat down on his bed.

She looked old – not so young as he'd remembered. What first flickered in his mind was just that; it was as if she were an acquaintance he hadn't seen for some time. Then in an instant this detached response vanished and he was flooded with anxiety, with a shocking fear that she must be ill.

She was stroking the coverlet where it rose over the pillow. Then her hand became motionless. 'I slept with him,' she said.

'I see.' The words didn't represent his first impulse. He wanted to cry out, strangely and indecently, that at least she might have enjoyed it, at least not come back looking like this. More strangely and indecently still, there rose before him the face of Jane Petford-Smith, renewed and radiant from her wretched amour, and he felt a bitter helpless anger that sprang from he didn't know what and directed itself at he didn't know whom – a mere incoherence of emotion that left him trembling.

'It wasn't pity,' she said.

This time his thought came clear. 'I hope it was passion. Otherwise it's a muddle – a mess.'

'Passion?' She shook her head. 'I don't think I'd call it that.' Her hand again strayed across the coverlet, and again checked itself. 'I was his wife, I suppose.'

'You're certainly his wife.'

She looked at him as if he had said something puzzling. 'I didn't say that,' she said. 'Not that I am his wife. Just that I was.'

'Last night?'

'In the past, I was meaning. But, yes – last night too.' She raised her exhausted face and gave him a long look. 'Have I lost you? It can't be true. Rupert, it can't be! It doesn't make sense.'

He saw that she hardly knew what she said; that she had come back shocked as from some ghastly accident. And suddenly Arnander was almost physically before him – the blind, meagre man. His anger returned and took direction. 'Is it your idea,' he asked, 'that you might shuttle ... commute, as they say?'

'I don't understand.'

'It used to be all the go, here in Italy. They called it *cicisbeism*. A husband and a lover.'

She stood up – and he realized that he had said a meaningless, unforgivable thing. 'Of course not, Rupert.' She made a helpless gesture. 'But it's happened so suddenly!'

'Yes – thanks to that incompetent old woman. I take it she must have approved your coming together again?'

'Yes, Rupert. She pretty well took the money at the door.'

The wild joke might have left him gasping – but somehow it drew him towards her unbearably. 'And I thought,' he said, 'she'd be jealous of any other woman!'

'I think she is. But she has strong orthodox feelings, I suppose, about who's who – with husbands and wives, I mean.'

'No doubt. Do you know that, the day before yesterday, she was all for conspiring with me to keep you ignorant of John Arnander's existence?'

'So you told me. But, I suppose, once I was there –' Jill broke off. 'But the Marchesa isn't – is she? – important. What's important is' – she looked at him in grave desperate appeal – 'that I've done something final?'

He found no reason to hesitate for an instant. Jill herself didn't yet know; her confusion was deep and real. But he knew – knew that an absolute of her character was concerned. 'Yes,' he said.

She looked straight into his eyes. Then, unexpectedly, she smiled – so that his heart was pierced and uplifted at once. 'I'm glad,' she said, 'that I'm not a fallen woman.'

There was a roar and a clatter from below. The man with the motor-tricycle was back on the job. Underneath the wall of San Francesco – the very wall on the other side of which, like the symbolic obverse of a medal, the sons of Adam cried out their timeless woe – the common business of Arezzo was being achieved with a bit of heave and sweat. Craine went over to the telephone which stood between their beds. He waited till the noise had stopped. 'I suppose they can get me Rome,' he said.

'Rome?' She had turned to her suitcase, opened it, and begun to pack; and now it was with a flicker of her familiar comradely mockery that she spoke. 'Do you want to talk about us to the Pope?'

He shook his head. 'I'll leave that to Marchesa Forni. But what I won't leave to her is Arnander's eyes. I got the impression that only some local man was consulted. Probably his opinion was sound – and even if anything could have been done, it's now likely to be too late. But you never know. We'll get hold of their best people here. The world's best people, if there's a shadow of doubt.'

Jill stared at him, and then slowly nodded. 'And you'll find out how to do it?'

'Of course. It's the least I can do for him.'

He picked up the receiver. Quietly, so as not to disturb him, she continued to pack.

PART TWO

THE ARNANDERS

CHAPTER ONE

'Do you remember,' Charles Arnander asked, 'how I used to be terribly keen on clouds?'

'Yes, I remember.' Tim Arnander glanced tolerantly at his younger brother. Charles, he was thinking, had immature notions of what constituted a large passing of time. Although of course – and Tim's gaze went back to the veranda of the clinic upon which it had been fixed – quite recent parts of one's life can seem a long way off when important and transforming events have happened since. 'But what about it?' he asked. 'What makes you think of your old clouds now?'

'Simply that it wouldn't be any good – not, I mean, here in Italy. Because there aren't any.'

'That's just a matter of the season. At other times of year there are tremendous storms here. Mummy was talking about them this morning. They go growling and muttering through these hills.'

'From crag to crag leaps the live thunder?'

'That sort of thing. There's a pine tree behind this villa that's been blasted by lightning. So if we come back to Vallombrosa at Christmas you can have clouds to your heart's content.'

'Shall we come back?'

'I suppose it depends on how Daddy gets on.' Tim gazed out into distance, frowning. There was a tremendous view from the terrace. That was one reason why their villa was considered the grandest here. You can't deny – Tim said to himself – that it's useful, this being rich enough to have what you like. Only it would be dangerous if what you liked wasn't really at all nice, or the thing. Aloud, he said: 'Of course there's to be the second operation. Then we'll know. But I wish we could have Daddy at Pinn.'

Charles straightened himself on the chair in which he had been lounging. 'But it wouldn't be proper. Would it?'

'Not if Rupert were there. The whole situation's difficult.'

'I suppose it is.' Charles let his attention wander – as he was prone to do when talk of difficulties turned up. He got to his feet and strolled to the edge of the terrace. There was a sheer drop – it must be hundreds of feet, he thought – and beyond this the sunlit valley lay like a great golden beaker. He stretched out his arms as if proposing to pick up the whole spectacle and drink; discreetly switched this to a gesture of mere laziness; and wandered back to his brother, gazing upwards as he did so at the line of dark trees behind the villa. 'Thick as autumnal leaves,' he said. 'Tim – you know? Thick as autumnal leaves that strow the brooks in Vallombrosa. And here we are. Isn't it extraordinary?'

'Is it?' Tim was still watching the clinic. 'You can write an essay about it when you get back to school. Poets I thought about on my holidays.'

'And that line – it's mysterious. Thick as autumnal leaves that strow the brooks in Vallombrosa. It *is* mysterious, isn't it? You agree?' Charles asked his question with anxiety.

'Certainly it's mysterious. It would continue mysterious however tiresomely you went on spouting it.' As usual, Tim was fair even when irritated. 'But it isn't more mysterious than Virgil. *Tendebantque manus ripae ulterioris amore.*'

'I suppose that's all right,' Charles said doubtfully. And he repeated at once: 'Thick as autumnal leaves that strow the brooks in Vallombrosa. Tim, don't you think this is a most extraordinary country?'

'I like it very much.'

'No – I *mean* extraordinary. The journey didn't seem to me through part of the ordinary world at all. The towns on the hills, the poplars and the cypresses, the light – ' Charles broke off. He was in a state of simmering imaginative excitement. 'All really there,' he went on, 'but more like what you just miss seeing before you go to sleep.'

'I've told you nothing of that sort happens to me before

126

I go to sleep.' Tim's impatience persisted. Virgil was much more to him than stuff to construe, and he would grow up with quick responses to whatever life offered him. But there was something in Charles – an imprudent degree of involvement with the touch and sight and sound of things – that it was his instinct to hold off. 'Here he comes,' he said.

Their father had appeared on the veranda opposite. He was fully dressed today, and they knew that it was something he had insisted on. His eyes were still bandaged. There was a nurse at his elbow; she guided him to a chair and began to arrange his pillows. But he had hardly sat down when he waved her away with a quick impatient gesture.

'Have you noticed ?' Charles asked. 'He doesn't like her.'

'Sister Barfoot ? No, I don't think he does. Perhaps she won't come with him, after all.'

'Come with him ?'

'Over here – when he's ready to leave the clinic. She's a private nurse, you know, and the idea is she'll stay on for a time. She's frightfully pretty.'

'Yes, isn't she.' Charles agreed quickly, but only because he thought Tim's remark strange. It was like a clock striking unexpectedly and telling you the hour is later than you'd supposed. 'Shall we go across ?' he asked.

'Better wait till we're called. Mummy's over there now. She'll come out in a minute. You can see he's waiting for her now.'

'Yes, you can.' Charles had sat down again, and now he lay back in his chair with a careful appearance of relaxation. 'Wouldn't you say,' he asked, 'that Daddy's frightfully dependent on her ?'

Tim nodded. 'He hasn't much use for anybody else. But that's quite right, you know.'

'I suppose it is. But aren't you jealous of him ?'

'Yes.' Tim, although he disliked the question, didn't hesitate to give it a straight answer. 'Rupert said there must be an awkward period of readjustment all round.'

'Rupert says quite absurd things. But he's the most civilized person we know.'

'He'd certainly never wave anybody away like that.'

Charles sat up again. 'But you must remember Daddy's had a frightful time.'

'I'm not criticizing.'

'Are you sure?' Charles was challenging. 'What do you honestly think of Daddy?'

'Oh, shut up!' Tim was now really disapproving.

'I think it's a proper question. It's not as if he'd always been there. He's new. So one has to make up one's mind.'

'I think perhaps you're right.'

'But probably one oughtn't to talk it out in a hurry.' Charles often executed rapid retreats before his brother's open-mindedness. 'Not while he's almost *quite* new. Not that it isn't months and months since we were first told about it. Why are the doctors so slow?'

'There has to be rather a long interval between the first operation and the second. And there was delay over the first. Don't you remember? Far the best man to do it was in New York. But Daddy wouldn't go.'

'Daddy was difficult at first – queer, almost?'

'I think so. Certainly he wouldn't go to America. And Rupert had a tremendous business persuading the surgeon to come to Italy. The second operation is going to be just as difficult. But fortunately the right man for it is in Rome. Look, there's Mummy.'

Charles sprang up. 'And she's waving us to go across.'

'Then come on.'

Although it was Charles who was eager, it was Tim who had been waiting, and who already led the way. He strode forward – his legs were really lengthening – with his lips compressed and the frown that gathered on his forehead on stiff occasions. They were a family, the Arnanders, and it was proper that they should be together. But the thing shook him, all the same, every day. And he said to himself openly that his heart was at Pinn, with Rupert.

And they weren't, this time, together for very long. Almost at once, their mother went away – leaving the boys sitting on the veranda, on either side of their father's knees. Tim was displeased by an action that had too much design in it. It had happened two or three times before, this man- oeuvre like a match-making, a leaving together of persons whom it is designed to make lovers. Tim felt his body go stiff, and he knew that if he wasn't careful his voice would go stiff as well. But that wouldn't do; it wouldn't be at all fair. For their mother was right in the efforts she made to bring them together. Tim had it clear in his head that his father wasn't ever going to be really important to him, al- though it might be different with Charles. But he knew that, on the other hand, he might be important to his father – and that his mother might much want him to be. His father was certainly short of human beings who meant much to him.

And there was something more. Their mother might well feel the need to share the burden so suddenly reimposed on her. For there was something here that Tim had no difficulty in seeing. Presumably it was a joy, getting back a husband from the dead; presumably it was a joy, even when you had one already. About that, Tim didn't certainly know; it was outside his range. But he did know that you had only to look at John Arnander to realize that he was a burden and a problem and a responsibility as well. Most of all, perhaps, a responsibility. That, at least, was how Rupert would feel about it : Rupert who, quite early on, had said abruptly that Arnander was a man in a million. Tim didn't at all suppose he was a father in a million, or that his mother's anxiety to bring them together proceeded from any calculation tend- ing that way. Although again it might be different with Charles, there was no doubt about himself. His mother would be using him to help with some sort of support of his father – distinctly that, and not the other way about.

As Tim arrived at this perception, he felt his stiffness leave him. He'd resent, in this relation, being planned for. But he didn't mind being used. And provided it was clear that he carried on with Rupert Craine as a stepfather, he didn't at all mind having a shot at being John Arnander's real son. Having got thus far, he felt prompted to speak. 'It's a perfectly gorgeous day,' he said.

Most unexpectedly – for he had never done it before – his father laughed. 'Do you know what you sound like, Tim? A civil servant – a high-up civil servant – who has cleared what's called his "in" tray and feels that he can conscientiously look out of the window.'

Charles giggled delightedly. He couldn't have made much of the joke, but he liked his father's voice: the foreignness on the surface, the faint cockney underneath. Tim didn't smile. He knew that his father, from the darkness in which he still lived and must, perhaps, go on living, was exercising some special power that went along with his being not an ordinary person. He was exercising it rather clumsily, as if for long he hadn't exercised it at all. Tim knew that it was something to be welcomed. He understood – although, in fact, nobody had put it to him that way – that his father would recover his sight in vain, unless he recovered other possessions as well: faculties or powers such as flickered in him when he said these rather raw perceptive things. Understanding this, Tim felt that any lead must be followed, any sort of talk kept up. 'And what about Charles, Daddy?' he asked. 'What does he sound like when he talks?'

'Something fizzy. It might be champagne, or it might be lemonade.'

'And what do *we* think about *you*?' Charles almost shouted this – shouted it through laughter, so that Tim looked at him in reproof. Charles was going full tilt into this new relationship, just as, at home, he would take those reckless headers into the swimming-pool.

'Yes, what do you think about me?' Their father had spoken after a moment's silence. But it wasn't that he had been disconcerted by Charles. It was simply that his mind had taken a dive after their mother; he was wondering where she had gone, when she would come back. 'Charles, what do *you* think I'm like?'

'Well, we don't know what you look like, to begin with. It depends on your eyes.' Charles was so wound up that he let himself be checked only for a second by the way Tim froze at this. 'But you're small, with a very thin neck; and you're almost bald, and there are wrinkles on your skull. So I think you're like a tortoise. Your head comes out – an ageless sort of head. It moves to and fro, and takes in an awful lot, and then goes in again under a very hard shell.'

'There's something else about a tortoise, that fits in.' Their father's voice was suddenly harsh. 'A tortoise moves intolerably slowly. And so do I. God, how slowly!'

'It isn't true.' Tim hadn't meant to speak; and now he didn't know whether there was warmth or coldness in his voice. 'Of course I know that the doctors need a lot of time. That's slow. It has to be. But you've come a long way, all the same – for instance, just to be sitting talking with us now; just to be bothering with us.'

'You're quite right, Tim. And I think it's a habit you're forming.'

'A habit?'

'Being quite right – or the next thing to it.' Their father's voice was gentle again, and quite untouched by irony. 'Stick to it.'

There was a silence. John Arnander had a small glass on a table beside him. He reached for it and drank. Tim didn't know whether it was medicine or an aperitif, but he noticed – now for the second or third time – the certainty with which his father's hand found it, picked it up, and set it down again. There was satisfaction in watching the small action performed – and moreover, although so small, it was somehow rather largely significant.

'Supposing I see.' Arnander's voice had changed again. This time it was spuriously casual, was almost comically like Charles's voice when approaching something serious. 'Supposing I see. Shall I be able to jump on a bicycle and ride away on it? Or shall I always wobble a bit, even if I don't take positive tumbles? That's the question, you know. Tim, you understand me?'

'Yes, Daddy.'

'Good boy. It's a matter of what happens to acquired

skills.' Arnander's voice rose again. 'It's quite devilishly a matter of that.' He paused. 'I was in very poor fleece, you know.' He paused again. 'Until your mother came. You see, I'd thrown up the sponge. And sheep get in desperately poor fleece when they do that. I don't know how it is with tortoises.'

Charles's laughter rang out across the veranda – to be checked as his father's hand came to rest for a moment on his head. 'Sorry,' Charles said. 'Am I disturbing the other patients?'

'Bother the other patients. There aren't any about, are there?'

'I can't see any.'

'And that tiresome English nurse – she's cleared out?'

'Yes. She's probably making herself tea.'

'Then for two or three minutes we can be serious. That's what your mother would like: that we should be extremely serious – the three Arnander men.' Arnander raised a hand – so that it was exactly as if he had seen Tim's lips coming firmly together. 'Wait. Wait until you hear what I say. It's about painting. Neither of you is going to be a painter, thank goodness. Of course I expect that Tim, when he goes up – isn't it? – to New College, will take with him a nice talent for sketching in oils. But that isn't painting. Charles, poor chap, will never do more than swim in ink. So there's no call to exhibit painting to you – well, in glowing colours.'

'You mean,' Tim asked, 'as inspiration, and tremendous joy in making things, and so on?'

'It's an immense labour of learning. You know, Tim, what faces a Chinese if he wants to learn to read and write? Painting's worse. There are not thousands of small intricate things that you must learn, but millions. You have to paint and paint – until you're blind, pretty well.'

'You mean,' Charles asked, 'that it's frightfully technical?'

'It's frightfully technical. You have the void and you have chaos: a square of canvas, say, and a mess of pigments. And you have to go ahead. It's a great sweat, and

I've often thought it astonishing that painters have any energy to spare to talk about it. But they do, endlessly – about all the brute hard work of it. What they don't much talk about, because it's useless and perhaps dangerous, is the something else.'

'There is something else ?' Charles asked gravely. He was looking at his father's shrouded face round-eyed.

'There's the small still thing at the centre, the mystery it's all about. Nobody has ever so much as caught a glimpse of it – not of the thing itself. But there are shadows of it. And one of the shadows is all that one can hope to have the tremendous luck to meet.'

'A person ?' Tim asked in a low voice.

'Yes. And the queer thing is that it may be so without one's very clearly knowing it. A person may be carrying the mystery, whom you think of as carrying no more than some of the fairly common desirable things of life.' Arnander was silent for a few moments. 'A priest,' he said, 'carrying the chalice. And you treat him as a wine-waiter bringing a sound claret.'

The boys sat quite still. Neither of them could have moved a muscle. Then their father turned his head as if listening. 'Where's your mother ?' he asked.

'I think she's gone over to the villa,' Tim said. 'But she'll be back in no time. Can we get you anything ?'

'Can we get you Sister Barfoot ?' Charles asked this apparently as a slapdash means of relieving tension. And he added – as he wouldn't have done except from the same motive : 'Tim says she's frightfully pretty.'

'No doubt she is.' Their father received this indifferently. 'But she's a nuisance, all the same. The only mistake your mother ever made.' He drained his glass. 'Shall we go back to being rather serious ?'

'Yes, certainly.' Tim spoke at once. He still felt sure that he was going to go on observing his father from a distance. But this didn't mean that he mightn't grow to like him. Some things he liked already. John Arnander didn't have the common affectation of treating young people absolutely

133

as if they were grown up. But he didn't talk down or patronize either. And his jokes – although they might have something lurkingly cruel in them – were jokes and not facetiousness.

'You said I'd come a long way, Tim. That's frank and true. You might have added that it wasn't under my own steam. The question seems to be whether it's likely to be worth it. All round, I mean. Because there's a heavy bill.'

For a moment Tim was astray – thinking of what it cost, for instance, to bring a surgeon across the Atlantic. Then he understood. 'There's Rupert,' he said coldly. 'And the children.'

'Exactly.' Their father spoke unemotionally. But he had turned his head and was listening again – almost, Tim thought, as a man might do who feels the approach of danger. 'I suppose,' he asked abruptly, 'you've been told all about how it began ? Rupert will have told you all about the bridge, and so forth ?'

'Yes, of course.' Charles answered eagerly. 'Rupert told us – although we knew a little already. He told us how you volunteered for something frightfully tough –'

'A sort of Commando job,' Tim interrupted.

' – and how you were badly knocked out, trying to carry it through.'

There was another silence, and then John Arnander nodded his bandaged head. 'So I was,' he said. 'Very badly knocked out indeed. And that's all Rupert said ?'

'Yes. He didn't explain what happened afterwards. He said you might care to talk about it one day, but that we mustn't expect you to. He told us about a friend of his, a fighter pilot with a wonderful record in the Battle of Britain, who would never say a word about the war.'

'I see.' Arnander's hands had been on the arms of his chair. Now they rose restlessly in the first groping action that Tim had seen him perform – rose, and then dropped idly on his knees. 'But you are both old enough, I think, to realize that this noble silence has to cover quite a lot ?' He paused. 'You haven't, I imagine, many friends whose fathers have let their mothers marry again and have children, and then bobbed up on them out of the blue – or the dark?' He had hesitated on the last word – and now he made another pause. But the boys said nothing. They were looking straight into one another's eyes, as was their habit in crisis. 'The fact is,' their father went on, 'that if you are to accept me at all, it must be as the sort of person I am. It's hateful and vulgar to talk about being an artist. Still, an artist I am. And my art and myself are one thing. That's a hard saying – but there's more truth in it than in your Rupert's tactful picture of me. I've always been far too interested in that one thing – far too absorbed in it, commanded by it – to be any sort of Horatius when a bridge comes along. Or to be any sort of husband when a wife comes along, or any sort of father when sons come along.' His voice had risen and gone harsh again. 'Or even to behave with ordinary responsibility under the impact of a dire calamity. Tim, what's the disposition, above all others, that a boy wouldn't choose in his father?'

'I don't think that's ever a good sort of question – a general question like that.'

'Well, I think I can give a pretty good answer myself. It's that he should get easily frightened. And I get easily frightened. I live in fear now.'

'Do you mean,' Charles asked in a careful voice, 'that you're afraid the second operation isn't going to go right, after all? For it is, you know. I'm certain it is. And they all say so.'

Arnander shook his head. 'No, Charles. It's something different. And there's one point of comfort about it. The moment they have to tell me the surgeon has made a muck of things, that fear dies. Others, I suppose, may come along. But not that one ever again.'

'Here's Mummy,' Tim said. 'She's coming over from the villa now.' He got to his feet. 'And I think Charles and I will go back. They still say, you know, that you oughtn't to have a crowd.'

'Do they? But I'm never likely to have that.' Their

father's mood had changed abruptly, and he was almost gay. 'Is she bringing a book? She reads to me from all sorts of young geniuses I've never heard of.'

Charles, although without alacrity, had got to his feet too, and was preparing to follow his brother. 'Yes,' he said, 'she's got a book. Shall we come back in the afternoon?'

'Certainly come back in the afternoon.'

'And – Daddy – will you, some time, tell us all that happened on the bridge?'

'You've rather missed the point of what I've been saying, Charles. I'm not very confident that I know all that happened on the bridge.'

The boys were back at the villa before either spoke. 'Sometimes,' Charles said cautiously, 'he's difficult to understand. Don't you think?'

Tim didn't reply to this, but gave a moment to watching, with serious attention, the Italian girl who was laying the table for lunch on the terrace. 'It wouldn't be true,' he said presently, 'to say he dramatizes himself. Or not badly.'

'What does that mean?'

Patiently Tim explained. 'But I think,' he went on, 'that most of his thinking *is* about himself. When his head goes back into his shell – and I agree that was a good picture of yours, although I don't know that you should have come out with it – it is himself that he carries on with. That's why he's so different from Rupert.'

'Rupert's more civilized. But what's really important about Daddy is his knowing about the mystery – the small thing at the centre. When you know that – know it even in what he called a shadow – you can do it.'

'Do it?' Tim frowned.

'Thick as autumnal leaves that strow the brooks in Vallombrosa. What if he paints again – like that?'

'And what if he does?' Suddenly Tim's eyes blazed as his mother's sometimes could. 'Do you think another whole gallery of the things will mend Rupert's heart?'

They looked at each other, awkward and flushed and silent, before they turned together to the table and sat down.

CHAPTER TWO

'In a way,' Groocock said, 'it would be easier for a younger man. A broken heart is at least a simplification. Just sign in each of the places where there's a pencilled cross.'

Rupert Craine signed the unimportant papers before him. Groocock, he was thinking, came out unexpectedly strong in this situation. He had his bachelor's acrid slant on it, and moreover seemed to have decided that it couldn't be handled in terms of his usual professional manner. In fact he was uncommonly good – much better than the lawyers, who were collecting substantial fees simply for expressing despondency and alarm.

Craine pushed the papers away. 'I must admit,' he said, 'that I had a moment in which I cast myself in young Troilus's role. But of course it didn't do. I saw it didn't do, as soon as I'd got the measure of the thing. Which, mind you, took a little time. I hope the story ends with Arnander sighted – if only to balance its having begun with me blind. I hadn't a glimpse, that is, of the ruthlessness required.'

'Not to fight?'

'Not to fight.'

Groocock pressed papers back into a file. 'You must have been conscious,' he said calmly, 'of choosing what might conventionally be called an unmanly course.'

'Decidedly.'

'It would add to the difficulty. And I gather that your wife didn't herself set any emphasis on the special circumstances of Arnander's being a man of genius?'

'If she had, I think I'd almost have contrived not to do so myself.'

'And it wasn't, on the other hand, his helplessness?'

'She expressly said it wasn't pity. And it wasn't religion any more than it was concupiscence. It was – well, whatever it is that is deepest in that sphere.' Craine paused for a fraction of a second. At once and quite without hesitation, you see, she did an entirely definitive thing. I state the sufficient truth when I say that she went back to her husband – not to the artist but to the man.'

'She'd be clever if she could go back to the one without going back to the other. Particularly in view of what I understood you to say.' Groocock gave Craine a glance less appropriate to an important client than to a doubtful column of figures. 'Didn't you maintain that she had been much more than a wife to the man; that she had been, in fact, a powerful inspiration to the artist?'

'In a queer fashion – yes. He would take a good look at her, and then paint a tremendous landscape.'

'Then she's not likely to have forgotten it. In fact it may be something rather more important to her than she was prepared to admit to herself while feeling some irritation before your own artistic enthusiasms and interests.'

Craine was silent. He hadn't realized that he had told Groocock so much. The fact of his having done so was a measure of the uncertainties by which he still felt himself to be surrounded. 'I don't know,' he presently said, 'that anything ambiguous or unrevealed in Jill's motive matters, really. Here we are.'

'Waiting.'

'What's that?' Craine hadn't understood.

'Waiting for the result of this second surgical operation. It's extremely important to all three of you. The whole complex of your relationships depends on it. Incidentally, I find it hard to believe in.'

'Hard to believe that anything can, after all those years, be done? I assure you that I thought it a very long shot myself, when I took it up. And it's a long shot still.'

'And you're gambling on it – all of you. If he doesn't see, if he doesn't paint, it will be a terrible sell all round.' Groocock paused grimly on this homely expression. 'Or am I wrong?'

Craine considered this. 'Well,' he said, 'take Arnander first . . .'

'Yes, take Arnander first. The man brought back from the dead. For it seems virtually to have been that. And it's something, I'd suppose, that the dead don't always like. Did Lazarus?'

'Somebody certainly wrote a play suggesting he didn't.' Craine looked curiously at Groocock. You never know what may turn up in a chap – he was thinking – when you get him in a new relation. 'Obviously it will, for Arnander, be a terrible sell. Nothing can express, I imagine, the intensity of his suspense, his expectation. If it's not unbearable to him, that's because he's got a strain of strength, you know, as well as certain notable elements of weakness. I don't care, myself, to think of failure. Still, can his last state be worse than his first? He'll still have, after all, his wife.'

'Yes – the Lord help her.'

Craine took a deep breath. But he didn't speak.

'And finally there's yourself. I suspect you've been prompted, and I'm sure you've been sustained, by the notion of this fellow getting down to the production of another set of masterpieces. It's a civilized way to take the thing, of course. But, in the way of being civilized, we can easily live beyond our income, if you ask me.'

'I'm not thinking of myself as a generous donor.' Craine felt himself to have flushed. 'And I'll thank you, my dear man, not to travesty me as a fellow willing to cuckold himself in order to give a leg up to the National Gallery. The plain fact is that I wasn't a chooser. Jill chose. But I'll admit that before she chose – or before I was certain she had chosen – there did come to me a glimmer of what I must do, if I was going to keep any proper pride. And the glimmer came – it will amuse you to know – among some pictures. Not that I was very conscious of them at the time.' Craine paused. It still seemed queer to him that it was with Groocock that this conversation was taking place. 'You see, I've always set store by painting. It's a liking that has found quite commonplace expression with me in various ways. You know how it drifts into my talk. Remember, for instance, my jawing away to you about that Amico I was buying. Well, it's a real enough devotion in its way – and when I was a lad I even had other dreams about it. They came to nothing, of course. They weren't sensible in a banker's son. But I've always kept a sense of what's what. So there you are. What glimmered at me was the perception that – very strangely – I had come on ground where I just mustn't thrust forward with violence or self-will. There were other interests at stake. And it would be a good thing if I could advance them.'

A telephone purred on Groocock's desk; he pressed a button on it and it fell silent. 'And the children?' he pursued remorselessly. 'Both families. How will it bear on them?'

'I don't think Tim Arnander will be greatly affected. He's launched, and he's an intellectual sort of lad, I expect I'll always be by way of having a word with him. Charles is different, and might take a fairly heavy impress from the change – although just of what character I don't know. In any case, Tim won't be useless to him. My own children, of course, are very young. Still, they're a tougher aspect of the problem, I'll allow. At the moment, their main impact is on the profits of the air lines. Jill and I do rather a lot of Box and Cox. She comes to Pinn. I go to London. It isn't one of those absolute muddles, you know. We haven't been in bed together since she went to bed with him.'

'Quite so, quite so.' For a moment Groocock had a relapse into his tactfully abstracted manner. He might, however, have been reflecting that the ruthlessness which his client had found himself obliged to practise was reflected in certain more direct ways of speech. 'And your decision to continue keeping it quiet for a time; is that going all right?'

'It worries the lawyers. They're terrified that something may happen which will have the effect of making us parties to a fraud. That, of course, is why Weidlé had to be told at once. He was in the middle of a big operation with Arnanders, and I had to persuade him to bring it to a standstill. Clearly I couldn't let him sell as by a dead man paintings I knew to be by somebody who is alive. As it happened, he was on the verge of tumbling to something like the truth. He's been very decent about the whole thing.'

'There are circumstances in which he stands to lose a lot of money?' Groocock's voice quite failed to take on the tone customary in it when he turned to the consideration of important financial affairs.

'Certainly there are. If Arnander has a second innings as a painter, every dab of pigment he sets on canvas will bring down the value of the canvases Weidlé already holds.'

Groocock was amused. 'It seems then, that even in those rarefied spheres one doesn't escape the operation of common economic laws. But surely counteracting factors might come into play? If the second innings was so brilliant that Arnander's reputation soared even higher than it has done . . .'

'Yes, of course. But, even so, it would mean that Weidlé was facing a desperate gamble where he believed himself to have engineered a comfortable certainty.'

Groocock laughed outright. 'I'm blessed if I feel like letting my heart bleed for him. If he really were caught out in that odd way – his dead painter, I mean, coming alive on him and turning disastrously prolific – it might come hard on his pocket, I don't doubt. But no spectator would find more than the merest light comedy in his situation. Whereas yours' – Groocock paused – 'might conceivably come to hold a pretty large dash of irony.'

'Tragic irony, as they say? Chucking a boomerang?'

'Well, yes – more or less that. Acting powerfully, as one thinks, to secure something – and in fact landing oneself with the opposite. I hope it doesn't come at you like that.'

Craine looked at his watch and stood up. 'As a matter of fact, I'm going along to see Weidlé now. So I'll tell him you judge him merely a figure of fun.'

Groocock shook his head. 'He won't be impressed. I don't collect pictures.'

'I don't know that I shall, ever again.' Craine smiled. He didn't want to close his interview with Groocock on a portentous note. 'As a matter of fact, Weidlé bustles around in the matter after a fashion that could be represented as comic enough. He's just back from Saltino. That's why I'm dropping in on him.'

'Saltino? That's where they are?'

'Yes, close by Vallombrosa. Weidlé was good enough to bring the boys back at the end of their holidays.'

'They wanted to come?'

'I don't think that Charles did. But, of course, they can't miss school. And probably it's best that they shouldn't be on the spot – just at the moment of crisis. Or so they thought.'

'They?' Groocock asked.

'Yes – the Arnanders.'

'That's what the parents are to be called, no doubt.' Suddenly, and with a gesture that would certainly have astonished the young accountants lurking behind their glass partitions, Groocock threw up his hands. 'My God, Craine – what a mess!' He got to his feet and moved to open the door. 'The crisis has come?'

'They should be operating any day now. And then almost at once – perhaps in about ten days – we'll know.'

Groocock looked very sober. 'I'm sorry that bridge didn't get the fellow,' he said. 'But, as it is – well, I can only say I wish him his eyes. And much good may they do him – and the National Gallery as well.'

CHAPTER THREE

Once before, Craine thought, he had gone on from Groo-cock's to Weidlé's. But on that occasion there had been another engagement in between. Lunch with a German banker – that had been it. Well, today too he had seen a German banker – a younger man this time, who had talked not about the wickedness of putting another generation into uniform but about its near impossibility. They had ex-changed views which would have been sombre if they hadn't been merely and grimly practical. It remained the devil, this carrying of the big collective headaches, and Craine couldn't be sure that his own share of that wasn't going to grow. Mungo's flair was as strong as ever, but it was operating, progressively and to a point of danger, in a void – or at least in a world that the old man could no longer intuitively size up. In twenty years Craine would be on that hazardous sort of shelf himself – and it would be younger men's hair that he would set tingling on their scalps. Mungo was talking the 'dash for freedom' stuff which Craine had thought of as the natural idiom of Tories so elderly as to be virtually in the Bath-chair bracket. It was harmless on the home front – Demos being only too damned good at setting trip-wires nowadays. But let the same sort of nostalgia loose in the F.O. and there might be the devil to pay. Dispatch a gunboat, send in the Marines, organize a punitive expedition. Roberts and Kitchener and Jackie Fisher. If Mungo went badly atavistic in that way it wouldn't do at all.

Not – Craine told himself as he waited for a bus – that the general grimness of things necessarily bore hardest on those, like himself, on whom it bore most directly and openly. It wasn't amongst bankers and industrialists, or even in the gibbering crew at Westminster, that one commonly met the really angsty boys. Dons, B.B.C. producers, National Service subalterns, louts in a dance hall, Arts Council daubers, Faber and Faber songsters, old Tom in the kitchen garden and young Bill at the garage: you never knew on whose back the dog clung. It was a lurking social malaise – if a dog could be a malaise – that lowered vitality, here of the gentle and there of the simple, and made the purely private rubs and bugs more formidable.

Or did it? Climbing to the top of his bus, he took himself up sharply. When war comes along, people lay off committing suicide; and even a cold war should perhaps, if anything, help the better-informed to balance up on their private anxieties. He might look at what lay on his desk, and think of what was building up at Saltino, and then sweep the whole thing together and complain that he really had too much on his plate. But it was probably sheer fallacy to suppose that the private life would be more endurable if lived amid conditions of unshakeable public security. Suppose that all this – all this of Jill and Arnander and himself – were happening just fifty years ago; was there the slightest reason to believe that it would be less disagreeable?

Craine sat down with a frown. He liked a speculative question, but this wasn't one in which he seemed to take much satisfaction. Nevertheless he must have continued to muse on it in considerable absence of mind, since he was presently quite unreasonably startled by a voice that spoke in his ear.

'Hullo, old boy,' Jim Voysey said. 'How are you getting along?'

It was a moment before Craine could account for the distaste he felt at this encounter. Voysey had undoubtedly spoken across a semantic chasm, since there existed a highly conventional Craine who froze at 'old boy' but would have taken 'old man' as venial. But this wasn't, of course, the idiocy at work; Voysey existed pretty freshly in his mind in a context that explained any lack of enthusiasm at running into him. 'Hullo,' he replied civilly. 'How are you?'

'Just starting to surface, I hope.' Voysey, although adopting a facetious idiom, took the inquiry seriously. 'It's the devil of a business, you know, that sort of thing – however smart the fellows you set to work on it.' He paused, glanced round the top of the bus, found it almost empty, and moved himself over to Craine's seat. 'Technically, you see, I'm still poor old Hugo's C.O. So it doesn't look too good, from an old-fashioned point of view.'

'But one mustn't hesitate to march with the times.' Craine, who was now sufficiently orientated, spoke with what he hoped would be a dissuasive irony.

'That's damned true. But, of course, there are regiments and regiments, after all.'

'And co-respondents and co-respondents too, you may say. They don't all wear the same shoes.'

'Ha-ha! That's deuced good.' Voysey had no appearance of being offended. 'But one has to fake it all up pretty carefully, as I say. One· mustn't give some dirty-minded old judge any chance to take a passing crack at the women involved – our women, I mean. Not the thing, eh?'

'Not the thing at all.' It's you who wear co-respondent's shoes – Craine thought uncharitably as he glanced at Voysey – but I'm damned if your grandfather wore boots.

'My wife's been a brick, I need hardly say – an absolute brick.' Voysey paused and looked puzzled, as if repetition had revealed something ambiguous in this image. 'But it's a frightful mess, all the same.'

'How,' Craine asked with simple curiosity, 'were you found out?'

'We weren't. I just came to feel, somehow, that I must get it off my chest. And it's really a ghastly muddle. Not that Jane hasn't been an absolute – hasn't been marvellous. Still, I can't help sometimes wishing that it hadn't happened at all. All the kids, you know. And so on.'

'Yes, of course.' Craine suddenly felt a strong and wholesome self-disgust. He resented Voysey as a sham member of his own class. This was absurd, for half the fellow's kind in the City were just the same. And he resented him – what was not absurd merely, but ignoble as well – because of the way in which he and his Jane Petford-Smith had popped up in Arezzo to spotlight an unbeautiful incipient wandering of his own spirit. In point of fact he ought to be grateful to Voysey for a certain bracing action on that bad day – the day things had come unstuck. 'But I expect the worst's over,' he said. 'Jane's got character – as well as other things. You'll be all right.'

'Yes – I'm sure I shall.' Voysey rather pathetically brightened. 'And, as I say, we've got hold of a good man. Not one of those smart chaps that spend all their time in the Divorce Court. I knew better than to go after one of them. The old fellows on the Bench like to score off them, you know. And you may get one in the eye by the way.'

The bus swung into the Strand. It wasn't very clear to Craine how this conversation was to be continued. He didn't, looking at Jim Voysey's florid face and indecisive mouth, find himself in command of any further reassuring remarks. 'Have you been to Italy again?' he asked at random.

'No, but I think we'll go. When it's all over, that is.' Voysey might have been referring to some protracted attendance upon a deathbed. 'What about you, old boy?'

What – Craine thought – indeed. And aloud he said: 'I can't keep away from that sun for long. A sign of old age, I don't doubt. And, of course, it's a bit of a release from the troublesome way things tend to go nowadays. Business things, I mean.'

'That's dashed true.' Voysey was as impressed as if an oracle had spoken. 'And, of course, the one sort of trouble makes the other worse.'

'Do you think so?' Craine's generalizing bent made him incautious. 'I've been wondering, as a matter of fact. Would one's private world be easier to cope with a couple of generations ago – in Ivy Compton-Burnett's set-up, say, rather than in Angus Wilson's?'

'That's pretty neat.' Voysey was at least aware that there was some highbrow reference in this, and was flattered at having it pitched at him. 'You couldn't put it better.' He paused and looked sharply at Craine. 'How's Jill?' he asked.

'She's very well, thank you.' Craine cursed himself. There was nothing like Jim Voysey's sort of predicament for giving a fellow a nose.

'Did I hear from somebody that she's abroad still?'

'Yes. We're lucky – just at the moment – in having a household that runs pretty smoothly. Let's us skip about when we want to.'

'With those friends of hers near that place – Arezzo, wasn't it – still?'

'No. She's at Saltino – along the road from Vallombrosa. We had another piece of luck: a decent villa with a marvellous view. But quite soon, of course, it will be a bit late in the year to be so high up.'

Voysey said nothing, but it was clear that some interesting conception was forming itself in his mind. Craine was determined not to be chased off the bus. It didn't escape him that Voysey had seen him buy his ticket. But the situation made him sharply doubt his and Jill's policy of reticence. It was John Arnander's ease that had been in question. His was a name sufficiently famous to make his resurrection a first-class sensation. And it had seemed wrong to let him face it blind when he had a chance of presently facing it with, so to speak, his eyes open. But gossip wasn't, in the circumstances, a thing at all easy to avoid.

'Saltino?' Voysey said. 'I don't think I've ever heard of it. Quiet sort of place, is it?'

'Well, no – it's something of a resort. But for Italians, perhaps – Florentines mainly – rather than foreign visitors.'

'Ah, Italians.' For a moment Voysey appeared almost alarmed at the pace at which his knowledge grew. He nodded towards the pavement. 'Odd hats they're wearing this year,' he said. 'But then when don't they?'

The foreshortened figures of a good many women were in evidence on the pavement; and as far as their heads went, it seemed to Craine, one wore this and one that. But he responded civilly to this new and impersonal topic. And presently Voysey turned to a more fundamental aspect of his subject. 'Have you noticed,' he asked, 'that some quite decent girls walk about nowadays waggling their behinds like a movie tart's?' Again he looked round the bus and made sure that he was not overheard. 'Sex,' he said darkly, 'is a deuced queer thing.'

Craine told himself that what he didn't like about this was the adverb. It was another imposter's word. 'Yes,' he said, 'deuced queer.'

Voysey made a pause during which he sucked the handle of his umbrella. 'Do you think it's true,' he asked, ' – what they say? That when a man gets old, however much he's managed to bring off at this and that, it's only what he's had in bed that he looks back on with any satisfaction?'

Craine shook his head. 'I doubt its being a universal truth. But I've no statistics.'

'Quite so.' Rather curiously, Jim Voysey appeared to take encouragement from this reply. 'It sounds as if it may be true. But if it is, one feels that it's – well, all a bit of a sell.'

Groocock had said something about a sell. 'A sell?' Craine said. 'There's a sense in which one's personal life will certainly be that. The last act's bloody, however rich the fun earlier on.'

Voysey looked disconcerted. Perhaps Pascal was beyond him. Or perhaps he was surprised to hear his inhibited companion swearing. 'I suppose it's true,' he said vaguely, 'that we're in the same boat.'

'We certainly are.'

'Well, I'm deuced sorry, old boy. Rotten luck.'

It was decidedly Craine who was disconcerted this time. 'We've got rather at cross-purposes,' he said. 'I wasn't . . .'

'I guessed there was a spot of bother. There is, isn't there?'

'Nothing to speak of.' Craine paused on this ambiguity, and didn't like it. 'Or rather,' he went on, 'a fresh one every day. Look at the bank rate.'

Blessedly, Voysey was on his feet and preparing to dismount. His flushed face shone with genuine benevolence.

149

'Look here,' he said, 'I know you must have your own solicitor, and so forth. But if you find you want a really high-class chap to get up on his hind legs in court and talk, just give me a ring.'

'Thank you very much,' Craine said. 'And please give my love to Jane.'

He had arrived at Weidlé's. There was a Tissot in the window, and a card announcing Minor English Masters of the Later Nineteenth Century. Minor English masters, he thought idly : it was a title suggesting the most insignificant of conceivable categories in a public school. But what the actual fact suggested was something more relevant; Weidlé's active business operations at present were still conceived on economical lines. It wasn't necessary to feel solicitous about him, since Craine couldn't imagine that he wasn't enjoying himself. Hadn't it been with large relish that he retold Mark Lambert's bizarre story of the painter who had gone in for an unexpected second innings ? Weidlé was now facing involvement in an actual situation very like that. But if the situation pleased his fancy, caught his imagination, he wouldn't regard it exclusively in terms of his till.

Craine spared a moment for the Tissot – it was a jolly affair of girls with parasols on board a man-o'-war; a period equivalent, he thought, of blondes in the bomb-racks – and then went inside. The young man was hovering – so alertly that Craine felt he might himself have been a ball coming out of a scrum – and he was conducted straight to the proprietor.

'Would you care for an Etty ?' Weidlé had raised both hands in a gesture of welcome which was at once theatrical and charming. 'Really a peach of a girl. Literally, you might almost say, rather than metaphorically. You feel you could pluck her from the bough.'

'Is she on a bough ?'

'She's on a swing – having climbed straight there, it

seems, out of a pool. Her clothes are on the bank, very nicely painted.'

Craine laughed; he liked Weidlé's beginning on this accustomed note. 'No,' he said; 'I don't want an Etty, thank you.'

'A pity. There are two ways of seeing them, you know.'

'Ettys?'

'Girls in general. As if you'd just taken the clothes off them, and as if they'd never had any. Profane and sacred art. And I'd feel life was the poorer for me if I had any settled notion which I prefer.'

'I've a definite preference myself, but I'd be very sorry if you had.' Craine sat down with a great sense of ease. 'And the boys?'

'They'll go to Pinn on the six-five. Meantime, I've dropped them into the National Gallery. It's only prudent in me to give an eye to forming the next generation of connoisseurs. And they can go downstairs and get a capital tea.'

'So they can. But not, my dear fellow, such tea as yours.'

Weidlé made his gesture again – but this time with an admirable restraint, as if he had been paid a compliment by some royal lady. 'You can't believe it hasn't been ordered,' he said. And then he added at once: 'They were going to operate this morning.'

Craine was silent for a moment – the famous tea was in fact being brought in with admirable promptness – and then he asked: 'Did you see any of the doctors?'

'I had a talk with the surgeon when he arrived from Rome.' Weidlé appeared slightly hurt that it could be supposed he had done other than go straight to the top. 'He was non-committal.'

'He would be, wouldn't he?'

Weidlé hesitated. 'I'd say he was very non-committal.'

Craine accepted his cup absently. 'I've a feeling it will be all right.'

'So have I.' Weidlé had a rare moment of hesitation. 'But it's a feeling I distrust. I'd call it a literary feeling – a feeling for a story. If Arnander doesn't regain his sight, the climax goes wrong. Therefore he'll regain his sight. But life isn't like that.' He frowned, as if the triteness of his conclusion didn't please him. 'Or is it?'

'The story will go on, all right – one way or the other. But tell me – well, tell me first about Arnander. He hasn't fallen back into any sort of apathy?'

Weidlé shook his head – gently, but so that the fine silver of his hair stirred and lifted. 'That's an ending I hadn't thought of there,' he said. 'Arnander gets back his sight, and employs it – we'll say – to arrange a collection of postage stamps. Painting is the last thing to enter his head.'

'But it won't be so?'

'It won't be so. Planting himself in front of a canvas is the one thing supremely before him. He'll paint, all right. Or try to.'

'And he'll succeed?'

'You know, my dear Craine, that I know nothing about painters. In fact, you've teased me on it.' Weidlé made a disclaiming gesture that wasn't wholly easy. 'So your guess is as good as mine.'

'That's not true.' Craine was very serious. 'What do you think?'

'That it will depend on character – on guts. He'll be an art student.'

Craine put down his cup. He was really startled. 'No!' he said. 'It can't be. You exaggerate.'

'He'll be an art student – absolutely. I'd exaggerate if I said he won't know how to hold a piece of charcoal, or draw a line. But the labour of conquering *his* technique again! Hercules isn't in it.'

'You've talked to him? That's how he feels himself?'

'I've talked to him.' Weidlé considered. 'I doubt whether he himself has taken the measure of it. But he had more than a glimmer. It's one of his fears, poor chap.'

'One of them? And continued blindness is the other?'

'I'd call it one of the others. There are more. But I can't distinguish them. Perhaps he hasn't got them in any sort of conscious focus himself.'

'I see.' Craine stirred his tea – although it wasn't the thing to do with it – and then looked up. 'But perhaps you confound him with – well, ordinary folk. *I'd* distrust myself – if I had to look back on having gone so queerly to earth for so long. But he has his drive still, hasn't he? His daemon, or whatever one calls it?'

'I'd suppose so. But it's a hard question. And inspiration isn't guts.' Weidlé glanced curiously, almost cautiously, at his companion. 'You very much want him to paint?'

'It would somehow represent – just for me, personally – something saved. And I think it would be easier for Jill.'

There was a long pause. 'That brings us to another aspect of things,' Weidlé said.

Craine had caught something evasive in this. 'Wouldn't it?' he asked. 'Wouldn't it be easier for her?'

'You treat me as a sibyl.' Weidlé gave the faint shrug of the shoulders in which one seemed to glimpse his father, Prince Schwarzenberg's adviser. 'Do you want me to give my impression of their relations?'

'Yes.'

'Arnander is extremely dependent on her. When he hears her voice, he vibrates to it. I can't think of another word.'

'It's probably a good one.'

'She is very unhappy. She realizes a tragic situation.' For the second time Weidlé hesitated. 'Tell me,' he asked, 'when she came back to you at Arezzo that morning, did she look as if she'd been through hell?'

'Yes.'

Weidlé peered into his teapot. Then he thought better of this and looked straight at Craine. 'That,' he said steadily, 'mustn't make you think she isn't devoted to him.'

'It doesn't.'

'One would suppose, then, that she'd want him to find happiness in new and absorbed creation. No doubt she tells herself so every night. But – well, we end, I suppose, with some platitude about the human heart.'

'I think,' Craine said, 'that you said something about a

tragic situation – about Jill's recognizing a tragic situation ?'

'Yes.' Weidlé stood up and walked over to the easel which had once supported Arnander's self-portrait. What stood there now was William Etty's almost innocent girl. He stared at it and then turned round abruptly. 'Take it,' he said, 'in terms of simple biological drives – or whatever jargon makes least nonsense in our context. What – at that level where she's next to helpless and driven – does she need ?'

Craine remained seated. He looked at Weidlé as a rider might look at a stiff fence. 'My children and her husband,' he said.

Weidlé gave an odd sigh. It might have been of relief. 'My dear man,' he exclaimed, ' – go away ! You need to be told nothing.'

'I need to be told about *their* children. You've seen something of Tim and Charles, there on the spot.'

'She wants them to become attached to their father, and their father to them. She doesn't in the least believe he's a good buy for them. But she's frightened of the void – the void in which he spent all those years. She feels that Tim and Charles might somehow become a bulwark against it one day. But *that* want in her isn't a deep want. I'd call it, if it didn't sound fantastic, something rather conventional. Tim and Charles are Arnander's children, and she scarcely sees beyond Arnander. Yet those two boys simply don't mean to her what her younger children – your children – do. Is that queer ?' Weidlé shrugged again. 'I'm afraid that I for one, just don't know. But she has told me that she thinks of Tim, at least, as very akin to you.'

Craine too had got to his feet. 'Do you mean,' he demanded, 'that in certain eventualities, and as a matter of practial accommodation, *they* might end up with my children, and *I* with theirs ?'

'I certainly think you would be well advised to see to it that you end up with Tim. About the little one – Charles – I don't know. But he'll make up his own mind – I believe with a good deal of passion – the one way or the other.'

'My God!' – Craine had a bewildered moment in which he echoed Groocock's judgement – 'what a mess.'

'Count your blessings, man.' Weidlé's voice was gentle. 'Count your material blessings, if you're not too proud. They can help, you know, when there's a mess to tackle. But tip in anything you were born with or bred to. You'll need the lot.'

CHAPTER FOUR

For weeks Craine's news came only in a sort of journal from Jill. The instalments neither began nor finished like a letter. They were like pages copied from a diary – the sort of diary, candid within controlled bounds, that a reticent person might keep for his own eye alone. They were such that he could have taken them to Weidlé – to whom he had grown curiously close – but scarcely sent on to the boys at their schools. Jill, however, was writing separately to them. So Craine kept the record to himself. And every few days he sent a similar but shorter report to Saltino, devoted almost entirely to news of the children at Pinn. It was all provisional. It couldn't be otherwise for a time.

Saltino-Vallombrosa
8 October

I hardly knew what I was doing when I sent off my cable. I hope it wasn't as wild as the Marchesa's famous one about little Nino.

It is, they say, a great triumph. What bewildered me – and I am still bewildered – was the suddenness. I had expected, if anything, a sort of slow dawn, a groping, a seeing things darkly, men as trees walking, permission to take a short low-lit glimpse each day. There was even some bit of pseudo-science, of muddled reading of psychology in my head. The infant laboriously constructs his world, distinguishes self and not-self, disentangles in a kind of creative act the chair from the table, the earth from the heavens. . . . John took a stick and walked out of the clinic within a couple of hours of the bandages coming off. He walked away down the road in sunshine, not much looking to right or left. I saw, on the table in his room, the dark glasses with which they had provided him. I was terrified and picked them up and thought to run after him. Professor Pirelli – he had come back from Rome – laid a hand on my arm as if I were an impulsive child. He was smiling, and I could see that it was his moment. But he hasn't, they explain to me, made any sort of medical history; he has simply done some recently discovered thing supremely well. The triumph is in that.

John stayed away for hours. When he came back, he said he'd been to the old monastery, the place that is now a forestry school.

He comes across to the villa tomorrow.

12 October

He is very quiet. He walks in the Pratomagno, or sits on the terrace looking at the view. I have to tell myself that it is true, that John Arnander who painted the La Verna is sitting in a high place in Italy – looking at the view. This morning I joined him. He talked a little, almost idly, and pointed here and there with his steady finger. He was amused when there were colours I couldn't see.

He is quite often amused. His mood is sunny. His only impatience is with Sister Barfoot, and there seems no reason why she should not leave us quite soon. I have a notion he knows whose idea it was that there might be advantage in having an English nurse on the spot, and that his impatience with the poor girl proceeds from this. It occurred to me today that the boys might, in the exceptional circumstances, get *exeats* and be flown out just for a few days. But John says that they had better stick to their books – particularly Tim, who, he says, is clever. He said, ironically but not unkindly, that Charles will one day be in danger of pursuing unremunerative enterprises, and that he should be kept away from infection a little longer. I supposed him to mean that Charles might become a painter. He said at once that Charles wouldn't be a painter. I remembered his old manner of being surprised at one's unawareness of self-evident things.

14 October

I am still bewildered – and don't know whether it is simply

because John so strikingly is *not*. Or certainly not by the world at large around him. He is taking it very quietly – that world. Not, as one might almost expect, wildly carrying on with it. A second marriage, a second honeymoon, with the pleasures the keener for being known about in advance.

Sometimes now I seem hardly to exist for him. It's an abrupt change, that – but like old times, after all. And in a way it's a nervous relief – to become the frame again, not the picture. During all these months I have felt his concentration on me to be intense. It extended to my physical presence; I felt he knew precisely how I sat or stood, or moved, all the time. It was a strain. Now, really, he is seeing less of me than when he was blind. Or that's how I often feel. And yet he doesn't ever steadily ignore me, as he used to have spells of doing. Almost, he studies me. And *that's* new. He may be looking for something no longer there. Those years, after all, have passed.

I haven't got this right. I puzzle him. When I said that nothing bewildered him, I was missing that out. Sometimes he looks at me surreptitiously – which was never a habit of his – and at once something flickers in him. I can imagine some natural, some very natural reactions in a man of his temperament in our situation. But why should something flicker in him ? I get from it some unnatural image – as of a child, perhaps, who seeks to turn out the light and find security in the dark.

15 October
The last page could be read, misread, as piping a plaintive note. But there's no injured feeling behind it – only a puzzle and, perhaps, some disturbing intuition. I'm seasoned to coming, for long periods, a poor second to a pile of cabbages on a table, or an old gnarled stump. That was all in the day's work. And such working days they were ! When I look at John today, I have to remind myself that he was no more physically robust then than now. Meagre, unexercised, he was yet capable, day after day, of achieving those tremendous labours. Joseph Conrad somewhere has a passage about

the toil of writing one of his books – *Nostromo*, perhaps – and he likens the labour to the everlasting sombre stress of the westward winter passage round Cape Horn. I remember just such days with John. Is the capacity for them in him still? I strain my ears and think I hear, through the thin wall of flesh, the deep, deep throb of the machine.

And he spent some time this morning poking round the big wooden hut that has been built on top of the old stables. It was put up during the war, when the villa housed wounded Italian officers. At lunch he referred to it as the studio. I could hardly look up from my plate. He spoke as if nobody could ever have thought of it as anything else. He wondered whether the single partition could be knocked down, so as to make one big room. It seemed a forward-looking plan, and I tried to test the strength of it, mentioning the winter climate up here, and the fact of its being essentially a summer resort. He took in what I said, but went on at once to talk of putting in a skylight and a fire-place. He could have, he said, a tremendous log fire. But he didn't actually speak of painting there, and he has made no move to secure any of the materials of a painter's work-shop. I return to the question: how much am I in anxiety about all this?

Sometimes I feel I don't care twopence for his painting, old or new – that I'm anaesthetic to the art in general, like Marchesa Forni; and that in point of what John is to me, it's neither here nor there. But his work was nearly all his happiness and torment, and if he is to have any sort of future it must be that all over again, and any sort of snag would surely be his final tragedy. He went – well, as at Castelarbia he did go, I suppose essentially because he hadn't eyes to paint with; and if now something else failed him, mightn't he go like that again?

I don't think I'm talking about a real anxiety, so far as his will goes. He will try. That pulse is really there to hear. But does this pause before he makes the beginning of an effort indicate ease and confidence, or does it speak of some distrust or fear? I don't know. My reason tells me that what one would at first expect is just what I have evidence of now: a long passive communion with what has been restored to him. But Weidlé spoke of terrific toil ahead, of a vast labour of rehabilitation in the whole field of technique. The stiffest of all the passages round the Horn. Perhaps John is brooding over that.

17 October

He has had the skylight put in and the fireplace built – all in two days. The workmanship of both is, in consequence, skimped and wretched. But John is pleased. Or rather, I said to myself: 'Look at his childish pleasure.' And then I realized that it is nothing of the sort, but the tremor of a deep excitement which he won't much longer control. I feel *de trop* – but it's a familiar old feeling, as I've said. May his bride be fruitful.

The Marchesa came up from Florence today. There is a car at the disposal of the innumerable shelved Forni ladies down there, and her share works out at about a day every three weeks. It was good of her to come up, particularly as she begins to get mountain sickness at about this height, it seems. I was prepared not to be surprised if John lived up to old form – not bothering his head, I mean, about somebody he felt he was through with. It isn't among my illusions that he had bobbed up with a larger armoury of the minor personal virtues than he went to earth with. But I was quite wrong. There is affection between them. The Marchesa inspected the studio but passed no comment on it. She has been in distress at the thought that she and her husband didn't make proper efforts about John's sight. I did my best to assure her that their own doctor had been right at the time, and that surgery has overtaken such cases only recently.

20 October

Poor Miss Barfoot is to leave us at the end of this week. She has of course no function now, and John continues to make fun of the idea that an English nurse was desirable during convalescence. He isn't, he says, a disreputable old man with gout and a fondness for a pretty face. I believe

160

she will be glad to go. It's very dull up here, and she isn't made for that.

Marchesa Forni seemed to set John's mind running on Italians – the sort I used to take him among long ago. He said he'd like to pay a visit, see a great house again. I wasn't sure what to do. We still, I think, want a little to defer the plunge into publicity. Certainly he does. Then I thought of the Perinos. They are utterly discreet; no conceivable surprise would make either of them turn a hair; and their villa would be a show place if they had the slightest disposition to show it to other than a few respectable old persons like themselves. So I rang up – the old lady didn't sound surprised even by that – and we drove over yesterday afternoon. Conte Luigi is certainly very much a man of one idea – having given all his days to fostering some impracticable innovation in viniculture which he once explained to me but which I didn't understand. But he must certainly have been quite aware that John had *died* – and so, equally, must the Contessa. So it was all dreamlike and comical, and exactly as I'd predicted. I'd played in their garden as a child – but that wasn't a familiarity that would license resurrection as a suitable tea-table topic. The old lady runs all sorts of activities – clinics and kindergartens and so on – on the spot; and she told me about these. Her husband showed John a great many jam-jars containing, I suppose, blights, pests and other diseases of the vine. It was all entirely pleasant. And then we took a little stroll through some of the rooms. People like that think it courteous to turn on a sort of modified showmanship; it isn't supposed one wants to do a tour, but one might care to renew acquaintance just with this or that. The old gentleman, although his mind was really still on the jam-jars, thought it mightn't be burdening us too much to take us just one room farther and glance at the Mantegna.

It is of course their grand thing – the great Agony in the Garden of which there is a smaller version in London. John looked at it for a long time – first at the whole composition, and then at the canvas here and there. It was

when he was looking at the two white herons fishing in the
stream that he responded in some way that eludes and
haunts me. Some very small thing, at once familiar and
strange, happened; something I didn't like. Then he was
impassive. But he must have caught me looking at him. For
he said quickly: 'God has not died for the white heron.
God has not appeared to the birds.' I remember how he used
to read occasionally in modern poetry, although always
declaring that it was incomprehensible to him. As we drove
back to Saltino I mentioned the painting again. I asked him
if the herons were very well painted. He laughed – perfectly
naturally – and made no reply. But half an hour later, and
when we were just going to get out of the car, he said
casually: 'Of course it takes Mantegna to make, entirely
parenthetically, a statement like that.' And at dinner he
said, very gently: 'Do you remember the Maremma, Jill?'
It was almost the first time he'd used my name. He was
quite silent for the rest of the evening.

24 October

Autumnal. Autumnal and oppressive and silent. Pine needles
and a mush of chestnut leaves thick underfoot. I should
have insisted on our getting away. He has had his great
log fire kindled as he promised himself, and he sits in front
of it, with his hands on his knees. This afternoon Celia Barfoot took him up tea. She was very silent when she came
back – and indeed she has been for some days. I don't know
whether she has some professional instinct that worries her.
Probably it is just the effect of the place and the season. She
has worked a lot in Italy – and I should imagine with depressing old people, as often as not. But in places with shops
and cafés and cinemas.

25 October

Autumnal and ominous. I keep remembering something else
in the Mantegna – another bird, the strange bird in the
dying tree. Celia said something strange about riding a
bicycle again after being long out of practice. Clearly something she had picked up from John. I have a terrible

foreboding that he won't, he can't, face the slog – the long days at the frozen ropes, driving round the Horn. We're at a nadir, a zero. The blood scarcely moves.

26 *October*

But it's happened!

This morning – it was mild and sunny – he had gone out for a walk. He was whistling and swinging his stick. It was very queer. About noon I thought I'd better stoke his fire, since it would turn chilly again later on. I went up the little outside wooden staircase to the hut. I had nothing else consciously in mind. But I was excited. My blood was racing. And there it was, tossed carelessly on a table. He'd got paper and a fine pencil, a hard fine lead. It was crowded: the whole hut, the whole studio, and Celia holding a tray. I stared and stared. I told myself nobody could be in a worse condition for making anything approximating to a detached aesthetic judgement. But I was certain, all the same. It had precision. But that's mild. Picasso round about 1920 was doing about as well.

It hadn't been concealed. But it hadn't been shown me. I came away.

29 *October*

He has done Celia Barfoot again. This time, you could count the lines on one hand. I asked him for it, and he didn't seem at all put out. I send it.

Celia isn't leaving.

CHAPTER FIVE

FYODOR WEIDLÉ dropped the drawing on his desk. 'You'll have to come out with it,' he said. 'The newspapers, and so forth.'

'At once?' Craine asked.

'Certainly. It's not a private event.' Weidlé refrained from looking again at the drawing. He had the appearance of proposing no further acquaintance with it. 'I don't make it as a material point,' he said. 'But I put it on record that I feel a fool.'

'You wouldn't have believed it possible?'

'I wouldn't have believed it possible. I almost want to suspect a trick – say, that he got it out of an old portfolio. But of course he didn't.' He paused. 'Miss Barfoot is a versatile young lady. At least she's changed her profession most obligingly.'

'It's certainly an unusual use to which to put a nursing sister.' Craine looked curiously at the drawing. It didn't strike him as an object for the exercise of delicacy. 'She was my idea. And he was said to dislike her.'

'He very well may. One can't tell if she's good-looking. He has scarcely given her a face.'

'It's modish.'

'That's true – or would have been true when Matisse was doing his illustrations to the *Poésies de Mallarmé*. There's a feeling of time-lag about such extreme simplifications now. But make no mistake, Craine. That' – and Weidlé pointed at the drawing again without regarding it – 'is no sort of pastiche, no sort of art-school stuff. It's the line of a master.'

'Then that's fine.' Craine spoke simply. But there was a cloud on his brow as he added: 'It would be amateurish, I suppose, to reckon it a shade ominous on – well, the personal side?'

'My dear chap, Arnander felt like making a start that way, and he simply grabbed the first wench available. At least we can look at it in that fashion until we've had further information. And you haven't, I take it, had that?'

'Not about this Barfoot girl. But I've had another letter. The place is certainly a studio now. Everything under the sun has come up from Alinari's in Florence. And Arnander's making studies for a big composition. He's working with as much energy as he ever did – and what that means you very well know.'

'Yes – I know. And he's not all that old. He may have a long working career before him.'

Craine smiled rather grimly. 'And just how,' he asked, 'does this news affect your own little affair?'

'It depends. I don't know that I've really thought it out. Or, rather, I've envisaged a restored Arnander as doing only one of two things. He might take to his brushes again and be unable to do a thing with them – nothing, I mean, that any competent person could see as counting. In that case, and with what I have' – Weidlé made a gesture that might have been in the direction of his strong-room – 'I'd be quite all right. My other thought – really quite a wild one – is that he might come out with something utterly new. I mean, you know, a sort of efflorescence, one of those personal styles of old age which the very great sometimes manage.'

'Donatello.'

'Quite so. Or Rembrandt. Unmistakably another, a terminal, phase. That would be wonderful.'

Craine couldn't help laughing. 'But – ideally – it wouldn't be too esoteric a development. Everybody would know that John Arnander was simply the greatest living artist and that Fyodor Weidlé controlled what might be called the central period. It would be wonderful, as you say.'

'But what I haven't really faced is a third possibility. Arnander picks up where he was, and continues to do what he did. A great painter with a unique vision – the painter of the Maremma, say, and of my self-portrait. But a great painter simply keeping it up. That would be, for me, mildly unfortunate. But at least I should have one consolation.'

'And that is?'

'And that is,' Weidlé said seriously, 'that I believe it would content you.' He paused. 'No, that's wrong. You're not going to emerge with any sort of content from this history. You'll get your crumb of comfort, say, by feeling that you've contributed simply to a large *œuvre*.'

'I shan't have contributed. The word's an absurd one.'

'Oh, I don't deny it must all be done by Arnander himself. The success or the failure will be his. But he's got it all in the bank, you know.' And Weidlé once more tapped the drawing. 'We just have to wait and see how he uses it.'

Craine sat silent for some time. There was nothing more to say to Weidlé, but somehow he was reluctant to get up and go. 'I've had one odd thought,' he said presently. 'There may be more paintings. There may also be more children.'

Weidlé smiled – rather cautiously, so that Craine was oddly reminded of Groocock. 'It's certainly true,' Weidlé said, 'that with Arnander the one sort of creation doesn't seem to exclude the other.'

'As it so often does.'

'Quite so.' Weidlé seemed to meditate giving the talk a discursive turn. Then he sat up – with an effect of addressing Craine more directly than he had yet done. 'Look here,' he said, 'ought there not to be a limit to your chewing over the whole thing?'

'It's natural that I should chew over *that*.' Craine was almost defensive. 'It would be queer, would it not? My own children as the centre of the sandwich.'

Weidlé ignored this. 'Do you want,' he asked, 'to receive that journal from – Saltino every few days? Ought she to be writing it? She had to choose, and she went to him. Nobody can criticize. But – well, wasn't that' – Weidlé gave his shrug – 'precisely that?'

'Since there's no help, come let us kiss and part? It's not

so simple. Don't you remember how it goes on? Nay, I have done: you get no more from me. I couldn't say that. And – strangely enough – I don't know that Jill could, either. Our instinct seems to be against that large gesture. Even although, as I've told you, we haven't met since it happened.'

'You don't propose to go out and investigate?'

'No.'

'Not even during one of those times when she comes to Pinn?'

Craine hesitated. 'I think not. Arnander, remember, has never set eyes on me. There seems no reason why he ever should.'

'But you'll go' – Weidlé was faintly ironic – 'to his first one-man show?'

'If it's said to be a good one, yes. If not, not.'

Weidlé sighed. 'I think, you know, if I had the power to persuade you, and if I were concerned, in the first instance, with your happiness, and, after that, with a general clear-up on the whole affair – '

'You'd insist that it had all ceased to be any part of my business. Perhaps you're right. But I simply don't – so far, at least – feel it that way.'

'I can't assert that there isn't plenty of practical business that's your pigeon still. The fact that they're economically independent – or at least that she is – doesn't alter that. For instance, are they all – all three layers of the sandwich – going to be legitimate? And is there any legal authority likely to be so inquisitive that they'll have to be convinced the whole strange story doesn't involve collusion and bigamy?'

Craine laughed. 'For what the point's worth, both Jill and I are certainly in the clear. There might be trouble for Arnander. But he was in a queer way. I've no doubt we could get the right sort of doctors to swear to the right sort of thing.'

Weidlé sat back. He appeared pleased. 'I believe that,'

he said, 'to be the first honestly unscrupulous proposition I've ever heard you advance. Such parsimony is a novelty in my field.'

'I'm not in your field, my dear man, except as an occasional guileless buyer. As for the children's position, the lawyers will look after that. There was quite a crop of such things – back-from-the-dead affairs – after the war. But you spoke about going out to investigate. I take it that it's in your mind to do that again yourself?'

'Lord, yes. I propose to keep very well up on it all. There's my bread and butter in it – or at least my quite celebrated tea. Which reminds me. Would you care . . .'

Craine shook his head, and stood up. 'No, thank you. I've one or two things to do – and then I'll be getting down to Pinn. The pigs are giving a spot of trouble. The children, fortunately, are flourishing.'

'I'm delighted to hear it. And my own particular friends, Tim and Charles?'

'The same, I think. Work and games unaffected by our perplexities. And one mustn't hasten to suppose there's going to be any deep disturbance.' As so often before in this room, Craine picked up his hat and umbrella. 'When shall you go out there next?'

'Not – unless something untoward happens – for a couple of months. The man must have time. Too quick a look might result in drawing false conclusions. And I still, you know, can't believe he hasn't the devil of a lot to learn again.'

Craine considered. 'That will take us to the holidays. Could you bear the boys again? They must go, I think. And I'd like it to be under your wing. So would they.'

'Then that's settled.' Weidlé was pleased. 'Do you know, I'd very much like, at the same time, to take them on a dash to Rome? Would it be all right?'

Craine advanced to shake hands. 'You must ask their parents about that,' he said.

CHAPTER SIX

Saltino-Vallombrosa
28 December

LOOKING back over all those weeks, I'm chiefly surprised,
I think, by the extent to which I had no notion of what
they were going to be like. And what they were going
to be like in – well, so many different aspects of the
thing. I ought to be grateful, I believe, for this multifarious
queerness. Some of them make others of them easier to
take.

Tragedy, or triumph, or a mixture; these had all seemed
possible. But who'd have expected a large infusion of
comedy? And the sensation side of John's return to life –
which was so large a side until, some weeks ago, it began
a little to die down – was certainly in the key of comedy
in the main. When the news broke, the first people to arrive
were straightforward journalists. They had open minds
about the *size* of the story, but unshakeable convictions as
to its *kind*. It was human-interest stuff, and their job was
to extract from it everything of that order that they could.
You'd think they'd be unbearable. But in fact, and once
you'd granted their bread and butter was impertinence,
they weren't a bad lot. Painting was the very last thing they
knew one end of from the other – which is probably why
John found it easy to get on with them rather well. I don't
mean that he was expansive. From what I could see – and,
not being mistress of these ceremonies, I didn't see much –
he was reserved and courteous and impeccable. He had very
little time to give them, but what he had to give he gave
graciously. That went down very well. It was amusing to
see them arriving at the notion that he must be important
as well as sensational. Presently the correct approach among
them became one of awe. John might have been Leonardo
– always the lay notion, it seems, of the greatest painter of

169

all time – risen from the dead. Not just Arnander risen from the dead.

Naturally there were awkward bits. On one occasion, for instance, two men were competing – literally with brandished cheque-books – for the right to reproduce, in one popular magazine or another, the first painting that the resurrected genius should consent to release. John enjoyed being indifferent to that. And Celia was furious with him. I'm bound to say I sympathized with her. They had only to hold an auction there and then, and the money would be in the bag. In *their* bag. And it was something honest in her, surely, that made her feel they ought to *have* a bag. She's living on me, after all. But nothing of that sort means much to John – and I don't know whether it's something very perverse in me that has always made me rather sympathize with that too. But Celia, poor child, knowing next to nothing about him, made a row. At least that's what I conjecture from the fact that I heard him pitching dishes at her. *La vie de bohème.* I was a little relieved, at that moment, that Tim and Charles weren't in residence with Papa and Mama.

This is a wretched hard-boiled vein. But the comedy – to get it down more clearly – is something to which, at moments, I've had to cling. I remember it being like that, long ago. Yet, this time, it's different. It's fundamentally different. Something has vanished from the other side of the account. Temporarily or permanently ? That's the question.

29 December

Yet all this – that he's living openly, a stone's throw away, with a silly girl; and even that, perhaps, something final has happened between us – all this is so plainly not the significant thing, the real thing, that's going on ! She hasn't had much of a buy. If she has ten minutes of his time – day or night – I'd be surprised. And when Weidlé brings out the boys, off she'll go. I haven't a doubt of it. He *does* have certain middle-class proprieties very strong.

But I was writing about the journalists. They faded out.

Or at least the ordinary undifferentiated ones faded out, and then we had those of the artistic persuasion. They were much more difficult. One had heard of some of them; they expected lunch; they were disgustingly and smoothly discreet. John loathed them. He'd have nothing to do with them. But he took it for granted that they'd be adequately handled and informed by me. They did, however, a little infect him, and he turned on a certain amount of discretion himself. Perhaps he locked that girl up in a cupboard. Certainly she wasn't much seen. But he was never any good at being *really* close about such matters, and they went away, I don't doubt, with as much gossip as they wanted.

It's funny to be back in such a world. At least, I suppose it is.

30 December

I see that my conduct, my attitude, is inexplicable – perhaps even revolting – in terms of anything I've yet got down, ventured to get down. I've been hardly at all in the studio – and, when I have been, nearly everything has been face to the wall. He's very close with me. I have to piece together what's happening. I've done so with sufficient success to know it's a tremendous, an incredible lot.

But, if he's close *with* me, he's close *to* me too. That's the whole key to the situation as something that can endure for a day. It's desperately hard to see, let alone to describe. This morning – although it was very cold – I walked up and down the terrace for a long time, trying to remember a word the psychologists use. As if there could be illumination in a word! It turned out to be – for what it's worth – 'ambivalent'. It's in one of the Latin poets, surely, in a more concrete phrase. *Odi et amo.* Is that it? But that isn't right, either. He makes desperate assaults upon me, as if I were a barrier that he must at all costs force his way through. And I feel that if he doesn't get through, the *odi* will come terribly in. I wrote, I remember, about his looking at the Perino Mantegna. That moment keeps coming back to me.

The snows are tremendous, but it is very still. I walk to Vallombrosa and back. Shuttered villas, lifeless hotels.

A few of the forestry people seem to have jobs out of doors, and there are a few sportsmen with guns. But it all isn't gay. Not even for Celia Barfoot, I'm afraid.

4 January

Today we had our first great man, Otto Frink. He must be about a hundred. He was already an old man, and already a great one, when he discovered John, long ago. He was the first man with world authority to speak up about the quality of the earlier paintings. What made that so impressive, of course, was his being an art historian and not a chatterer about the geniuses of the day. He is now very doddery, and I was afraid it was going to be too much for him: both the ascent of these polar regions and what he found when he got here. He came out of the studio weeping, and told me he'd seen what he'd never hoped to see again.

So this is the place to say, to try to say, what has been happening, what beneath all these private pains and perplexities has really been happening, at Saltino.

It is, as Charles likes to say, very technical. I'd forgotten painting was so technical – and indeed I don't think it ever was so much so with John before. He's obsessed, quite obsessed, with the idea of making up for lost time. He has said to me that he mayn't, after all, have long now. I don't know whether he was thinking of his life, or of his eyes. He knows the doctors say his sight will now be as lasting as any part of him. But it's understandable that he should find that hard to believe, sometimes. So he works like a man possessed. No, that's feeble. He *is* possessed. But still, it's technical.

Otto Frink talked his art history to me for half an hour before he drove back to Florence. It was a wandering talk – he was tired out – but its general theme was the recorded instances of spells of preternatural productivity among painters. The most striking belong, apparently, to the Renaissance and not to modern times. And there is, Frink said, a rational basis to it. Ever since the end of the seventeenth century the technique of painting has been more casual than during the Renaissance. This was a surprise to me. I'd supposed it would be the other way. Briefly, he said that modern painters put in a lot of time and energy messing around, whereas the older ones had everything organized and systematized from the start. It's only quite recently that there has been a bit of a change. And John has pounced on it, he said, with an astonishing grasp of its possibilities. For instance, since he began in October he hasn't spent ten minutes squaring up; he has simply chosen from among his sketches, and let photography and a sensitized canvas do the donkey-work. And he's been using a scaled palette as if he'd been familiar with it all his life. And a great deal else. That it all adds up to a tremendous lot, I don't know. Frink was plainly just getting a little way towards accounting, on those sort of grounds, for what had staggered him. In the studio there are a score of substantial oil sketches, two large finished compositions, and a third composition on the easel.

Just before he drove away, Frink told me – with a Germanic solemnity contrasting comically with his ancient quavering voice – that the two finished pictures are accessions to the body of European art. I watched his car disappear into a snow-storm. But I think it was tears, and not snow-flakes, that obliterated it so quickly.

5 January

Yes, I was very much moved. And that rather surprised me. For the thing that chiefly seemed to come to me after the first shock and strangeness of John's return to life was a conviction that there could be nothing but confusion in basing any course of conduct on the fact of his having been a great artist. And I stuck to this conviction even when there came the further strangeness: the possibility that he might be a great artist once more. If he had a claim on me, it wasn't on the score of his talents, however transcendent. But it hasn't been so simple. For I have been more significant to the artist in John than the artist in John has ever been to me.

But there is more to tell about yesterday – after Otto Frink
had departed like an Ancient of Days. John came in to
dinner. He might have or he might not have. I simply
haven't been recording the minor tiresomenesses and awk-
wardnesses of this wench-in-the-stables *ménage*.

He came in to dinner – and I looked at him and saw
that he had been under more strains than I knew. He is, of
course, under a constant stress one just can't begin to
estimate: the stress of getting on canvas what he is getting
on canvas – and at a tempo he's never touched before. But
he has been, too – I could now clearly see – under a further
heavy stress of uncertainty, of doubt. And Frink – as I say,
his first discoverer – had released him from it. He didn't
look at me, but he spoke at once. 'I say,' he said, 'I'm sorry
about that girl. She's gone, though.'

It was, with an absurd preciseness, a remark out of the
past. I gave him his *pasta* – we live very simply – and said
nothing.

'You see,' he said, 'I've been living in rather a cloistered
way for some time. But there was nothing to her.'

It was excruciating – by which I mean that it was another
flare-up of the comic in our affair. I thought I could remember exactly the same words – prompted by an occasion
on which they had shut him up in hospital with scarlet
fever. But something moved me to say what would never,
I realized, have been particularly apposite before. 'Nothing
to her?' I said. 'Why, you thought her ravishingly beautiful.'

He was disconcerted. 'No doubt she was a pretty piece,'
he said. There was a consciousness of virtue in the very
tense he used. It was as if he had merely had to tear her
up and toss her into the waste-paper basket. 'However, I've
turfed her out.'

I suppose I'm getting old and soft. Anyway, for a moment
I was on the verge of being revolted. For all I know, Celia
Barfoot may have been a virgin. He had seduced her – in the
first instance no doubt by employing the nasty little trick

of getting her to pose for him with her shift off. And here he was, taking the largest credit for having ejected her – quite literally into a snow-storm. I was, I say, nearly revolted. And then – can it be called anything but hysteria? – I had a queer sense of exhilaration, as from the years falling away. But I knew it was something illusory and treacherous – like what an old man gets, I suppose, from some queer glandular operation. So I was sufficently impassive. 'Have some *sugo*,' I said.

He had a lot. He twirled his fork in the *tagliatelli* with a gusto I hadn't seen since our early days; it carried the past with it as absolutely as did this brisk closing down on an exhausted amour. And I felt my heart melting before it. I wanted to give him pleasure – nothing in the world but to give him pleasure. 'What did the great Otto think?' I asked.

'He's an incompetent old ass – blind and deaf and with his head full of rotten old pictures.' John took the Chianti flask and tilted it recklessly over his glass. 'But he thinks things aren't too bad.'

He looked at me confidently and inattentively. But although he was really absorbed in some unspeakable release he's gained – and, I felt, some consequent opening prospect of further unrelenting and utterly satisfying eternally tormenting labour – although he was really absorbed, he suddenly wanted to give me pleasure in his turn. Of course he knew precisely the figure he'd been cutting, and from moment to moment how I'd felt about it. But he took it all in his stride – and now, wolfing his food and making a large luxurious business of drinking what wasn't so very much wine after all, he talked about Tim and Charles. I had to rub *my* eyes, almost, to realize that *his* eyes haven't yet rested on either of them. He seemed determined to convince me – as if I needed any convincing! – that he was as inescapably a perceptive father as he was an unreliable one. And, almost immediately, the unreliable side came out – triflingly and in terms of a dip, this time, into the mildest comedy. He is genuinely looking forward to Fyodor

Weidlé's bringing them to Saltino for the end of their holidays. They attract him both as individuals and as products of an environment and education that are strange to him; he finds it amusing, I mean, that *his* sons should be in process of what he calls *that* sort of togging up. I wish that there was, as yet, more to it than this. But to listen to the largeness of the plans he was now making for their visit, you'd suppose he intended to devote the greater part of his days to them. I endorsed one proposal after another – and at the same time told myself to tell all that to the Marines. Ten minutes at a time will be as much as he's likely to take away from whatever's going on in that studio. But there's to be a whole day, if you please, in the Uffizi. Tim, he says, will take it all in a composed and discriminating way, and seldom be seen to pause unbecomingly before mediocre achievements. But Charles will quickly turn childish and outrageous amid such acres of junk, and Charles will be right. At this, I had a curious moment of apprehension, a glimpse of the risks that – if we have arrived at anything permanent at all – Charles will run as the result of the resurrection of such a father. They're of a worth-while order, I suppose. But there they are.

John talked on. At least while eating his *dolce* and drinking another third of Chianti – he seems to have a quite automatic control over anything that might cloud his eye or make his hand tremble – he talked on, and this time about plans on a larger scale. Somebody, it must have been one of the art scribblers he'd barely speak to, has told him that Brazil is the only place where painting is really happening – and so to Brazil, he announced, we shall go. 'It's lucky you have all that money,' he put in parenthetically, and then off he went again. He returned to the Uffizi, and to galleries in general, and talked about pictures being put inside and doing time. The subject ought to be taken up, he said, by the people who go in for penal reform. Completed paintings should always be exposed in the streets – 'under some sort of awning', he said – and carted off by anyone who took a fancy to them. But every five years there should be a Feast of the Grand Combustion, when into the bonfire everything that was over five years old should go.

And so on. He wasn't exactly repeating himself. Still I'd sufficiently heard that sort of gay senseless talk long years ago to be much disposed either to weep or to throw a bottle at his head now. Then, quite suddenly, he stopped off. Perhaps he felt that he'd done his stuff, put on a turn for me, and could now be getting back to business.

Well, that was all right – and I smiled at him as he gave me a long look before grabbing his overcoat and plunging out of the villa. I went into the *salotto*, and sat down by the stove, and told myself I was wondering what sort of work he got on with by artificial light. But his look came back to me as something that cancelled the whole intended effect of his talk. He might have been a man turning away from a shattered mirror, or from a familiar window that has been reglazed with frosted glass.

7 January

Fyodor Weidlé and the boys have arrived safely.

9 January

Wonderful sunshine. One might be in the Alps. I took another long walk with Weidlé. He has been rather a surprise to me. There are things about him that I hadn't got hold of at earlier casual meetings, or when he was here last. Even that he should be capable of tramping over snow! I'd thought of him as characteristically sitting in a car and wearing a coat with a big fur collar. He did in fact arrive like that – and he'd rather outrageously provided Tim and Charles with astrakhan hats, which pleased them enormously, although I suspect Tim of a lurking suspicion that they're not quite Italian, even in winter. But he's not – Weidlé, I mean – flamboyant in a manner I'd somehow supposed. Of course he has the graceful ways and the reserves of guile that go with salesmanship at his level. But underneath, he is uncompromisingly austere. I imagine he could be what's called ruthless. Of course he plainly puts in time combing his hair. But it occurs to me that if he didn't he would be in danger of looking rather like a minor prophet – and who would venture to buy pictures from one of them?

He spent the first evening with John in the studio, while I played Charles's favourite Snakes and Ladders with the boys. But since then he's been chiefly with me. He said at once that John's command of his craft is a miracle, and that if he'd made any rash bets a little time ago he might have had to eat his own astrakhan, which is old and probably very tough. I haven't heard him say much to John – except to tease him about his labour-saving devices. The studio, he says, is like a kitchen in the Ideal Home Exhibition. As if Weidlé had ever been at that.

He's very quiet and thoughtful. And he doesn't look well. I've an idea that he is a sick man, who has got beyond pictures and so on meaning all that much to him – he's had a long spell of it, after all – and that he's finishing off by taking a good look at people. But this may be quite deceptive. Though I don't think it is. No, I think that what he's looking at up here is some human problems, and that he doesn't terribly like what he sees. He did tell me today how he got a first inkling that there was something very strange about John's supposed death. An elderly woman called Morrison, the mother of an American painter who died a few years ago, sent him her son's collection of drawings to sift through. There was a small portfolio endorsed – I think he said – 'In mem. J.A.' He told me that, after he had discovered the truth, he got Mrs Morrison's permission to destroy its contents. I was rather startled. 'They were better gone,' he said. 'There oughtn't to be any curiosities of art; it's enough of a curiosity in itself.'

This was deep in the woods, and the silence around us was oppressive. I could feel that he was troubled by having appeared to offer me an empty epigram. 'Of course I know about the drawings made in blindness,' I said. 'Rupert told me. And they must have had, certainly, a rather overpowering pathos. But weren't they also, as it has turned out – '

He interrupted me – which isn't at all his habit. 'There are kinds of pathos,' he said, 'that are best for the dark.'

I just don't know what this was a streak of in Weidlé. But I think that many men who get along notably on *élan* have somewhere a melancholy vein. He isn't in the least given to being consistently enigmatic. That would repel me – whereas in fact he has drawn me into a feeling of real intimacy. I have talked to him unreservedly – even saying things that I haven't set down here. Like John, he is a very noticing man.

This evening he made us all play Snakes and Ladders – including John, whom he amused by declaring the game to be the perfect emblem of the human condition. But Charles, when the meaning of this had been explained to him, said it would be so only if played under the bed without matches. This outlandish remark pleased John even more.

10 January

Fyodor Weidlé has left us. He spent the morning with John in the studio, and on returning to the villa rang up London, as is his custom. An hour later, he had a call from New York – and then he came and told me he must go. It is some unexpected business crisis. He has perfect tact, and didn't make too much of his regrets. But I could see that he really was upset. He is attached to the boys – and they showed their disappointment naïvely, so that I was afraid he felt he was letting them down. But there is no difficulty about their getting back to England; at Florence they can be put into a sleeper for Calais, and being on their own will delight them. Weidlé went straight off without lunch, as he had to do if he were to make Malpensa in time for the night flight. I was sorry to see him go.

Tim told me this evening that he had seen Sister Barfoot. I suppose it must be true. He spoke with a carefully calculated degree of casualness that startled me. Then I remembered that he had judged her very pretty, and I thought that the embarrassing factor might be in that. But I couldn't be sure. You never know where John may let you down.

Quite apart from his having said the girl was gone, it's another small ominous note so far as the future of this reunited family is concerned. Plenty of children, I suppose, stumble upon queer facts about their parents, and are none the worse. Still, I shall be relieved, I'm afraid, when Tim and Charles do set off on their return to school at the end of next week.

CHAPTER SEVEN

MARTIN CRAINE threw back his head in peals of laughter. 'Go-go!' he shouted. 'Go-go!'

The fat pony went. Martin's heels drummed on her back; they couldn't be said to reach anywhere near her flanks. Rupert Craine walked alongside. Considered strictly as equitation, it was indecorous. But at least it was a start. 'Elbows in,' Craine said conscientiously. 'Back straight.'

Martin shouted with laughter again. He too knew it was a start, and he was triumphant. Hazardously, he turned his head and looked at the ground, which was a long way off. It was a critical moment. 'Go-go!' he commanded emphatically. 'Go-go!'

They came back between the mulberry trees, and then in front of the dining-room. Rachael Craine sat up in her pram in sunlight, solemnly observant. She was wearing a bonnet – for Nannie's ideas were inevitably antique – and this added to the composure of her appearance. It was impossible to believe that that button of a mouth would ever utter, or that anything would deflect that round blue stare.

'*Rach* ... *ael!*' Martin shouted as they came up. He hadn't yet any vocabulary for boasting, but he was boasting, all the same '*Ra ... chael!*'

Incredibly, Rachael opened her mouth – but it was only because she had decided suddenly and prodigiously to yawn. She was unimpressed. The pony pawed with a mild impatience, being aware that the proceedings were over. Nannie came forward, and Craine lifted Martin off. 'He may do,' he said.

'I'm sure he'll be a credit to you, Mr Rupert.' Nannie was as little impressed as Rachael had been. She had, after all, no doubt seen Craine on his first pony too. And her responses were always uncompromisingly conventional. 'But what a lot of noise!' She turned to Martin. 'You'll have shouted yourself hoarse,' she said sternly and informatively. 'And in such a raw air, too!' She shook her head. 'I think he'd better gargle,' she said.

'Nonsense, Nannie.' Craine was momentarily impatient. But then he nodded his head good-humouredly. 'As you think best, though. He must be fit for a tougher lesson tomorrow. Martin – more tomorrow?'

Martin nodded his head. 'Go-go!' he said dreamily. 'Go-go!'

Craine walked away, and climbed to the little terrace. There he turned, and looked back over the garden and the paddock. You couldn't tell that the Pinn was over its banks; from the mist that swathed it only the pollard willows rose in an irregular line, like troops advancing through an inefficient smoke-screen. But beyond the little river Craine's seven Lombardy poplars, bare and gently swaying, rose into clear sunlight. A vapour trail scrawled the sky above them. The only sound – the only sound now that Martin had stopped shouting – was the faint throb of machinery from beyond Pagan Episcopi. Craine listened for a moment – if a fellow threshed as late as this, there should be somebody in a position to give him a rocket – and then walked into the house. His butler was in the hall.

'Mr Weidlé, sir,' the man said. 'I've put him in the library.'

Craine went into the long chill formal room, lined with his grandfather's classical texts and histories. Weidlé was looking cold and pinched, and the lustre seemed to have gone from his carefully tended hair. 'For heaven's sake!' Craine said. 'If it must be books, come in among my own. They're a ragged lot, but I keep them cosy. What's Evans been thinking of? He must have taken you for a philistine bigwig of the first order.'

Weidlé laughed, and made one of his most perfect gestures. 'Just that,' he said. 'The top man in the Civil Service. The Principal Secretary – isn't he? – to or for or in the Treasury. I felt your excellent Evans make the identification instantaneously. Sir Fyodor Weidlé, K.C.M.G.'

Craine led the way into the other room. Weidlé was unnaturally vivacious. And he was certainly very tired. Craine, as he presently poured sherry, looked at him curiously. 'I heard you had to come back,' he said. 'It was in Jill's last budget.'

'Ah – so you've had that. I might have got here first. But I found, after all, that I needed a couple of days to recover my breath – and to make sure I knew what I was talking about.' Weidlé had sat down close by the fire. His vivacity had dropped from him with an awkward abruptness. He sat staring sombrely into the flame.

'Did you really have sudden urgent business?' Craine was fishing for cigarettes. 'It didn't, somehow, come through like that. Not that Jill doesn't seem to have been convinced.'

'Certainly I had sudden urgent business.'

Craine became quite still. 'And nothing to do with Arnander?' he asked.

'You know very well it was to do with Arnander.' Weidlé spoke the words gently – so that the immediate challenge with which he followed them up was surprising. 'What does come through?' he demanded. 'What does she tell you – in her letters, or whatever they are?'

'What Jill writes is disturbing,' Craine said. He spoke cautiously. He might have been opening a tricky conference with gentlemen from Ankara or Buenos Aires. 'Or perhaps it's what she doesn't write.'

'She speaks of some change in him – towards herself?'

'Yes. But it seems to have a basis that's natural enough. During his blindness, he was almost morbidly dependent on her. Do you remember telling me that, when she spoke, he positively vibrated to the sound of her voice? But now, when he's back at work, she has to play – and rather abruptly – second fiddle. She keeps on saying that it's something she was used to, long ago.'

'An abrupt change, but explicable. Is that all?'

'No, it's not – or I wouldn't speak of something disturbing at the back of it. She seems at times to feel that it precisely *isn't* like long ago; that something has gone from their relationship. She puts no name to it. It's only an intuition.'

'I think she knows more.' Weidlé pushed away his glass. 'You want the truth about them – out there?' He waited for Craine's nod. 'There are times when he can't bear her.' He waited again, but Craine was mute. 'That's what it has done for him, and for her – his gaining his sight.'

Craine managed to speak. 'It's madness – what you're saying.'

'You know it's not. But put it, simply, that she baffles him. And that means that she must eventually find the situation – not him, mind you, but the situation – insupportable. With Arnander blind, she could have made do – although it would have required all the devotion she has. But with Arnander sighted – well, it's hopeless.'

'I say it's senseless, what you're telling me. It isn't in Nature – a change like that.' Craine turned away, walked the length of the room, and came back. 'Or might you be saying, with equal truth, that he can't bear himself?'

Weidlé nodded. 'Say that he can't bear the suspicion which his response to her – or his lack of response – threatens to bring to his consciousness.'

'You're talking nonsense.'

'You know I'm not, Craine.' Weidlé's voice was suddenly urgent. 'You understand it. I know you understand it. Good God, man, your only chance is in understanding it!'

There was a long silence, and then Craine sat down. He sat, or sank, down – but his voice when he spoke had steadied itself. 'Arnander's work,' he said. 'Tell me about it. Tell me what's in that studio.'

Weidlé took a deep breath. 'I can do that easily. Nothing at all.'

For a moment Craine seemed to feel that he had listened to a literal statement. 'Empty?' he asked.

'No, no. The sketches, the big compositions – they're all

there. Everything that old Otto Frink saw. And they look very like Arnanders. Not a new sort of Arnanders. Just the old sort. But they're not even that.'

'Not even that?' Craine's mind was still groping. 'In heaven's name, what do you mean? Forgeries?'

'Nothing of the sort. Something much simpler, although much stranger. The man's recovery of his technique really has been miraculous. It's nothing like a hundred per cent – but it's miraculous, all the same. I'm not surprised that Frink in his near dotage – Frink, who was the first person to proclaim what John Arnander was – didn't look beyond it. If he had, he would have found – well, what I've told you. Nothing at all.'

'You mean . . .'

'I mean that – thanks to you – Arnander has recovered his sight. But he hasn't recovered his vision.'

There was another long silence, and then Craine came back fighting. 'Sight . . . vision? That's mere word-chopping.'

'It's nothing of the sort. Shall we go into your drawing-room and look at the Maremma?'

'I don't need to look at the Maremma.'

'Of course you don't. And we needn't argue over the right word for what John Arnander has lost. I talked about vision because I think of him as a visionary painter. You can call him a transcendental painter, and say that he's lost that dimension. Or you can express it quite differently. Think of that Mantegna.'

Craine slowly took this in. 'The Perino Mantegna?'

'Yes. You heard about his taking a look at that. Think of it, I say – Christ and Judas, and then the birds and the small creatures, there in a complete otherness, and yet a part both of the picture's rhythm and of its thought. It's a great intellectual statement, Mantegna's picture. And it scared him. So perhaps, in a last analysis, it's an intellectual power he's lost. Anyway, the thing has happened.'

'And Jill scares him too?'

'At least she puzzles him. There's a very simple turn of

words for the situation.' Weidlé paused. 'He can't imagine what he once saw in her.'

'Yes.' Craine took it squarely now. 'His sense of her was part of the very process of his genius. Now, when he searches for that old sense of her in vain, his confidence flickers and he knows himself to be on the verge of some unbearable discovery. Jill's presence – perhaps the strangeness of her beauty that he sees he no longer sees – whispers to him, can't but whisper to him, of the nullity that has come over his art. So he can't bear her. Isn't that it?' Craine scarcely waited for Weidlé's slow nod. 'And Jill herself?' he asked. 'What does she know about his painting? You told her the truth?'

Weidlé shook his head. 'She knows nothing about that. She hasn't connected up. And I didn't feel I could tell her. I felt that job to be yours.'

'Good God, no!' Craine was on his feet again. 'Do you realize how I've let her down?'

'I can't say I've heard of it.' Weidlé spoke suddenly with a sort of weary dryness.

'Her, him, me.' Craine reached for the sherry decanter. It was a futile gesture prompted by the perception – which came to him thus oddly in the middle of his crisis – that Weidlé was indeed a sick man. 'Her, him, me,' he repeated. 'The boomerangs I've sent singing round our ears!'

'The boomerangs?' Weidlé asked.

'I fought for his sight, Weidlé – I fought for it! There was a sense in which his blindness was a deep, deep refuge – a shell, you might say. And I winkled him out of it. It was his chance, Jill's chance – even my own. The roof had been whipped off and everything gone sailing. But there was at least the possibility of retrieving something. And it was something pretty big.'

'Well – it all hasn't answered,' Weidlé said. His fatigue was growing, and beneath his sympathy there lurked something bleak and chill. 'Plans do miscarry in a way that suggests a malign skill. That's the moment to talk about boomerangs, no doubt. But I don't know that there's much to be done.'

'Him, her, me. I brought him back from the dead – and to a disillusionment which, when it comes, he'll never forgive. Blind, he had a wife to whom he at least – '

'Be quiet, man!' Weidlé had raised his head and spoken with authority. 'Pack your bag and shoulder your responsibility.'

It pulled Craine up. 'I should go out?' he said.

'At once. Don't you remember in what state you found him at Castelarbia? Can you tell what morbid turn he mayn't take, once the truth breaks on him? And your wife's there, and the boys.'

'My wife?'

'She's a woman with two husbands, Lord help her. Such things don't cease to be facts, you know, simply because they seldom obtain among the clergy.' Weidlé shrugged, as if not caring for his own feeble flicker of humour. 'You might at least get them moving. It's an absurd place to spend the winter in. Perched on a precipice, with a view that isn't there! There's no sense in it.'

'That's true enough.' Craine got to his feet again and walked to the telephone on his desk. 'I'll get on the next plane. If you stay to lunch, we can go up to Town together.'

Weidlé nodded silently. He appeared relieved; and while Craine made his call he sat forward, his hands stretched out to the fire. 'Where's the Amico?' he asked, when the booking was concluded.

'The Amico?' Craine had to make an effort. Then he smiled. 'Oh, I gave it to Tim. I was wondering whether he'd consider such a present thoroughly foolish, when he asked me for it. He would like, he says, a small painting every birthday.'

'Didn't I know I'd make a collector of him?' Weidlé brought his hands away from the fire in a small triumphant movement. For a moment his gaiety had returned to him.

Craine smiled. 'Then save up something good for his twenty-firster,' he said.

'I certainly will – if I'm about.' Weidlé's smile answered Craine's, and he reached idly for a cigarette. 'I'd like just to walk round your pictures,' he said. 'If it wouldn't be a bore for you. And if there's nothing more that we can usefully discuss.'

'Clearly one can talk unprofitably. And I'm grateful to you for telling me, a little time back, that I'd do better to shut up. But' – and Craine hesitated – 'you *are* quite sure ?'

'Well, even if I am, I may be wrong. Otto Frink, after all, has his own absolute certainty, just the other way. Then again, I was wildly astray about the time and effort that it would take Arnander simply to recover the use of paint. So you've good reason not to take my word as decisive.'

Craine shook his head. 'I can't believe you are wrong – not about what is, or is not, on those canvases in his studio now. But mayn't it come ? Mayn't it yet come back – the vision, or whatever we are to call it ? Isn't the very speed with which he has recovered his technique perhaps significant ? If he has put such concentrated effort into that . . .'

'No.' Weidlé looked straight at Craine. 'For what my conviction is worth : no. The thing isn't in abeyance. It's lost. We can, you know, lose things. It's another hard fact.'

'But when . . . how ?' Craine brought out the words rather desperately. 'And why ?'

'The sibyl has no answer to give.' Weidlé clicked a finger and thumb; it was another of his ways of showing that he disliked his own words. 'Of course, there was the bridge.'

'The bridge.'

'Yes, man – the bridge. He went to pieces on it. And, when he took himself off, there was perhaps some small vital piece that he failed to pick up and take with him.'

For a moment Craine stared at Weidlé in silence. And, when he did speak, it was rather weakly. 'But art doesn't work like that !'

Fyodor Weidlé was on his feet and producing the first flash of anger Craine had ever seen in him. 'So you know how art works? Then you ought to be giving lectures on it. You're wasted – believe me – in that damned bank.' He took a step forward, and for a second held Craine lightly by both arms – surprisingly, since he had never come to other than the most formal handshake before. 'No, no! We don't know much about it, you and I.'

CHAPTER EIGHT

THE plane dropped into Italy on the tail of a storm. It had been bumpy going over the Alps, and beneath a film of twilight there had appeared only a kaleidoscope of darknesses, with here and there a savagely upthrust fang of rock and snow. Travelling thus in the twentieth century, one can be caught by the sort of horror the region held for one's earth-bound ancestors: the horror of sterility and formlessness and the void. The young woman in charge of the flight sold large quantities of cigarettes. It was a ritual of reassurance, an assertion of the continuing consequence of economic man amid all that silence and all that cold. Craine, acknowledging himself in the same boat, absorbed the *Financial Times*.

When one reads the geography of Europe at such a pace, he thought, the punctuation marks accent themselves with an unnatural heaviness. The bus to trundle the little group of passengers across the airfield was late in turning up, and they seemed to wait interminably in a wind of ice. The same wind blew through the sheds as they shuffled past officials, and pounced on them again after the long drive into Milan. The small discomforts of travel in a bitter season took on a disproportionate persuasive force, so that there seemed to be temerity and futility in the whole modern assault upon man's immemorial measures of space and time. We're up to no good, Craine told himself, in all this demand upon the freedom of the continents. Politicians, for instance. If they hadn't the means to hurtle from capital to capital, confusing and irritating each other, we'd conceivably be in a less desperate way.

The train was luxurious, and the dinner timed to occupy the greater part of the smooth swift run through darkness to Florence. He ate it conscientiously, and exchanged a few sentences in his careful Italian with an elderly man in the opposite seat. When the train stopped at Piacenza, he could glimpse on the platform people still buffeted by the wind.

It was his own journey that he distrusted, and nothing else. Weidlé had dispatched him on it. But it had been Weidlé who, not so long ago, had been hinting that he ask himself whether the Arnanders were any longer very substantially his business. Did the nullity of John Arnander's recovered art really alter that ? And was it going to help Jill so to arrange things that it should be Craine himself who would reveal it to her ? If it were true – and he didn't doubt its being true – wasn't the right thing to hope for some merciful gradualness of disclosure ? But Weidlé's sense was all of urgency; was of the sort of situation upon which, whether by any apparent logic of events or not, crisis is likely to supervene. No doubt he felt that Arnander might at any moment *see* – a sudden moment of revelation bringing home to him, too, that absoluteness of difference between abeyance and loss. But in such a moment – as far, at least, as Arnander was concerned – Craine supposed himself to be the very last man likely to be helpful. Unless it came, no doubt, to clearing up the merely practical aspects of a real mess.

The train hurtled through Parma, and he thought fleetingly of Stendhal. All that exquisite mathematics of passion; it's as irrelevant to you and me – he said to himself – as is an elegant but arbitrary geometry. He almost said something about Stendhal to the man opposite, a professor, it had appeared, from Bologna – but he thought better of it and continued to pick in silence at his *pollo*. He became aware that he was carrying with him on this dash south a great load of apprehensiveness and anxiety. Perhaps it was the passing shade of Stendhal that had released the knowledge to him : the mercilessness, the tearing of illusion to the quick. Or perhaps it was simply this journey through a wild night. The train was moving very fast. He thought he felt the wind flick at it, as if urging it to yet greater speed towards some fatal terminus. The wine swayed gently in his glass – and then the coffee in his cup. The meal was

taken away and the sound of the train changed – the purely
subjective change that announces the last stage of a
journey in the dark. The lights of Prato flashed past. They
were in Florence.

There was still the wind. Blasts of it blew through the
great station where bright cold light beat down on muffled
and huddled passengers waiting for trains. It was cleaner
than Birmingham or Leeds – but it might have been Birmingham or Leeds apart from that. It was hard to believe that
Santa Maria Novella lay just outside, baked by centuries of
sun; that into this turbulent air rose Giotto's tower and
Brunelleschi's dome. Craine picked up his bag and walked
down the platform. There might be deep snow at three
thousand feet, but none of the taxis outside would make any
bones about driving up to it. He had passed the barrier
when a voice spoke respectfully in his ear. 'Signore Craine ?'

He turned in surprise. It was a chauffeur. The man had
no sooner made sure of his identity than he took his bag and
led the way to a closed car. He opened the door – with a
subdued drama appropriate to the successful accomplishing of a mission – and invited Craine to enter. There was
already an occupant: a woman clothed entirely in black.
And Craine was in doubt about her only for a moment. She
was Marchesa Forni.

He kissed her hand, and she spoke unemotionally as the
car drove off. 'I had no doubt it would be this train. Nevertheless I am relieved. We can drive straight out.'

'It is very kind of you to meet me, Marchesa.' Craine
was puzzled. He had sent no message ahead of him. So
presumably this was Weidlé's work. 'But surely you don't
mean to venture up to Saltino tonight ?'

'To Saltino ? No, no – there is nobody there.'

'Nobody there ?' He was bewildered – more bewildered,
he realized, than the Marchesa's words required him to be.
There would be nothing unnatural in the Arnander household's having decided, after all, to pack up, to descend from
its unseasonable aerie. He saw that his response to this

192

small mystery was bound up with his own suppressed anxieties – and moreover that beneath the Marchesa's calm there lay something very far wrong indeed. 'Why.' he asked, 'should there be nobody there ?'

'You don't know ?' she, in her turn, appeared surprised. 'The villa went too. The wind. The terrible wind.'

'The wind !' For a moment a wholly grotesque image rose in Craine's mind, that of a massive house whipped from its foundations by the gale, and floating down like a spinning leaf into the valley of the Arno.

'But my cable – that has brought you here. You understood it ?'

This time, Marchesa Forni's voice was almost alarmed. She might have been recalling that cables were not her strong line in intelligible communication. He hastened to put her out of doubt about this. 'I received no cable. I haven't come in response to one. It must have reached my home just after I left it. So please explain. For instance, where *are* we going now ?'

'To my very old friends, Luigi and Laura Perino. I have myself, you understand, no accommodation. And I knew they would much wish to help. Your – the *signora* knew them as a child. Tim Arnander, too, will go there. He will rejoin the others as soon as he leaves the hospital. I have just come from the hospital. It is terrible.'

The old lady's coherence was faltering, and he was afraid that she might break down before he had made sense of the situation. 'What is wrong with Tim ?' he asked urgently. 'Is he in any danger ?'

'No, no – not that. He has only broken a leg.' Marchesa Forni braced herself. 'And it was while behaving with courage. It is something he may have from his mother, no doubt. From his father – I think we are agreed – he could hope only for other qualities.' Unexpectedly, she laughed – and he sensed with alarm that she was violently trembling. 'It is Nino !' she cried. 'It is Nino who is perhaps in danger. They could tell me very little. It is terrible. But his – but the *signora* and Charles, at least, are unharmed.'

Craine drew a long breath. The car — he supposed it, from its amplitude and antiquity, to be the vehicle shared by so many Forni ladies — was nosing its way eastward out of the city. It was late, but there were still some shops and cafés lit up; and two glances would have told him, somehow, that it was Florence he was traversing. 'Was it a fire?' he asked. 'Was that it?'

'A terrible fire. Everything, everything destroyed. And with snow on the roofs, on the ground! But they could not control it. The wind. The terrible wind.'

'But there has been no loss of life?'

'Not yet.' In the gloom of the car he could see her shake her head — and again he knew her to be trembling. 'There was a woman. She might have died. But Tim saved her.'

'I'm very glad to hear that.' Craine managed to speak calmly. 'Is it known how it began?'

'It was in the studio. There was a new, a badly built fireplace. Nino would kindle great fires in it. And he grew more and more careless, it seems. And last night it happened.'

'You say everything was destroyed?'

'Nearly everything. The fire had spread to the villa and gained a hold there before the danger of it was realized. They did, I believe, drag a few things out.'

'But from the studio?'

'Nothing. Nothing was saved.'

There had indeed been severe weather, Conte Luigi agreed. Something like a blizzard was reported at Bibbiena. One might as well be in the Abruzzi. But what he himself feared was a long succeeding frost — one of those wicked winters in which the threat to the olive and the mulberry advances beyond the Apennines.

Craine hoped it would not be as bad as that. The old gentleman thanked him, and pursued his theme for a few minutes longer. He had already expressed welcome, solicitude, concern — all with the discreet vagueness appropriate to his not quite knowing what it was all about. His wife displayed an equal composure. It was impossible to tell whether they were aware of being in the presence of marital complication; it was only apparent that they had guests. Marchesa Forni, Craine saw, had chosen her emergency haven well.

And Jill might have been a daughter of the house. Craine didn't himself readily kindle to such places – they were apt to touch off his deep squirarchal distrust of a nobility – but he saw how perfectly she stood composed amid these mellow measured splendours. With her head turned away from him against the background of an old silk screen in faded aquamarine, she suggested nothing so much as a profile pricked out in the great age of the city now slumbering below them. She had said hardly a word on greeting him, but a glance had told how much she acknowledged the need of his support when matters looked to be getting out of hand. And they had very much looked to be doing that, he gathered, when she had allowed the Marchesa to send off her cable. Tim's leg had been one thing; but for a time his head had threatened to be quite another. It was no more than concussion, however, and it had lifted; so he was in no worse condition than, say, the scores of English boys now in Swiss hospitals as the consequence of over-enthusiastic slithering about on ski. Jill herself produced this comparison with a faint incongruousness that suddenly pierced Craine's heart. She was more or other than that sort of forthright mother of English public-school boys. But it was a part she played well. Hadn't he always acknowledged that everything became her? If John Arnander's resurrection had prospered, he oddly thought – if, for the first time in history, an Englishman had become indisputably the greatest of living European painters – then Jill would most admirably have filled the role of that painter's wife.

But now she had once more come over to him. 'Will you,' she asked quietly, 'go up and see Charles? I'm sure he's not asleep. He's been hoping – he's been hoping against hope – that you might really turn up tonight.'

He smiled at her. 'That's very handsome of him. I'll go at once.'

But it was with gravity that she returned his glance – even though it was a gravity that acknowledged gratitude. 'I'm afraid you'll find him disturbed still,' she said. 'He had a shock.'

Craine nodded. 'Tim's injury – and his father's?'

Rather oddly, Jill hesitated. 'Well, yes,' she said. 'These things too.'

And she didn't offer to go with him. A servant showed him the way. Charles was sitting up in bed reading, or making a show of reading, *Bevis* – a romance the provision of which was a singular testimony to the resources of the household. The chamber in which he had been accommodated was vast and shadowy; it would have looked like something on a stage, if it hadn't more resembled a contemporary illustration to Dickens – one designed to furnish with a maximum of pathetic suggestion the figure of a single forlorn small boy.

'Rupert!'

Charles had thrown down his book, jumped out of his gigantic bed, and flung himself into Craine's arms. Craine lifted him in air, set him down again, ruffled his hair. It was all common form between them – until he realized the boy was convulsively sobbing. It was something Charles hadn't done for a long time.

'Bad sort of day, old man.' Craine produced a handkerchief. The tears weren't of a sort you could pretend not to notice. 'But it's coming straight. Tim's all right – the old donkey. And so will your father be quite soon, I hope.'

Charles took the handkerchief and blew his nose. He was making a big effort after self-control. 'I've got to the fight,' he said with a gulp.

'The fight, Charles?' Craine was puzzled.

'Where Mark and Bevis fight in the jungle. But of course, I've skipped.'

'Of course. One does – the fifth time.'

'It's the sixth. I think it's the sixth – counting your reading it aloud.' Charles paused, and seemed to concentrate upon decorous breathing. 'It wasn't even a day,' he said. 'It was a night. A *very* bad sort of night.'

'A big fire can be pretty startling.' Craine heard his own voice, firm and informative, and was reminded of Nannie at Pinn. 'The first time, that is to say. It's probably not the same a fifth time – or a sixth. Firemen scarcely notice, I suppose.' He sat Charles on the edge of the bed. 'There were firemen ? They came ? I've hardly, you know, heard about it yet.'

Charles nodded. The sense of having something to communicate steadied him. 'First some of the foresters. And then the engines from Pontassieve. They came charging up the hill. But it all happened so quickly. They say it was because of the wind. Wasn't that queer ? Because you blow out a candle, after all.'

'Think of a bellows.'

'Yes, of course. And is become the bellows and the fan to cool a gipsy's lust. That's mysterious, isn't it ?'

Craine laughed. 'Well – it's complicated. Too complicated, I've always thought, for a simple soldier. What was his name ? Philo, was it ?'

'It's mysterious.' Charles wasn't interested in the dramatic context of his scrap of Shakespeare. 'But how important are things, simply because they're mysterious in that way ?'

'It sounds a big question.' Craine looked curiously at the boy, and realized that he was obscurely grappling with some urgent moral issue. 'We might have a go at it at breakfast. You can't have had much sleep last night.'

But Charles shook his head impatiently. 'Tim hadn't any doubts. He made up his mind at once.'

'Tim's good at that.'

'Of course, Tim knows more. He hasn't read more than I have – at least, I don't believe he has. But he remembers what they teach him. Virgil. *Tendebantque manus.* You know that ?'

'Yes, I know that.' Craine saw that Charles's eyelids were

dropping. It should surely be possible to get him off to sleep. 'I can say more of it, I think – although it's a very long time since I learnt it.' He repeated the few lines of the *Aeneid*, and then, when his memory failed, switched to another piece. It was a kind of cheating, but perhaps that was pardonable. 'What about tucking up?' he asked presently.

'Yes. Yes, please.' Charles remained passive while Craine got him under the blankets. His eyes closed, and he seemed to be asleep. But suddenly they opened again. 'Rupert!' he said urgently.

'Yes, Charles?'

'She was screaming, you know. Screaming and screaming.'

'Yes. But it's all right now.' He put his hand on the boy's forehead. 'It's all right now.'

'Yes,' Charles said. 'Yes, please.' He sighed. He was really asleep.

Craine sat beside him for some time, listening to his light breathing. Tim, Charles, Martin, Rachael. He thought of them simply like that. He got up, turned off the light, and went downstairs.

CHAPTER NINE

JILL was alone. They might have been two country-house guests, of nocturnal habits, attracted into cautious confabulation in the small hours. But Craine's first words were aside from such a fancy. 'He's asleep,' he said. He remembered how often he had said it before.

'I shall be next door – if he wakes up later. But he won't. Not now that he knows you're here. There are drinks on the table.'

'What about you?' Craine didn't want a drink – but a glance at Jill suggested she might be the better for one. He thought he had never seen her so pale. And he wondered whether this now so startlingly appeared only because they were undistracted and alone together. Or had something happened – some fresh news come – while he was with Charles? He was about to ask her, and then changed his mind. 'Brandy?' he said.

She shook her head. 'But have you got a cigarette?'

It was a familiar reply, and with a familiar movement he produced his case. 'Are the old people coming back?'

'No. Maria Forni has driven home. She was uneasy, poor dear, about having swiped the car for a whole day, out of turn. And I persuaded the Perinos to go to bed. They said various discreet things, and went off. They're nice, don't you think?'

'Yes, they're very nice.'

There was a silence. 'You came – without knowing?' she asked.

'Yes. Weidlé thought it would be a good idea.'

She nodded. 'He left, didn't he, in order to send you?'

'Yes.'

'And because of something about John's work? That was why?'

'That was why.'

'Otto Frink was wrong? It's no good?'

Craine hesitated. But he understood that Jill's mind had caught up with a great deal. 'Well, Frink was rather wrong. The technique is pretty well all there. But the real thing isn't. Not, that's to say, if Weidlé's judgement is to be trusted.'

'Of course it's to be trusted. You know it is. The thing's true. It fits too well not to be. John, me, everything.'

'Yes.'

Again they were silent. Jill gazed at the tip of her cigarette. Then she turned her eyes to him and he was startled. 'But I can't tell you,' she cried, 'how strange the certainty of it makes everything last night!'

'I don't yet know much about last night.'

'You might call it just the queerest of epilogues.'

He walked across the room to her. 'Look, Jill. You must tell me. Now. We can think up a name for it later.'

She smiled – although her eyes still held some final trouble he felt he didn't begin to understand. 'I know,' she said. 'I'm sorry. I must talk sense.' But still she hesitated. 'Charles didn't come out with much?'

'I didn't want him to, if he could be got to sleep. But he did get one thing off his chest. Indeed, as soon as he'd mentioned it, he seemed to feel he needn't stay awake any longer. He said there had been a woman screaming. A woman screaming and screaming.'

Jill nodded. 'Yes,' she said. 'Celia.'

Just for a moment, Craine was actually at a loss. Celia Barfoot, presumably, had not struck him as other than very much a super in the affair. 'That wretched girl!' he exclaimed. 'Hadn't he turfed her out?'

Jill shook her head. 'No. Or perhaps he thought he had. John was always able to persuade himself of the strangest untruths. He had, in fact, more or less hidden her away. He may have thought it the same thing.'

'Yes. I see. You wrote that Tim thought he'd seen her.

You hadn't supposed John would really keep her about, once the boys came.'

'Well, I was wrong. He had some real infatuation for her, I think. It was something new in him. Of course fornication, a mistress, wasn't new. But this was different. John had seemed much the same, you know. But I've sometimes had a feeling that the whole basis of his personality has changed.'

'Like his art.'

'Like his art, it seems.' Jill stubbed out her cigarette. 'But his deep attachment to the person of Miss Barfoot proved, after all, not to carry very far.' She paused again, and Craine knew that this irony preluded the core of what she had to tell. 'He let her roast, you see, while he rescued his paintings.'

'Really roast ?' The words sounded absurd to Craine even as he uttered them. 'Go on roasting – and screaming ?'

'Just that. She might have perished. It was a deliberate act of choice. What they call a judgement of value, I suppose.'

Disconcertingly, Craine found himself almost moved to laughter – as he might have been by some neat savage farce, some abominable outrage perpetrated upon Pluto or his kind on a screen. 'It has given Charles something to chew on,' he said – and noticed that there was nothing remotely like laughter in his voice. 'The importance of what he calls mysterious things. Set over against the importance of a screaming girl. Good God !' – he was now staring at Jill round-eyed – 'you had this as – as positively a spectacle ?'

'Yes, last night. And certainly as a spectacle. It might have been a stage – a stage upon which the curtain had gone up very suddenly indeed. I hadn't known that fires – well, worked at that pace.' She looked at him strangely again. 'It was in every sense an *éclaircissement.*'

'No doubt. But just how did it happen, Jill ?'

It pulled her up once more. 'Do you know, I don't think I can run to much of a narrative ? Perhaps it will come back to me more coherently later on. At present it's a series of flashes, as if it had all happened under the beam of a crazy lighthouse. And I've forgotten what you know, what you remember, about Saltino. There is – there was – a range of stables, a stone's throw from the villa. And a wooden storey added on top.'

Craine nodded. 'Yes, I understand about that. The place John turned into his studio.'

'And into his own independent establishment, as you know. I went there only by invitation. But that was like old times. So much was like old times – and yet wasn't. He slept there, as often as not – I mean, since he began to work again. And at one end there was a third storey, more or less. Or not quite that. The studio ceiling was lower, and a sort of attic had been fitted in. I'm explaining this badly, but it's all not important after all. The things that happened are what's important.'

'Yes ?'

'Well, it was into this little attic that he must have shoved the girl – shoved her when he didn't want her to be about. She was prepared to take a lot, I must say. But, of course, people are, quite often – with John.'

Craine was silent.

'And she slept there, I suppose, when he couldn't be bothered with her. Which would be most of the time, poor child. He had this rather new sort of infatuation for her – I believe he thought her ravishingly beautiful – but when a man is working as John was working, it would take a Phryne or a Cleopatra to get much of a look-in. Well, that was the set-up. And then, in the small hours, it was suddenly blazing. There's another thing I didn't know about a fire – that it makes such a noise. I woke up imagining that great animals were roaring outside the villa; and I was still half in that dream, I believe, when I looked out of my bedroom window and realized the truth. Or part of the truth. For I didn't realize that the fire had actually got a hold on the villa itself. That was something I discovered only when I'd run downstairs and got outside. It complicated the next

– well, I suppose the next fifteen minutes. There were the boys, and there were our servants – four of them, and all women. Why should we want four servants? How absurd Italy is.'

'And then?'

'I had to get them out, of course. And meantime, over the way, was John – rushing up and down this staircase. I haven't told you about the staircase.'

'You did actually mention it when you were writing, as it happens. The way up to the studio was by an outside wooden staircase.'

Jill nodded. 'That was it. Like a fire-escape, only not in the least likely to escape a fire itself. Not, of course, that it made the place any sort of death-trap – or not to anybody who was remotely keeping his head. And John couldn't be said not to be doing that. He was simply hurrying frantically up and down, carrying his precious canvases and everything else to safety. It was strange and alarming, but I had other things to think about. I had begun to realize the pace of it all. The decisive factor was the wind, the really terrible and terrifying wind. It hurled fire all over the place. One might have been in the path of some horrible weapon, of a flame-thrower directed by a maniac. I got Tim and Charles into the open air, and then I had to see to the women. They slept quite high up at the back, and there really did seem some possibility of a death-trap in their case. I had to go through the house to get at them. There wasn't any flame the way I went, and it might have been easier if there had been. I might have seen my way. As it was, there was nothing but darkness and smoke. The lights wouldn't go on, and altogether it was quite a business. By the time I'd got up to the servants' rooms I wasn't at all sure how I was going to get them, or myself, back. Anyway, my rescue expedition ended absurdly. They had climbed down a trellis to the roof of the loggia, and from that lowered themselves without any difficulty to the terrace. When I got to a window, there they were – and they started shouting and waving when they saw me. I can remember feeling absolutely furious with them. And then I climbed down the same way. When I got round to the other side of the house again, the situation had changed drastically.'

Jill paused as if for breath; she was now pouring out her story rapidly. 'Surely,' Craine asked, 'John must have got all his stuff away by this time?'

'No, he hadn't. He was still behaving in just the same frantic but purposeful way. Something, I suppose, must have held him up for a time. And then there he still was, carrying things down and stacking them near the foot of the staircase. What made the drastic difference was Celia. There she stood, at her attic window, screaming her head off. It wasn't perhaps unnatural, for there were actually flames licking up behind her. Then the really unnerving thing happened. John stopped and stared up at her – and at once carried on precisely as before. There was a great deal of shouting from not far away, and I knew that help couldn't be far off. I looked round for it, and what I saw was Charles. It was clear to me in an instant that he had seen precisely what I had seen. I hadn't time to feel this was unfortunate, for I was suddenly aware that Tim had vanished. And Celia – as Charles has said – was screaming and screaming.'

Again Jill was silent for a moment, and Craine gently prompted her. 'This attic window – was it really high up?'

'Of course not. The fool had only to lower herself from it and drop. Only she was helplessly in the grip of her hysteria. Then I saw Tim. He was on the roof of the studio. I thought I must be fainting, because the roof seemed to sway. But it *was* swaying – and flames were coming through. The hard bit for him must have been getting in at the window. But he managed it. What he did then, I don't know. Perhaps he punched her on the jaw, perhaps he only slapped her good and hard. Anyway, for a moment he got her passive. And then he must have gathered up every ounce of strength he had. He used it simply to pitch Celia out of the window.'

There was another silence. It represented a period during

which Craine wasn't very sure if he could trust himself to speak. 'Good show,' he said.

'The wretched girl landed in snow, and got no more than a shaking. Tim, when he jumped, was less lucky. His foot caught in something, and his head came a bad crack on the wall of the stable. But he might have been a great deal unluckier. The studio might have collapsed that way – and buried him and Celia together. As it was, it collapsed at the other end. Mainly, I suppose, it was the roof – three-parts burnt, and simply lifted up and over by the wind. It came down like a great torch hurled to earth by a giant. I hadn't much time to be horrified, because I was making a dash for Tim. We were rather isolated up there, you know, with most of the villas and the clinic shut up; and actually it was quite surprising how quickly things got organized. It was lucky, too – for John.'

'Just what happened to John ?'

'I saw nothing of it myself.' Jill was now speaking quietly and carefully, almost as if she were giving evidence in a court. 'But one of the foresters told me. Clearly, it took John in a queer moment – a very queer moment, if you add in the knowledge of what those paintings and sketches *were*. He was counting them.'

'Counting them ?' Craine was really startled.

'Yes. He was checking them over, quite composedly – supposing them quite out of danger, no doubt, and certainly without a thought for himself or any other living creature. It didn't quite square – did it ? – with his notion of a Feast of the Grand Combustion. And then it came down on him, and them.'

'The roof did ?'

'The roof – like the lid of an enormous flaming coffin. It took very resolute men to get him out. For seconds his head and shoulders lay in something like a furnace. But they managed it. He was half-way to Florence in an ambulance before I knew anything about it.'

There was a final long silence. 'But he'll live ?' Craine asked.

'Oh, yes – he'll live. You might call it a second resurrection.'

Craine poured brandy. It was certainly a good idea now. The great strange house lay all mute around them. No doubt – this being Italy – there were servants awake somewhere, ready to see them with any necessary ceremony to their beds. But the only sound came, very faintly, from outside : the bitter *tramontana* still sweeping south over Tuscany, Umbria, Rome, to lose itself in the Tyrrhenian Sea. Craine thought for a long time before speaking. 'You can't go on doing it,' he said. 'You mustn't.'

Jill let the brandy circle in her glass, and looked at him in silence.

'There's no reason why great artists shouldn't have women – and even wives – if the wives will rise to it. But I'm damned if they ought to have children. What sort of a thing is that for boys to remember ?'

'What, indeed.' She was quite still.

'You suspect that the whole basis of John's personality has changed. You know, you positively know, that his relationship with you has. When he was blind, he was utterly dependent on you; he was living on a memory – perhaps no more than a dimly recovered memory – of what that relationship had been. But, when he got back his sight, it was – well, the wrong sort of sight. It produces the wrong sort of pictures, and surely no sort of relationship at all. And he'll go on. He'll go on now, fighting his own deeper knowledge of what's become of him, reading what people say about his work, finally being driven into the open with himself. And you'll be involved. Fundamentally, it's all happened already. There have been moments when it has peeped out that – '

'Yes, I know.' She interrupted him calmly. 'When it has peeped out that he can't bear me.'

'I say you can't go on.'

Jill shook her head slowly. When it came to rest, her gaze was very steady. 'But you haven't got it all,' she said.

206

'Not quite all. There was a telephone message. It came while you were with Charles. They'll save his life. But they can't save his eyes.'

EPILOGUE

EPILOGUE

THE City had been knocked down; the City had been built up again. Soon – Craine thought as he walked through autumn sunshine – it would be complete: the last great lattice of steel sheathed in its glass or stone or concrete; the last acre of offices advertised for sale in *The Times*. It wasn't his, Craine's, idea of a City of London; no, it wasn't his cup of tea. But he didn't know that it was, after all, too bad. The needs it served, the drives it expressed, were nothing to be ashamed of. Yes – he supposed – it would do; it was all very much of a compromise, but after a fashion, it marched. And it was only of some very rare things in life that you could say more.

Craine walked, perhaps, a little faster than he used to. Old Mungo was definitely out of things; Craine had even more on his own plate; private business – such as today's – was harder than ever to fit in. Still, he didn't move sightlessly. As long as you avoided *that*, you had – well, some chance of a glimpse of something. Once, he remembered, just here, he had seen a red bicycle.

He turned into Watling Street.

Mrs Eggins continued in the best of health, and Mr Groocock was free at once. Groocock was going grey, Craine thought as he entered the inner office and shook hands. But not so grey as you might expect, in a man for whom life was presumably one long audit. He wondered whether this would be one of Groocock's reserved or communicative days.

The question answered itself almost at once. 'I saw the obituary of our friend,' Groocock said. 'Most interesting. And entertaining, in a discreet way, on the manner in which, as a youth, he emerged more or less out of the blue.

I hope you'll send in something of your own. They call them tributes, don't they? The affairs that appear a few days later.'

'A. B. C. writes that the late X had, above all things, a genius for friendship?' Craine shook his head. 'No, I don't think I could manage that – even about Fyodor Weidlé, of whom I had become rather fond.'

'Was it sudden?' Groocock asked.

'No, he'd known for quite a long time. I can't tell you much about his last weeks, or months. We didn't often meet. He was, in fact, rather avoiding me.'

'I'm sorry to hear that.' Groocock put out a hand to the papers on his desk – a sign of precipitate retreat upon discretion. 'Well, I think everything's ready, more or less, for the lawyers to come in with their rigmaroles.' He tapped first one file and then another. 'Here you are. The Arnander Trust. The Craine Trust.' He paused, suddenly self-convicted of having been remiss. 'I hope,' he asked, 'that Mrs Craine is well?'

'Yes, thank you – although she was as sad about Weidlé as I was. She hadn't been seeing much of him either. We neither of us had, since just after John Arnander's death. He didn't want much to discuss it, I suppose.'

'Ah, yes – a very sad accident, that. And after such an extraordinary escape.'

At the risk of the largest impropriety, Craine laughed. He was really amused. Groocock had even assumed his slightly abstracted manner. 'My dear man,' Craine said, 'you've been good enough to talk to me frankly about my strange fortunes before this. We needn't relapse.'

'No, no – that's true.' It was almost possible to believe that Groocock had flushed. He pushed his papers away. 'Tell me,' he said. '*Was* it an accident?'

'It may have been. But I don't think so.'

Groocock shook his head. 'I must say, suicide isn't surprising. It was a plight – a dire plight, poor devil. To have had it all in his grasp again, actually to have achieved his old heights, and then to be plunged into that second darkness – it doesn't bear thinking about.'

'*He* certainly couldn't bear thinking about it. He was Lazarus – brought back to live in hell. Perhaps because – because he had his wife still, he couldn't even relapse readily into the condition to which his first blindness had brought him. He raged. He wouldn't reconcile himself by one iota to his condition. He struggled at incredible things. He remembered that Degas, when nearly blind, had taken to modelling. There's a famous little ballerina. Arnander tried that sort of thing – in clay, in wax. In every sense, it was a terrible mess.'

Craine paused, and Groocock fished cautiously for an understatement. 'He can't,' he said, 'have been easy to live with.'

'No. And yet one mustn't exaggerate.' Craine's inexpungable fair-mindedness rose up. 'He got something from Jill, and that meant something to her. It was killing her, but he got something. Not much, to any mortal seeming. But such things can't be measured. And his hostility, remember – for hostility to her had been growing in him – sank back, with his renewed blindness, into a renewed dependence. She was right never to leave him.'

This time Groocock said nothing. He knew when to hold his tongue.

'He brooded – it was inevitable that he should brood – over the work he'd done in those few precious months before the fire and the catastrophe. If only those canvases had been preserved, he thought, it would all have been worth while, after all. Even the moment – I've told you of it – when he left that girl screaming.'

'But in fact, they'd perished – every one of them?'

Craine nodded. 'In fact they'd perished in the fire. If they can be said ever to have existed.'

Groocock sat up and stared. 'What's that?'

'It hasn't yet been made generally known, and I don't know that it ever need be. They were only, so to speak, dream-paintings – triumphs Arnander imagined that, during his period of miraculous resurrection, a relenting Fate had allowed him to achieve. It wasn't so. His genius had gone out of him.'

'And he didn't know?'

'He didn't – in any common sense of the term – know. No doubt the seed of knowledge lurked somewhere deep in his mind. If he'd kept his sight, it must have thrust up through the surface sooner or later and confronted him. As it was, it remained a seed – no more. When he didn't rage – which wasn't very often – it was because he believed that his genius had really flowered again in those months of recaptured vision. But then the thought that the fruit of that flowering had perished would catch him and throw him back into torment. And that was the point at which irrational processes began to come in.'

'You mean – insanity?'

'Well, he began to have times when it appeared to him incredible that his work – his work that he'd carried from the studio to safety at such fearful cost – *could* have perished. Rather it had been hidden away, stolen from him in his helplessness. There was a monstrous fraud, a conspiracy, a persecution. Somewhere, somehow, somebody else was holding an exhibition, was getting the credit for paintings greater, he believed, than the La Verna or the Maremma.'

Groocock considered. 'Then wasn't he,' he asked, 'a case for the psychiatrists?'

'Of course he was – in the sense that persons of that sort were consulted. They said these were merely episodes of aberration which might remain entirely manageable. They advised that Arnander shouldn't be argued with, or indeed addressed on the subject at all. That kind of thing.'

'And that was as far as they got in – what do they call it? – prognosis?'

'One of them supposed that, very slowly, he might sink back into the sort of state I'd found him in at Castelarbia. It would be a matter of years. And meanwhile, there he was: first in hospital with those fearful burns, then in the Saltino clinic when it opened again in the spring, and then in a *pensione* down the road. And there too was Jill. And there, from time to time, were his two boys. He was in torment, and might so remain for thirty years. And they all knew it.'

Groocock again briefly pondered. 'I don't know,' he said, 'how you feel about suicide, from the point of view of religious belief. But if ever a man was justified in . . .'

'Suicide?' Craine shook his head. 'Perhaps it was that. Or might it have been murder?'

'But I read about it!' Groocock was shocked. 'It seemed precisely the sort of affair that leaves one a little wondering – but certainly not about possible foul play. There was a very full account. The terrace of the burnt-out villa – he would go and sit there. It was said that he took satisfaction in listening to the workmen who had begun to rebuild or repair the place. There was a safe quiet walk to it, and nobody suspected the slightest danger. Wasn't all that true?'

'Perfectly true.'

'But in fact, beyond the terrace, or beyond one end of it, there was a sheer drop to rock below. And, just at one point above this, a balustrade or railing was defective . . .'

'And that's perfectly true, too. So was the testimony of the workmen up on a scaffolding. Arnander had sat on the terrace all afternoon, like a man gazing out over the view. Then he got up and took a turn up and down. He was very sure of himself physically, never troubled about his sense of direction. But suddenly he seemed to become disorientated – and without knowing it. Quite confidently, and simply holding his stick out before him, he walked straight to the gap and went over. Of course he was dead when they reached him.'

'That was something.' Groocock seemed to feel that his tone carried a satisfaction that might be misinterpreted. 'That there wasn't, I mean, some long final agony. And I agree that, as you tell the thing, it doesn't convey a convincing impression of accident. But how it could in any sense be – '

'Weidlé was there, you know,' Craine interrupted. 'They'd had lunch together.'

'Well, what if they did? Weidlé can't very well have poisoned the poor chap.' Groocock paused on this, frowning – so that Craine was reminded of how Weidlé himself had used to dislike sounding a dubiously facetious note. 'Unless he poisoned his mind,' he added sharply.

'I don't know whether telling him the the truth is to be called poisoning his mind. For that's what I think Weidlé did. He told Arnander the truth about what had happened to his powers, his genius. One might say that he uncaged the truth – for, as I've said, it was already there, prowling the darkness of Arnander's unconscious.' Craine looked up. 'Darkness. That reminds me of something that Weidlé once said to Jill. He said that there are kinds of pathos that are best for the dark. And I remember, too, something he said to me on what must have been almost the last occasion we met. It was again something that might be thought sententious. A gnomic habit was growing on him, towards the end. He said that there was absolutely no safety in the truth, but there was always liberation in it.'

Groocock stirred uneasily. 'Even so ...' He hesitated. 'Even so, his intention mayn't have been what you could call lethal. Say that telling Arnander this truth was a risk that nobody else was prepared to take. Once taken, its effect might have been of liberation other than in that fatal sense. Arnander might have faced that last irony about himself – the irony of his having elected to rescue those virtually worthless pictures instead of the girl – and survived, all the same.'

Craine nodded. 'Yes. Kill or cure. It may have been that. One can't tell. And, even if one could, it would be rash to bring in a judgement. Only I do believe this. It was something that Weidlé wouldn't have done, if he hadn't been facing the dark himself.'

The two men looked at each other seriously, and for some time neither spoke. It became clear that their topic was exhausted. Groocock put out a hand for his two files: the Craine Trust, the Arnander Trust. Then he changed his mind, and reached for some loose papers. 'By the way,' he said, 'before we go on, there's something else. Some signatures. In each of the places where there's a pencilled cross.'

And Craine signed the unimportant papers presented to him.

*Some recent Penguin Fiction
is described on the
following pages*

MY OEDIPUS COMPLEX and Other Stories

Frank O'Connor

1956

W. B. Yeats once declared that 'O'Connor is doing for Ireland what Chekhov did for Russia'. A patriotic boast, perhaps, but it doesn't take an Irishman to recognize the unpredictable liveliness and observant sympathy in these eighteen short stories. Their insight into Irish character and life never slides into sentimentality. Ranging from a child's confident misconceptions about sex to Sam Higgins, the honest headmaster, driven to exasperation and near madness by his slick and cynical rival, they are written with a freshness and fluency that is indeed Irish, but their appeal is world-wide.

'Frank O'Connor has long been recognized as one of the great short-story writers of this century' – *Time and Tide*

'Nowhere will you get so vivid, so humorous, and so deeply understanding a picture of Ireland as in these tales. . . . Anyone can enjoy his stories. All start with a bang and carry one through breathless to the end' – *Daily Telegraph*

'A miraculous technique which universalizes the stories without impairing their local virtue' – Muriel Spark in the *Observer*

THE FREE FISHERS

John Buchan

1954

When Anthony Lammas, minister of the Kirk and Professor of Logic at St Andrew's University, left his home town for London on University business he little imagined that in less than two days he would be deeply entangled in a web of mystery and intrigue. But then 'Nanty' Lammas was no ordinary professor, and his boyhood allegiance to a brotherhood of deep-sea fishermen was to bring about many other strange results, and involve him and his ex-pupil, the handsome young Lord Belses, with a beautiful but potentially dangerous woman. . . .

Set in the bleak Yorkshire hamlet of Hungrygrain, where work is afoot which threatens the safety of England herself, then engaged in the Napoleonic Wars, this stirring tale of treason and romance displays all the gifts of story-telling for which John Buchan is so justly renowned.

AFTERNOON MEN

Anthony Powell

1964

Life was hard in the thirties. Especially for a young man like Atwater, whose ill-defined work at a museum left long periods for vacant thought; or a girl like Lola (Atwater met her at a party) who read Bertrand Russell for inspiration. Fotheringham, on the other hand, worked hard, but with the growing suspicion that his talents were being wasted on that recondite (if not dubious) spiritualist magazine. Even Barlow, the much-admired painter, had his problems : he really must decide – over the next drink but one – which girl to marry. As for Brisket, Wauchop, Scheigan, and the rest, how bravely they managed to confront the abyss with a positively reckless gaiety.

This wickedly funny portrait of London's party-set between the wars was Anthony Powell's first book, and remains one of the most subtle and sparkling of them all.

'Like *Ulysses, Afternoon Men* is a cul-de-sac – nobody could write another novel quite in the same manner. . . . One of the most significant (and incidentally one of the funniest) novels of its age' – Jocelyn Brooke in *Time and Tide*

PAUL GALLICO

'In his own way he is something of a genius' – Peter Green in the *Daily Telegraph*

Four of Paul Gallico's charming fairy tales in modern dress are being published simultaneously in Penguins. They are:

FLOWERS FOR MRS HARRIS · 1944

In this extremely popular novel the author of *The Snow Goose* tells the story of the London 'daily' who visits Paris to buy a Dior dress.

MRS HARRIS GOES TO NEW YORK · 1943

The sequel to *Flowers for Mrs Harris* is a warm-hearted and comic tale of the famous London 'daily' on a chivalrous mission to the States.

JENNIE · 1942

His enchanting story of a boy metamorphosed into a stray cat 'has the same simplicity as *The Snow Goose*' – *The Times Literary Supplement*

LOVE OF SEVEN DOLLS · 1945

'There seems to be no limit to Mr Gallico's ability to produce small miracles' was *The Times*'s reaction to this story of the Breton girl and the puppet show.